Celebrations of the Zebra Storyteller

These stories are (or should be) classics; they're not merely extraordinary, but absolutely unique. Witty, magical, immensely strange, shimmering with paradox, Spencer Holst's stories oblige us to revise whatever it was that we thought we knew about the possibilities of storytelling.

Francine Prose

I tell you this is a wonderful book . . . for sheer and not-always-so-simple joy.

Beverly Lowry, *Houston Chronicle*

His gift is to a remarkable extent that of a storyteller in the oldest and simplest sense. It's not hard to imagine him telling stories on the street corners of ancient Rome.

W.S. Merwin

Spencer Holst invites us to fantastic new worlds; he opens up possibilities we've only dreamed of. Exquisite fiction from a great storyteller.

Raymond Mungo, *Mademoiselle*

His stories—written with the verbal and rhythmic preciseness of poetry—are witty, intriguing metaphors for the secrets of the cosmos.

Howard Kissel, *Women's Wear Daily*

T0294274

At first I thought *The Language of Cats* was just a book of wry, marvelous fables. But as I went further and began to *feel* entirely different, I saw that what we have here is a matter of ecstasy.

Muriel Rukeyser

His sense of humor and of the macabre have earned him a special place as wise jester of the vanguard.

The New York Times

Spencer Holst is a mad genius of a writer, a master of odd juxtaposition and surprises, a poet with a fresh view of the commonplace.

Jacqueline Shonerd, *Books West*

These are routines—something like fictions, something like jokes—of a stand-up tragic. Transcriptions of a spoken voice, their cadences linger beyond laughter.

John Hollander

Spencer Holst at his best is a goblin telling a story to an audience of spellbound magicians. His stories transform you into a man in an invisible coat seeing all the secrets of the world.

Diane Wakoski

Beautiful language . . . , a flexible syntax capable of limpid exposition and description, his utterance is often gnomic, his drive demonic, and his compassion angelic.

Robert Stock, *The Nation*

Stories that will last forever.

Donald Newlove

Spencer Holst has been called a "goblin" and a "demon," but he writes like an angel—an anxious angel, whose exquisite fiction has the power to move and even inspire people.

Joseph Catinella, *Saturday Review*

The author has been a favorite of the literary underground for a long time and his work should be more widely known.

Library Journal

Subterranean anonymous archaic Lower East Side Kafka prose-poems in mirror-universe — mysterious impersonality, not self seeking — in simple NY American lingo — City lingo — Empty Buddha centered fables — Lookback on present thru time Distance — Author by now like myself ageing wrinkled in Science-Fiction Wars & Dope Eras, Police State! — but still writing in pubescent youth's persona — Power of imagination goes back Poeesque thru late 1940's to Mailer's underground paranoiac trotskyite Monroe Street — Patient genius, triple quadruple twists & contradictions — old indian Aboriginal storyteller as inconsequential as life — Daggerotype Illuminations, Oracle's "little fantasies" — Silent monster — Storm on Bklyn Bridge — Mind puzzles — Charmant! Charming!

Allen Ginsberg

THESE STORIES

WERE WRITTEN BY PLAYING

THE TYPEWRITER,

THE AUTHOR IS A MAGICIAN, WHAT THAT MEANS IS

YOU CAN

READ

A STORY --

YOU CAN KNOW IT BY HEART --

YOU SAW HIM DO IT --

BUT YOU STILL CAN'T FIGURE IT OUT,

AND THE TYPEWRITER HE USES IS

JUST AN ORDINARY TYPEWRITER,

John Cage

The Zebra Storyteller

The author and his wife Beate Wheeler.

The

Collected Stories

Zebra

Spencer Holst

Storyteller

Drawings by Beate Wheeler

Photographs by Norman Saito

Station Hill

Published by Station Hill Literary Editions, under the Institute for Publishing Arts, Inc., Barrytown, New York 12507. Station Hill Literary Editions is supported in part by grants from the National Endowment for the Arts, a Federal Agency in Washington, D.C., and by the New York State Council on the Arts.

Distributed by the Talman Company, 131 Spring Street, Suite 201E-N, New York, New York 10012.

Front cover, detail of painting by Spencer Holst: *Blue Palimpsest*
Cover and book design by Susan Quasha, with assistance from Vicki Hickman. Back cover photo by Norman Saito.

"The Typewriter Repairman" first appeared under the title "¢%#&?! the Typewriter Repairman" in *Mademoiselle*; "The Adventure of the Giant Rat of Sumatra" first appeared in *Oui*; "The Language of Cats" first appeared in *Cosmopolitan*, and (in French) in *Cosmopolitan/Paris Edition*; "Miss Lady" first appeared in *Viva*; and "The Frog" was first published in *The New York Times Book Review*. Other pieces have appeared in various periodicals, including: *Scholastic Voice, Ear, East Side Review, Fireside Calendar, Athanor, Chelsea, Equal Time, Some/ Thing, Sumac, Transition, Magazine, Atlanta's First Annual Poetry Festival, For Now, Prospect, Rallying Point, Sou'wester, Red Crow, Roy Rogers, Green Mountain Post, Friends Seminary Review, El Corno Emplumado, WIN, American Way, Mixed Voices,* and *Resistance*. Stories have also appeared in numerous textbooks and anthologies—including: the *Norton Introduction to Literature; Norton Introduction to Fiction; Pegasen från Prärien* (in Swedish); *Fantastic Worlds: Myths, Tales and Stories; Self-Portrait: Book People Picture Themselves; Underground Anthology; Sudden Fiction International; Flash Fiction;* and *America a Prophecy*.

Library of Congress Cataloging-in-Publication Data

Holst, Spencer.
    The zebra storyteller : collected stories / Spencer Holst.
      p. cm.
    ISBN 0-88268-143-5 : $28.95 — ISBN 0-88268-124-9 : $14.95
    I. Title.
PS3558.O39Z43   1993
813'.54—dc20   93-4201
                                                          CIP

Manufactured in the United States of America.

To Sebastian and Dawn Holst;

and

to a stranger who will read aloud, and to one
who listens– this book is dedicated; but then . . .
to such a pair all of Literature is dedicated.

With the exception of a few pieces written in my youth, this book contains every story I've ever written, about a third of which appear in print here for the first time.

S.H.

Contents

VI

"... that, in general, from the violation of a few simple laws of humanity arises the wretchedness of mankind—that as a species we have in our possession the as yet unwrought elements of content—and that, even now in the present darkness and madness of all thought on the great question of the social condition, it is not impossible that man, the individual, under certain unusual and highly fortuitous conditions, may be happy."

Edgar Allan Poe
The Domain of Arnheim

The
Zebra
Storyteller

The Zebra Storyteller

Once upon a time there was a Siamese cat who pretended to be a lion and spoke inappropriate Zebraic.

That language is whinnied by the race of striped horses in Africa.

Here now: An innocent zebra is walking in a jungle, and approaching from another direction is the little cat; they meet.

"Hello there!" says the Siamese cat in perfectly pronounced Zebraic. "It certainly is a pleasant day, isn't it? The sun is shining, the birds are singing, isn't the world a lovely place to live today!"

The zebra is so astonished at hearing a Siamese cat speaking like a zebra, why—he's just fit to be tied.

So the little cat quickly ties him up, kills him, and drags the better parts of the carcass back to his den.

The cat successfully hunted zebras many months in this manner, dining on filet mignon of zebra every night, and from the better hides he made bow neckties and wide belts after the fashion of the decadent princes of the Old Siamese court.

He began boasting to his friends he was a lion, and he gave them as proof the fact that he hunted zebras.

The delicate noses of the zebras told them there was really no lion in the neighborhood. The zebra deaths caused many to avoid the region. Superstitious, they decided the woods were haunted by the ghost of a lion.

One day the storyteller of the zebras was ambling, and through his mind ran plots for stories to amuse the other zebras, when suddenly his eyes brightened, and he said, "That's it! I'll tell a story about a Siamese cat who learns to speak our language! What an idea! That'll make 'em laugh!"

Just then the Siamese cat appeared before him, and said, "Hello there! Pleasant day today, isn't it!"

The zebra storyteller wasn't fit to be tied at hearing a cat speaking his language, because he'd been thinking about that very thing.

He took a good look at the cat, and he didn't know why, but there was something about his looks he didn't like, so he kicked him with a hoof and killed him.

That is the function of the storyteller.

Mona Lisa Meets Buddha

Up in heaven the curtains fluttered, the curtains fluttered, the curtains fluttered, and the Mona Lisa entered at one end of a small hall, which was hung with many veils.

Up in heaven the curtains fluttered, fluttered, fluttered, and the Buddha entered the hall at the other end.

They smiled.

The Getaway Car

In the darkest hours of the night on the country road which passes the county prison, the jailed and the jailers alike can sometimes hear a ghastly cranking, as if a ghost were cranking a ghostly Model-T Ford; then they hear the motor start, backfire several times, and then depart; and as prisoners and guards alike are listening to the chugging of the motor fading out in the distance down the road, the fleeing ghost utters its cry: Ah-GOO-gah! Ah-GOO-gah!

The Largest Wave in the World

A hurricane sent the 200-foot radio tower dancing upright across the fields, its guide wires trailing giant blue sparks.

The suspension bridge split lengthwise down the middle. Each side of the highway was suspended by vertical strands to its single cable, and though the two great cables stayed firmly fixed to the towers, the two pieces of highway broke loose and were pushed mightily away from the towers and flapped horrendously in the great winds. Built of massive blocks of stone and steel sunk deep into bedrock, the bridge towers held firmly to the ground, but the tops of the towers began to vibrate like two buzzers, or more precisely: as the towers were sunk into a single great piece of stone, and as the towers themselves were perfect geometric replicas of each other, the bridge towers buzzed *in phase* like the prongs of a tuning fork, producing a single pure tone. For fifteen minutes while the eye of the storm passed overhead, the buzzing resonated inside that giant cylinder of still air, and a strange musical tone was heard around the world.

Every seismograph jammed, and it's judged that it was the loudest continuous sound heard on earth during the time since life began.

In the base of the bridge tower, deep inside, were a number of rooms where a hundred people huddled in more or less comfort, safe from the holocaustal winds. As the eye of the storm passed overhead, and as the wind suddenly died down to an uncanny dead calm, those people ventured outside to look around in wonderment. This is the largest suspension bridge ever built, and it is located on the Eastern coast of the United States, crossing the Hudson River at The Narrows, just before that river empties into the Atlantic Ocean. When those hundred people came outside onto a broad stone terrace, they looked out toward the nearby ocean and saw the sea hugely tossing though there was not a breath of wind, and they noticed an odd silence.

Some shouted at the top of their lungs and one raised a wooden chair into the air and crashed it to the floor, but those activities made not the slightest sound.

For the strange musical tone had "jammed" their ears, just as it jammed the seismographs. Their ears temporarily had stopped functioning. They were utterly deaf. Later they all said they could hear the mysterious musical note, not with their ears but with every cell in their bodies.

After several minutes had passed, they noticed that the waters of the ocean were receding. Where a moment before the waters had been hugely tossing, it was now dry land, and that place where the water met the land now seemed several miles away. The thick billows of clouds of the hurricane wall rose thirty thousand feet into the early evening sky and came down to a hundred feet above the surface of the ocean; the ceiling of clouds remained in place as the level of the ocean fell, so soon they had a view—beneath the storm—of the floor of the ocean, which was now dry land as far as they could see, and they say they saw before them a fantastic canyon cut into the floor of the ocean, which in the distance got deeper and deeper as well as wider; and they say they saw far off between the walls of the canyon a brilliant orange moon, *they insist they saw the moonrise*, that it bathed them in orange light, that the canyon floor and the bridge were bathed in orange light. And that it took several minutes before the glowing moon slipped up behind that whirling wall of cloud that by then was fast approaching. In sudden pitch darkness and wind they scrambled into the rooms at the base of the tower, and locked the doors tight.

And every one of those hundred survived it, the wave.

A Balkan Entertainment:
The Man Behind the Scene

For Margradel Hicks

He was an operator. He traveled frequently between Belgrade and Sofia, to Prague and Bucharest, and he was familiar with the famous, but nobody knew him.

He got things done. He arranged things. He knew criminals, he knew officials, he knew how to "fix" things. He was a specialist at covering up the mistakes of Managers. He was a murderer and practiced extortion and acted as middleman in dealings with stolen goods.

He carried eminent credentials, but he frequently changed them. He was known to different men by different names. Though he had encountered the Soviet Secret Police many times, he baffled them. Neither the police nor public knew his nefarious part in those multifarious plots — he was always the man behind the scene.

Since his youth he had loved the sport of racing camels.

One of his more respectable roles — it was more like his hobby, a relaxation from his more deadly endeavors — was being Commissar of Camel Farms in Eastern Bulgaria on the sands; at the immense State Farm he had lavish quarters and a stable of racing camels for his private use, and a swimming pool. His butlers were bodyguards. His accountants were forgers, and they kept the books at the farm impeccably — the place always showed a profit — so that his superiors in Sofia never had cause to investigate him, or to question the way he ran the place. And he was truly proud of his animals, who frequently won prizes in foreign fairs in Turkey, Egypt, Arabia and India, and abroad brought the Motherland much admiration.

It would be a slur to suggest that thieves in Communist countries are less intelligent or less successful than their American or European counterparts. As many shops are robbed in Moscow as in New York, Soviet safecrackers are as "cool with their soup," as many priceless paintings vanish from their museums, Soviet embezzlers are no less daring, vast frauds are successfully perpetrated — but these dramatic events are not reported in the daily press or the popular magazines.

His fingers were in many pies filled with the fruits of crime.

He had connections everywhere, and if there was anything he knew how to do, it was how to pull strings, to force people to do things, as often as not, things they'd never dream of doing.

So that when he sent out invitations to twenty very prominent individuals to come to the farm on a summer afternoon to witness a demonstration of camel riding like they'd never seen before, those people came.

They came in limousines. They flew in from Moscow, and some from Warsaw and East Berlin. The premier of Yugoslavia came accompanied by his country's finance minister, and they looked vexed and pale, their eyes protruding wildly as if they had not slept. A very holy man, the Patriarch of Constantinople, flew in from Istanbul with a look of hope on his face. A Chinese magician was there, a man revered by professional conjurers and stage magicians, and famous for his animal illusions. An eminent physicist came from Siberia. The museums of the Soviet Union were well represented, an elegant, bespectacled bunch. There was also a giant baboon on a chain; it is uncertain where he came from or what he represented, but by his side stood the crackerjack reporter from *Pravda*, talking to the man from *Tass* and the senior editor of *Izvestia*.

There they all were on the dot at noon at the start of a straight fifty-yard racetrack. This is the traditional length and shape of the camel-racing track. On the track itself was a huge table.

With athletic grace the operator leaped atop the table and addressed the notables, saying, "Gentlemen, I have invited you here to witness a demonstration of camel riding. I am going to ride a camel once down this track, and I want you to watch me. Of all my accomplishments, I am most proud of the way I ride. All my life I've been the man behind the scene, but recently I've discovered that at heart I am a show-off. After today I shall never again engage in behind-the-scenes activity. Today you will witness that I change my way of life. Today I shall be a show-off."

"First I shall show you my wealth (I am a multimillionaire) and the rare objects I have come to possess. And I make you a bargain! If I put these things into your hands—then you must not be overwhelmed, then for five minutes you must turn away from these treasures, then you must watch me ride! After that you may do what you will with what you see …."

And out walked what was probably the prettiest camel in the whole world.

Undoubtedly it was the prettiest camel in Bulgaria. It was led to the table, and the notables noted that it was cleverly laden with bundles. In a moment attendants unloaded the camel, spreading out boxes, briefcases, and unusual objects along the table. The attendants opened the boxes and half-spilled their contents of cash, gold, and jewels onto the table.

Strangely, it was the most timid man in that whole group who was the first to speak. He was chief of the rare manuscripts division of the Leningrad Library, he had found a manuscript on the table, and once he started talking there was no stopping him—"His lost play! His last play! The only copy! Look! Printed out in capitals and underlined twice, it says—

FINAL SCRIPT
(corrected by the author)

"And it's signed William Shakespear!" shouted the librarian, wagging the manuscript in the air. "Look at the way he spells his name! Look at the way he spells his name! Twenty years ago it was found in the stacks and that afternoon scholars pronounced it genuine, but by evening it had vanished. (We were warned by the authorities never to speak of it; the theft was hushed up.) But this is that manuscript! Look, everyone! The front page bears the stamp of the Leningrad Library! This is our book and it's been kept out too long, this play is long overdue . . . . Why, the first performance of Shakespear's last play shall be given in Moscow! Then perhaps it could be taken to London . . . and later to New York . . . for this play belongs to the whole world!"

"But this manuscript," he added, "belongs to the Leningrad Library."

The truth is that no one there heard a word this man had said, for each had found something separate on which to rivet his attention.

The museum fellows each had found a long-lost painting, and had anyone been listening, they might have been heard to whisper, each to each, "Our van Eyck!—Our Vermeer!—Our Velásquez!—Our Monet!"

Another whispered, "The Treasures of Troy!"

The premier and his finance minister found a bulky briefcase, took one look in it, and snapped it shut, and each got a grip on the handle and stared hard into the eyes of the other. The bag contained practically the whole treasury of Yugoslavia in foreign negotiable securities. But of all the objects on the table it is possible that the most valued was the splinter of wood about three inches long at which the Patriarch stared, startled and awe-struck. He moved toward the table so cautiously, so quietly, yet with such intensity, such was his curiosity, that the whole group finally turned to watch him, hand outstretched, hesitate to touch the splinter. It was just an old piece of wood, but it looked very, very old.

The old man touched the fragment of wood, and he smiled.

Everybody saw it—his face radiated happiness.

Whatever it was the old man hoped to find there, he had found it.

He looked up at the operator, who was still standing on the table, and he asked, "What *else* can you show us?"

"*This!*" answered the operator, and he held between two fingers a tiny object, brilliant lemon-yellow and strangely shaped. "We must now go to the other end of the racetrack," he told them. "You will be better able to view me riding my camel from there."

The operator leaped off the table and took a few steps toward three open limousines, and the chauffeurs started the motors.

"But what is that you have in your hand?" several of them asked. Obviously none of them knew what it was.

But the Patriarch said, "Young man . . . is that object in your hand something used in the game of golf? Is that not, in fact, a golf tee?"

"Golf! Golf! What is that?" asked those eminent men of one another. That golf tee mystified them, and fascinated them, for you understand, there is not a single golf course in the whole of the Soviet Union.

"Follow me," said the operator, holding the golf tee aloft so that they could all see it. "And leave my things there on the table. After you watch me ride, then you can do what you will with all that you see."

The group entered the limousines and were driven to the other end of the track to the finish line.

"Notice," said the operator, "that a tiny hole has been drilled down through the center of the golf tee, and now look at this."

He held in his other hand a short darning needle, and he dropped it into the hole so that the eye of the needle protruded over the top of the tee. And from a chauffeur he procured two magnifying glasses, which he presented to the magician and the physicist.

"Would you kindly assist me," he asked them. "Would you examine this needle, especially the inside of the eye, and notice that it is clean and unmarked." They did this. And after pressing the golf tee into the ground on the racetrack's finish line so that the top of the tee was just level with the surface of the track, he told the two, "When I finish my ride, without touching the needle, would you please examine it again."

And now he addressed them all. "You may wonder why I became a millionaire in the Soviet Union. If you ask a mountain climber why he climbs a mountain, he will answer: Because it is there, because it is possible. And that is why a criminal becomes a millionaire, because it is possible, that is all. And now I shall ride . . . . Drive me to the start of the track!" he directed a chauffeur, and he stepped onto the running board of a limousine and was driven back to where the camel stood.

From where they stood the spectators could see to their dismay that the attendants had put all the treasures back into the bundles and that the bundles were being thrown onto the camel.

The operator leaped onto the camel and held his arms out wide. Two attendants thrust into his hands two huge paintbrushes, and two more attendants held up two huge bowls filled with vermilion paint. He thrust the brushes into the bowls and swirled them around in the paint, and then shouted, "Go!"

Holding the brushes, his arms stretched wide, he rode with the reins in his teeth.

The camel got halfway down the track before the spectators noticed that unlike most objects as they approach us, the camel and its rider did not appear to be getting any larger. Indeed, by the time they were three-quarters of the way down the track it was quite clear that the camel was no larger than a Great Dane and the man was perhaps the size of a monkey. By the time they were five yards from the golf tee, the camel had shrunk to the size of a cat and the man was no bigger than a mouse. When last seen—a few feet in front of the tee—they were no bigger than an egg. And then they vanished, treasure and all.

The spectators looked at one another, while the magician and the physicist bent to examine the needle with their magnifying glasses. On the inside of the eye of the needle—one on either side—they found two dots of vermilion paint.

*

"I don't see why I was invited here," said the magician. "This was no stage trick."

"I don't understand why I was invited here," said the physicist. "This hocus-pocus is nothing a scientist would understand."

"I am sure what we saw was no hoax," said the Patriarch. "However, I feel I would be personally damned were I to proclaim it a miracle."

And the premier said that he would be damned if he was going to reveal that he had witnessed the entire treasury of Yugoslavia being stolen by a thief who rode off on a camel through the eye of a needle.

And it would soon be discovered that there were no camels at all on the farm, that during the previous month the men who worked here had taken all the camels abroad, never to be heard from again—*the man had stolen every camel in Bulgaria!*

Not a line has been published about it, and there is no record anywhere of this occurrence. Those men took a vow never to reveal even to their most intimate colleagues what they had seen with their own eyes. The whole thing was hushed up.

But of course they told their wives.

This report is merely the gossip of Belgrade.

If it had happened in America where they publish everything—Hah!—it would have been a different story.

The Adventure of the Giant Rat of Sumatra

A jar of olives in pitch darkness on the shelf of the restaurant kitchen in the small hours of the morning . . . the place closed and everyone gone . . . .

A large rat, fat and round as an olive, sat on its haunches on top of the jar.

It sniffed intently, and listened to the shrieking wind blowing a blinding blizzard into huge drifts. A 50-mile-an-hour wind in fifteen-below-zero weather boded death for the Traveler, and made even the restaurant kitchen unusually chilly, the water pipes having frozen, and there was ice in the sink.

High North Atlantic tides and the weather had forced the huge wharf rat to abandon its usual haunts—its nest was soaking wet—and seek shelter in this kitchen. He was a ten-year-old male from Sumatra three months off the ship from Rangoon, and it was his first experience of the Norwegian winter.

He sat on the olive jar and twitched his whiskers, and listened long, for surrounding him and coming at him from every direction was the odor of . . . cat. Two cats guarded this kitchen. For an hour the rat sat there in the dark, relatively warm, waiting quietly, and the rat heard no sound . . . except the wind, and in the distance the sloshing surf that had flooded his nest in the warehouse that faced the fjord.

A number of hours later, the owner of the restaurant entered the building with his wife. They discovered the kitchen in chaos, evidence that a fantastic fight had taken place, blood all over the place, and small bones in the middle of the floor that had been eaten clean.

"What's wrong with this cat?" asked the wife who had found one of her cats huddled in a dark corner trembling and mewing softly, whimpering in a state of shock. The old lady sensed that the cat was not even aware of her presence. "What could have frightened her so?" inquired the old lady.

"Whatever it was," answered her husband, kneeling and examining the pile of bones, "it ate the other cat."

2

Large tropical wharf rats are noted for their uncanny intelligence. There are many stories of a fabled cleverness at avoiding traps, and this rat was quite bright.

During his entire stay in Norway he was not seen by a single human being.

And one is tempted to assume it was his wharf-rat intelligence that caused him soon to climb a cable of a ship about to set to sea, no doubt with a notion to return to Sumatra and warm sunshine.

The rat obviously couldn't understand Norwegian or he would have heard the sailors talking, and known that this ship — it was the ill-fated *Matilda Briggs* — housed an Arctic expedition.

Shortly thereafter the ship entered the pack ice, the ship became frozen in the ice, and the men huddled in the icy boat barely clinging to life as hopeless months passed and their provisions eventually gave out.

The rat's whiskers quivered with cold, and his eyebrows froze.

The leader of the expedition, with three others, set off on foot across the pack ice with the intention of bringing back help for those who stayed inside the meager shelter of the ship; and of course they succeeded: they brought back help, and a number of those who had waited, suffering in the ship, survived.

Among those who survived was an old English seaman, not an officer or anything — an old salt. On his first day in a civilized port, as he sat in a fancy tavern eating kidney pie, he was interviewed by an English journalist, a lady.

"Did the men pray?" asked the journalist.

"God *answered* my prayer!" said the seaman seriously.

"It was a bloody miracle . . . about the rat!"

"What do you mean?" asked the journalist.

"There was a tropical wharf rat aboard, and I was determined to catch it. Many, many months I tried. I'm handy with tools, and I built a half-a-dozen traps, each more ingenious than the last. The men said I was mad, they said I was obsessed with catching the rat . . . but in the end they admitted I wasn't crazy. You see, it saved our lives. I'll never forget: it was in the middle of an endless night, the party had left on foot four months before . . . . Finally, in desperation, I got up on the kitchen table so that the other sailors could see me, and I knceled and clasped my hands, and I said out loud so that all could hear—I prayed to God that I would catch the rat. And at that moment . . . so that all could hear it, there was a loud click, the sound of my trap snapping shut. I had caught the rat alive. If ever there was one of God's creatures who was at the right place at the right time, it was that rat in my trap. After that we all knew that God was with us, was with us in the very room."

"You caught the rat . . . I see . . . ," said the bewildered lady. And then she added, frowning heavily, "But what did you do with the rat?"

"We ate it," said the seaman. "Tasted like Chinese food. He was a remarkably healthy animal. Can't figure out what he ever found to eat on the ship, but he was round and fat as an olive."

"Did you like the taste?" asked the lady.

He looked sharply at her, for how could she know how many traps he had contrived, what a battle of wits it had become, the wharf-rat intelligence at avoiding traps pitted against the human intelligence of the animal trapper. But the trapper, the human, had finally won out; after many months in an endless night the human brain surpassed the wharf-rat brain . . . with a little help from God . . . and how could this poor lady understand that satisfaction? Grinning broadly, he said, "Like Chinese food—it was delicious!"

3

Yet what does an old sailor know of the world?

What can he know of the life of the English journalist? Would it surprise him that a journalist would think nothing of eating a few mice on an afternoon?

Let us follow this lady as she leaves the restaurant and notice how, at the nearest garbage can, she disposes of her notes, and now as she enters a rather shabby deserted street along the waterfront she removes her pearls and rings, throwing these, along with her pocketbook, into another refuse can. Now her journey takes an unexpected turn as she slips between two abandoned buildings, and in those darkest shadows—is she taking off her clothes?

Now out of those darkest shadows comes a cat.

A skinny tomcat, all sinew and bone.

He pauses a moment and goes beneath a fence and now down deserted passageways, now through a broken basement window into what some might call a cozy apartment, though somewhat messy, and smelling strongly of pipe tobacco and chemicals.

A rather large, comfortable old gray cat who had been napping, stirred and said, "Eh! What! Is that you, Holmes? Where the devil have you been?"

"Watson, my good fellow! Don't bother getting up! I've been disguised as a lady journalist, and I've had an enlightening conversation with a sailor, and he told me everything I wanted to know. Watson, do you recall several years ago in a Norwegian port there was a brutal murder, and I said I would not rest until I knew the fiend had gotten his just deserts?"

"You mean the waterfront restaurant murder! Two cats, sisters, I believe . . . lived alone in the restaurant. One found brutally murdered, and *eaten*, and the other left a raving lunatic! A hideous business!"

"And do you recall, Watson, that I found at the scene of the crime a hair from a large wharf rat that had lived in Sumatra and come to Norway by ship from Rangoon? I learned that here in my laboratory from studying the hair. I could find no witness, neither cat nor human, who had seen such a rat in the vicinity. Yet I knew he had been there, and after a while I realized he had escaped. I studied the shipping lists, and the only boat he could have left on was the *Matilda Briggs*, Arctic bound. Well at long last, Watson, the ship has returned, and today I got positive proof that a rat fitting that description was indeed aboard, and was caught alive, and then eaten by the crew. So though no one in Norway ever once laid eyes on the murderer, even so, he is discovered and dead; he got his just deserts. Justice was served. I think we can call that case closed."

4

The gray cat fumbled with a key held awkwardly in his paw, trying to open his desk.

"Watson, allow me to assist you with that," said Holmes, easily opening the recalcitrant drawer, which held the famous files kept by Dr. Watson on the cases of Sherlock Holmes. "Watson, sometimes I think you're ambisinistrous," chided the great detective.

Watson blushed. "I was thinking of something else! Damnation about the key — I had an idea! The title! Imagine this in large letters in my Table of Contents: The Adventure of the GIANT RAT OF SUMATRA . . . . What do you think?"

"Watson, old friend, the world is not ready for this tale. You must not publish it."

"What's that you say! Not publish it! Tosh! Certainly I'll publish it, it's one of your greatest triumphs!"

"Confound it, Watson! Don't you see? You'll be revealing the Secret of Literature, and the world isn't ready for it. Especially the publishing world isn't ready for the Secret of Literature. There is no way you can tell the story without revealing that you and I are Conan Doyle's cats. When an author's cat wishes to dress up and act like a man, he becomes a character in a book, and in fiction no one can discern that we are not regular people. But it must remain secret! The publishing world—those editors, those critics, those literary agents of whom I know you are so fond—would be dismayed, Watson, *deeply* dismayed to learn you are a cat, that Lady Chatterley, Bloom, Scrooge, Robinson Crusoe, and Moby Dick himself were all cats! Cats all! And your friends . . . unquestionably . . . would grow to feel queer about their work . . . .

"Good Doctor Watson, don't you see? The Adventure of the GIANT RAT OF SUMATRA must never be published . . . ever. I, Sherlock Holmes, forbid it!"

The Frog

A frog that became addicted to morphine during experiments at the Federal hospital at Lexington, Kentucky, fell into my hands at the conclusion of their experiments. As a frog, he was a wreck. Unless he had morphine, he wouldn't eat or even look at a fly. I kept him as a pet and gave him a name, but it became rather a problem supplying him with morphine. Being merely a laboratory assistant and not a doctor or even a nurse, I had no access to the drug, which many doctors here are studying, attempting to discover a cure for human addicts.

However, I'd gotten to like him. He was a full-grown bullfrog, slimy and green, and I kept him in a fishtank cage in my room, which was on the grounds of the hospital in a building occupied by laboratory assistants, nurses' aides, and kitchen workers. All the fellows on the floor became fond of his voice. Ordinarily I believe frogs croak only in the evening, but our frog would begin to croak whenever he needed a fix. It was a mellow beautiful belch, mellifluous, euphonious, and strong, and I might add, very male, not as loud, but not unlike the bellow of a bull from a hilltop.

I'd been to the dentist several months previously, and I had some pills for pain, which I had never used, stuck away in my dresser drawer. I crushed them and added a little bit to his water, and he gulped it right down and was quiet. Because a frog doesn't weigh much, it doesn't take very much of an opiate to be effective, and by careful division of the dosage, the white powder I had made from my pills lasted several weeks.

A baker from the hospital kitchen whose room was down the hall from mine next furnished me with some cough medicine which had been prescribed for a throat infection. Actually he shared the medicine with the frog every day, depriving himself so the frog wouldn't get sick. But the baker got well, his hacking cough abated, and my frog was out of opiate again.

He croaked all night.

I wasn't sleeping myself, and about 3 a.m. I heard a slight noise outside my door. As I glanced in that direction, I saw a glassene envelope being slid under my door. I got out of bed and opened the door, but whoever had done it had vanished. Inside the envelope was — Lord knows what it really was, perhaps it was actually heroin, but more probably it was medicine someone had snitched from one of the wards. Anyway, it worked. I put a tiny fraction of it in his water and he gulped it eagerly, and then stared at me with a long grateful look. The pupils of his eyes were like pinpoints. Soon he closed his eyes and rested contentedly, though I doubt he slept. But everyone on our floor finally did.

He was a swell frog.

Everyone on the floor was familiar with his medical history and was discreet about his problem for otherwise I think I might have gotten into trouble if any of the staff nurses or doctors had discovered what I was doing.

Only men lived in our building but on weekend afternoons we were allowed to have female visitors in our rooms and frequently these guests were brought in to meet my frog.

He was our mascot.

One afternoon a laboratory assistant with whom I often worked, and who was a friend, was visited by his two teenage sisters, and he brought them into my room. They made a big fuss over the frog and one of them insisted on holding it in her hands. She was a terribly pretty young thing. She didn't mind that it was wet and she insisted on giving him some medicine herself. The frog was quite content and seemed almost especially friendly. He sat there in her hands as if he liked it. I had left the room for a minute, leaving the two girls and my friend and the frog in my room, when suddenly I heard what sounded like a peal of thunder and a brilliant light flooded the hallway, emitted from my room. I rushed into the room and saw a stranger standing there, a tall Italian-looking guy.

"What happened? And what are you doing in my room?" I demanded of the stranger. I gave a quick glance at the scene and added, "And what happened to my frog?"

The girl answered, "I kissed the frog — and this man appeared in a big flash of light."

"Allow me to introduce myself," volunteered the stranger to the girl. "I am Prince . . . ." and he rattled off some Italian name which I couldn't make out. He continued, "Many years ago I was transformed into a frog, to remain one until I should be kissed by a maiden. My dear, will you become my wife? I know where there is a great treasure, and you shall live in a palace, among beautiful fountains and great old trees where the weather is always like summer. Will you be my wife?"

The sweet child's lip curled into a sneer, and her eyes opened wide with astonishment. She answered, "You think I would marry a junkie? Never!"

"In that case, my friends, I bid you good day. My best wishes to you all—good-bye forever." And so saying, he stepped out the window, and I never saw him again.

I have since decided he was a burglar and that he stole my frog, because I never saw my frog again either.

It is true, however, that a couple of years later my friend, the laboratory assistant with whom I often work, showed me a picture on the society page of a New York newspaper. He said, "Look! There's that burglar who stole your frog!"

It is true there was a remarkable resemblance. It was a photograph of a princess of the Netherlands with an Italian prince, and they were soon to be married.

But you know how newspaper photographs are.

I don't think it was the same person.

I told my brother-in-law not to mention it because my wife likes to kid me about how she might have married a prince, and so I didn't even bother showing her that photograph.

...certif...
...miento, y re...
que tenía 47 años más
de lo que él creía. Ade-
más, según la certifica-
ción del Registro, había
nacido cuatro años an-
tes que su padre.

INMORTALIDAD

"La inmortalidad no
es deseable para el hom-
bre —dice Albert Eins-
tein—. La vida eterna
solamente conviene a las
piedras".

EXCESOS

De Jacques Decrest,
fallecido recientemente:
"A fuerza de purismo,
se termina por escribir
mal; por exceso de pe-
reza, se termina agota-
do".

Immortality, Circa 1954

Author's note: *History quickly overtook this story, and it was never published. Sputnik, the first object put into orbit, went up in 1957. When I wrote this story in 1954 I was living in the mountains of southern Mexico. I put the story into an envelope addressed to Albert Einstein, Institute for Advanced Studies, Princeton, NJ, USA, with a note saying — Sir, I am a writer of fiction, and last week I wrote this story, which I enclose because I think you will enjoy it — I never received an answer. However, three weeks later in perusing the Mexico City Sunday newspaper and in a column of quotations from around the world each no more than a paragraph, I saw one of those squibs was headed in boldface INMORTALIDAD. Hey, that's my title! I said and was fascinated to read further.*

INMORTALIDAD

"La inmortalidad no es
deseable para el hom-
bre — dice Albert Eins-
tein —. La vida eterna
solamente conviene a las
piedras."

Or roughly: "Immortality is not necessary for man," says Albert Einstein. "Eternal life is only suitable for the rocks."

1

The great scientist died.

He left a great will.

Documents of his life, historic scientific papers, the manuscripts of speeches, and a few fine musical instruments were bequeathed properly for the furtherance of astronomy, Israel and the arts; one terse sentence gave direction for his funeral — he said he wanted to be buried in space.

The General Assembly proclaimed a World Holiday.

Flocks of many-emblazoned Fighters escorted a refrigerated Flagship flying his body to Palmyra in the Pacific.

There a rocket was poised on its tail. It was silver, had twelve gold wings, red rings and green stripes with wartlike knobs and faucet handles; it hummed . . . .

There flew the thousand most powerful and most famous to attend to the history-making, peculiar ceremony. They slept on the beach that night in army tents.

Overnight—a giant antenna rose.

In the morning Eliot read his *Elegy*; Stravinsky conducted his *Dirge*; the Pope, great Jews, Buddhists and Brahmans prayed; presidents, premiers, prime ministers and kings spoke; and at the appropriate time, when ordinarily he'd've b'n lowered into a grave, six mysterious international figures, pallbearers, placed his body into the missile; the director of the Princeton Institute for Advanced Studies pushed the button: an immense cloud of blue smoke gathered; a roar from fantastic motors shook the air around radios from France to Shanghai; battleships bobbed nearby; faraway seismographs quivered; the World took off its Hat—and out of the smoke the rocket bolted like a blazing blasted beast past Pacific birds—breaking for space—bearing the scientist.

The rocket rolled through the stratosphere and at its height a second shell shot from inside it out—

Higher yet, a third missile broke away, and the second shell broke asunder and fell.

The last thing shot Outward was the man . . . naked.

2

When the huge numbrous cloud of radioactive blue smoke cleared, Palmyra was sterile, all flora and fauna perished, all objects vanished, and sand to a depth of 13 meters congealed to cobalt blue glass.

3

The funeral was greater than at Giza.

The force with which he soared away equaled exactly the gravity holding him back; so the body swung into an orbit around the Earth.

As he will be traveling in vacuum there will be no deterioration of his flesh, ever; a million years from now, when perhaps some new species has become dominant here, his body still will circle round the Earth.

And in the future, young scientists learning to use the telescope will practice sighting him, and predicting his orbit.

Calendars will have a mark: there will be there, with the phases of the moon, and eclipses, with Christmas, Thanksgiving, Easter — the day — and Exact Time when anyone with ordinary field glasses can look up and watch the great scientist float across the face of the full moon.

The Language of Cats

Once upon a time there was a gentleman.

He was a scientist. There were letters after his name.

He spoke a hundred languages, from Iroquois to Esperanto.

He was the author of several little papers on astral mathematics.

He was thirty-five, authoritative, and quiet-spoken.

His hobby was playing chess on a three-dimensional board.

His job was the most dramatic known to scholarship, and the most hectic. He was hired by the armed forces to break codes and during the war had done brilliant work, going days without sleep. The generals were awed by him because several times, they said, he had literally saved the war by breaking the enemy's master codes. And indeed, that means he saved the world.

But for the life of him he couldn't remember to put cigarettes in ashtrays, so all the furniture was scarred with little brown burns.

His wife was blond and small and thin and was a very neat housekeeper.

He drove her to distraction.

He was constantly making messes all over the house, eating in the living room, leaving his socks in the middle of the floor, his shoes on the windowsill; and flames, every once in a while, would burst from a wastepaper basket from an unextinguished butt, but luckily their house still stood.

He turned his wife into a nagger.

She'd shout at him ten times a day until finally he could stand it no longer; he could not, would not, argue with her about such trivialities; his mind was filled with formulas and figures and strange words from ancient languages, and besides, he was a gentleman.

One day he left her. He packed his bags and moved into a cottage nearby in West Virginia with a Siamese cat.

2

The cat hypnotized him.

It was a beautiful blue-point Siamese. It talked a lot; that is, it meowed, meowed, meowed, meowed all the time.

He'd sit on his bed and stare at it for hours while it stalked cellophane balls, bounced from bed to dresser, then to the sink, to the floor, and then back again and again to the bed.

Every once in a while, it would give the air a bat.

Suddenly it would stop and sleep.

He'd sit and stare at it, the pale gray, gently breathing ball of fur, and his thoughts would ramble over the dissatisfactions of his life.

Voltaire had once said he despised all professions which owed their sole existence to the spitefulness of men. Certainly his was such.

He had lost all interest in his friends, and women. He found most people shallow and vulgar.

Some evenings he made the rounds of the bars as if looking for someone, without the success, ever, of even getting drunk. Books put him to sleep.

And finally the cat became the center of his life, his sole companion.

One evening, as he sat staring at it, he developed a peculiar desire.

He wanted to communicate with it.

He decided to conduct some experiments.

So he lined the walls of his garage with a thousand little cages and placed a cat in every cage. Most of the cats he bought, others he just picked up off the street, and some he even stole from casual friends, so possessed was this scientist by his scheme.

On a tape recorder he began collecting all the cat sounds.

He recorded their howls of hunger, distinguishing those that wanted tuna fish from those that wanted salmon. Some wanted lung, liver, or fowl. And all these sounds he filed systematically in his growing record library.

He carefully compared the shriek when a *right* front foot was being amputated to that made when a *left* front leg was being cut.

He recorded all the sounds they made when mating, fighting, dying, and giving birth.

Then he quit his government job and began to study in earnest the thousands of shrieks and caterwauls he had recorded, and after a while the sounds began to make sense.

Then he began to practice, mimicking his records until he mastered the basic vocabulary of the language.

Toward the end, he practiced purring.

He had never experimented on his own cat. He wanted to surprise it.

One evening he walked into his apartment, hung his coat in the closet as usual, turned to his cat, and said, "MEOW!"

3

This was the way cats said "Good evening" when meeting.

But the cat did not seem surprised.

The cat answered, "Mrrrrowrow!" which meant, "It's about time!"

The cat gave him to understand that it would tutor him in the more complex subtleties of the language, that it was well informed of all his experiments, and that, if he did not pay attention to his lessons, the man would be Mrowr—sorry!

As the weeks went by, the man discovered to his continual amazement the fantastic intelligence of his Siamese cat.

Bit by bit, he learned the history of the cats.

Thousands of years ago, the cats had a tremendous civilization; they had a world government which worked perfectly; they had spaceships and had investigated the universe; they had great power plants that utilized an energy which was not atomic; they had no need of radios or television, for they used some sort of mental telepathy; and some other wonders.

But one thing the cats discovered eventually was that the importance of any experience depended on the intensity with which it was felt.

They realized their civilization had grown too complex, so they decided to simplify their lives.

Of course, they didn't want to just "go back to nature"—that would have been too much—so they created a race of robots to take care of them.

These robots were an improvement mechanically over anything nature had produced.

A couple of their greatest inventions were the "opposable thumb" and the "erect posture."

They didn't want to bother about fixing the robots when they broke down so they gave them an elementary intelligence and the power to reproduce.

Of course, we are the robots to which the cat referred.

And now the scientist understood why cats had always seemed so contemptuous of their masters.

The cat explained that cats were not afraid of death; indeed they led constantly passionate and heroic lives, and when properly prepared, when their time came, they welcomed death.

But they did not want *an atomic death.*

And the robots had developed a mean and irrational attitude toward *mice.*

"It occurred to us to merely wipe the race out, but then we'd have to go to all the trouble of making a new one," said the cat (in his own way, of course), "so we decided to try a thing which, frankly, many cats thought would be impossible—to *wit:* teaching a robot how to talk cat language so he could transmit our orders to the world!

"We chose you," said the cat in a condescending way, as perhaps our scientists would speak to a monkey whom they had taught to talk, "because of all the robots you seemed most promising and receptive and the foremost authority in your little field."

The cat gave the man a list of rules, which he copied on a slip of paper.

The rules were:

DO NOT KICK CATS
NO ATOMIC WARS
NO MOUSETRAPS
KILL THE DOGS

"If the world does not obey these rules, we will simply eliminate the race," said the cat, and then closed his eyes and yawned and stretched and promptly went to sleep.

"Wait a minute! Wake up! Please!" pleaded the man timidly, touching the cat on the forehead.

"Let me sleep!" growled the cat. "You have your job. Get going!"

"But I can't just take these rules to people and say some cat told me. Nobody would believe me!"

The cat frowned and said, "Suppose we give you a little demonstration of our power? Then people will believe this isn't just a joke. A week from today I'll have some cats go through Moscow and Washington spraying a gas which will drive everybody insane for twenty-four hours. The gas will release all their destructive impulses. They won't hurt each other, but they will destroy everything they can get their hands on, all the buildings, bridges, public works, all the documents, and even all their clothes."

Then the cat yawned again, and went back to sleep.

The man, with the slip of rules in his hand, walked out into the streets to do as he had been told, but first—and he hardly knew what he was doing—strange mischief lit his eyes as he thought of his neighbors. He opened the thousand cages.

4

An October breeze hit him in the face, flame-colored leaves crunched beneath his feet, the setting sun reddened everything with its final gorgeous rays, the street noises rushed into his ears as in a dream, and a Good Humor bell was tinkling pathetically at the approach of the black night and of winter, or so it seemed to him as he walked, dazed by the tremendous responsibility he had been given, his mind whirling in great circles, desperately finding poetry and beauty in the cracks on the sidewalk, in the stripes on the barbershop poles, in the snatches of young girls' conversations which he heard as he passed by them, in the outrageous odors of garbage cans, in the whole of the city scene which he had never really noticed, had walked through blindly before, his eyes turned inward on his work, but which now he gulped in with gladdened earnestness—but to escape! to escape his fantastic duty to the world he lost himself in all its beauties; but this new world he saw was seen by others, I'm sure, who were in very different situations, and as it is this strange world he saw which I am trying to describe, I shall digress a moment: Imagine a child in England, a couple of centuries ago, who had stolen a loaf of bread or a handkerchief or a half-crown and whom some stern and stupid judge had sent to prison, to grow into manhood in prison, never knowing the softness of a woman, never knowing a meal given with love, or never tasting candy, never seeing a show, or any of our most common pleasures—on his release we can easily imagine his awe, delight, and terror, his great yearning to touch each girl he meets, his need for patient love and endless explanations (for he would understand almost nothing of our free world) and that, not finding a person with such patience, he would soon be back in prison – but all that's beside the point – the point is that the world of this scientist escaping his responsibility and the world of the young man just rudely vomited from a prison would *look* the same; and so to understand how this October night appeared through his daze and confusion – imagine how the world would appear to a person after finishing such a ridiculously lengthy, pointless sentence.

5

The lights began to twinkle on as the darkness descended.

A cream-colored convertible, in which four drunken high-school boys were singing happily and shouting lustily at pedestrians, suddenly swerved off the road and cut the top off a fire hydrant, threw two of the boys through a jewelry store window, threw one of them twenty feet into the air so he landed flat on his back on the pavement, and left the other, the only survivor, moaning miserably with broken ribs against the steering wheel; flames burst from under the hood of the twisted wreck, which had stopped abruptly over the broken hydrant; the gushing water drenched the back of the car, but left the flaming front untouched.

An excited crowd began to gather around the catastrophe, hungrily devouring the spectacle.

The scientist, who was on the other side of the street, a witness to the whole accident, saw it as if it were a movie accident, and continued his aimless dreamy meandering; and he was clutching the slip of rules tightly in his fist, though he was not even aware of it, so lost was he in the beautiful movements, lights, and noises of the city.

Though he still walked, his mind turned itself inward again, and he wondered whom on earth he could take these rules to – he didn't know the President, and anyone in authority to whom he spoke would certainly laugh.

He pondered the problem for a long time.

He looked out at the world again and discovered to his surprise that he was in front of his old house.

The lights were on. He had not communicated with his wife since the day he had left. He walked down the narrow path and entered the house without knocking, from habit, as he had always done.

His wife had her hat on.

"You get out of here!" she screamed. "I have a date! I don't ever want to see you again!"

The scientist looked around at his old house. Everything was the same. The furniture was even arranged in the same precise, neat way.

The furniture! It was this furniture that had been the cause of their breaking up. She had loved her furniture more than she had loved him.

He picked up a vase. She loved this vase more than she had loved him. He threw it against the wall.

Smash!

His wife screamed.

Next this antique chair of which she was so fond.

Smash!

It broke into three pieces.

He threw the lamp out the window.

Crash!

"Stop it!" screamed his wife. "Are you crazy?"

He went into the kitchen and got a knife, throwing some ashtrays on the floor and tipping over the bookcase on the way, and began to rip the overstuffed chairs.

"Stop it! Stop it!" screamed his wife, now hysterical and weeping.

But the scientist hardly heard her. He was ripping, smashing, tearing, destroying utterly, utterly demolishing, in a frenzy of rage more overpowering than her tears, every piece of furniture in the house.

Then he stopped.

And she stopped crying.

Their eyes met and they fell toward each other, in love more than ever before.

The violent scene had somehow changed them both. The man's eyes were now clear, and his brow had lost its heaviness. Her voice was soft and warm.

Then the man remembered the cats, and what they were going to do.

"Look!" said her husband. "Let's get out of Washington for a while. Let's go on a second honeymoon. Let's take the car and go out west to the mountains and just get away from everybody and everything. We'll find some wilderness and live there. Now don't ask any questions. Just do as I say."

She did as he said, and an hour later they were driving westward out of Washington.

"Darling!" said his wife suddenly. "We'll have to go back."

"Why?"

"Didn't you have a Siamese cat in your cottage? He'll starve. You can't just leave him locked in there. And if we go back, you can pick up some of your clothes. It seems silly to buy new ones when all we have to do is go back to the cottage."

"Look!" said her husband, pressing his foot on the gas. "That cat can take care of itself!"

6

Driving in shifts, it took them three and a half days to reach the edge of the mountains, where they bought a rifle, knapsacks, sleeping bags, cooking utensils, and all the paraphernalia they would need to live away from civilization for a while. They began their journey on foot, sweating and groaning under the weight of their knapsacks.

They did not see another human being for a couple of months.

But once, when they were walking a short distance from their camp, they met a wildcat.

The wildcat snarled menacingly.

The man had left his rifle at the camp.

The wildcat was between them and their camp.

So the scientist pushed his wife behind him and began to snarl and meerrroooww.

For several minutes they spoke, and then the wildcat turned and ran off.

"Darling, what were you doing? You sounded as if you were actually talking to that wildcat."

And so the man told her the whole story of how he had learned to speak the language of the cats, and that now probably Washington and Moscow were in ruins, and soon the whole human race would be destroyed.

He explained that it had just been too much. The human race was not worth it. And so he had decided to get away from everything and get what little happiness he could out of these last few remaining days.

"I have no idea how or when the cats will destroy us, but they will, for they have powers we could never imagine," and his voice trailed off in sorrow. She took his hand, and they walked slowly to their camp.

Now she understood his flashing eyes, and this new energy he'd gotten, his new youthfulness—his madness was becoming apparent to her—and she found it strange that, even so, she loved him more now than ever before.

<h1 style="text-align:center">7</h1>

A couple of weeks later, they were sitting around their campfire. Snow surrounded them, and while the scientist stared silently at the stars, the woman grew cold and began to shiver. Finally she got up and began to pace back and forth.

"What date is today?"

"I don't know," answered the man absently.

"It must be around Christmas," she said.

The man glanced at her sharply and then grew thoughtful. A few minutes later he leaped to his feet and shouted. "What was that? I heard sounds!"

His wife listened for a moment, and answered, "I didn't hear anything."

"Listen! There it is again! It's like horses' hooves!"

"But darling. I don't hear anything."

"Well, I'm going out and see who it is!" said her husband determinedly.

And he walked out into the blackness.

His wife heard him talking, loudly, as if to someone, but she heard no other voices. She called out to him, "Darling, who's out there? Who are you talking to?"

He shouted back, "Oh, it's all right. It's just Santa Claus. Those were his reindeer we heard."

His wife said sadly to herself, "There's no point in telling him there is no Santa Claus."

8

He came back with a green plant, a cactus, which he had obviously just picked from the snow, and with a grand, old-world bow, handed it to her, saying, "Santa Claus gave this to me to give to you for your Christmas present. He came all the way out here, just so you wouldn't spend Christmas without a present."

She took the plant in her hands and moved nearer to the fire. These bursts of madness frightened her, or was he joking? Or was he being gallant? She looked up at him, staring out across the mountain ranges again, at those faraway stars. How noble and insane he looked. But then terror touched her again, and she said, rather timidly, "You know, dear, back there at the house—when you got so angry—it was very good of you not to hit me."

He looked over at her a moment, a little annoyed, but he was silent, and returned his gaze to the horizon.

"But then," she added, "I needn't have worried. You're such a gentleman."

9

They returned to civilization shortly after that.

Moscow and Washington were not in ruins.

And, much to his wife's surprise, it turned out her husband was not insane—the lunatic was that Siamese cat. They discovered the cat's corpse at the cottage—dead from starvation.

For there is a language of the cats, but all Siamese cats are crazy—always talking about mental telepathy, cosmic powers, fabulous treasures, spaceships, and great civilizations of the past, but it's all just meowing—they are impotent—just meows!

Meows!

Meows!

Meows!

Meows!

Meows . . . .

Pleasures of the Imagination
64 Beginnings

For Sally Gross

There are different kinds of writing. For instance, there's the kind of writing where you walk over to the typewriter, sit down, and write a first line. You go into the kitchen for a glass of water, light a cigarette, all the while thinking of what you've written. You return to the typewriter and write a second line, then you write a third line, and oh – all sorts of things happen, and there – you find you've written the last line, and if what you've written is any good, then it's all of a piece, as if the whole thing were implicit in the beginning.

As if you put your hand in the water and catch a fish by the tail.

However, there is a different kind of writing: you sit down at the typewriter, just as before, and write a beginning. But when it comes to writing more – nothing happens. You have many thoughts, your mind is aswim with phrases, but your hands don't move toward the keys. Finally, you begin again, and write a new first line.

I have a big old wire wastebasket which I never empty in which I put things that I think I might work more on, and over a number of years it's got chock full of beginnings, false starts, some might say – failures perhaps – but I've made a book of them, or what-you-might-call a book, of sixty-four examples of this nameless genre of writing. And I have given them names, just as if they were regular stories.

Sometimes I wonder whether there are real stories implicit in such first lines – you might say virtual stories, not unreal, but existing in some never-never realm not inaccessible perhaps to certain readers who do themselves indulge in the pleasures of the imagination . . . .

In London

In London yesterday a lorry lunged, sideswiped a fog light and plunged into the Thames. The plainclothesman who surreptitiously was following me broke cover, took a whistle from beneath his cloak and blasted the alarm, rushing to the embankment, abandoning me in the yellow fog.

The Miserable Ostrich

Walking down a desert road in a sandstorm, a six-foot ostrich with a painful broken toe staggered with the wind behind him, wagged his wings wildly each time his left foot touched the sand, until finally, for the first time in his life—indeed, for the first time in ten million years—the ostrich flew like an ordinary bird, rose two hundred feet into the air, soared for five minutes here and there . . . .

CROAK!

The red berries of Fall—each scarlet ball rebounds the colors of the call of the scarlet tanager. Green frog—CROAK!—the water lily on which he sits trembles, and a careful eye could see green rings radiate around it, startling a dozing dragonfly.

An iridescent insect walks by.

Gong

It's hard to hold a hammer with your arm in a sling while carrying a gong during the rush hour on the subway in Tokyo.

The Floodwaters

The floodwaters left a ring on the outside of the bathtub.

The Daymoon

A racing fog enveloped the ship for a number of minutes, a stinging mysterious mixture of mist and hail making haloes of rainbows around the golden white lights of the ship.

It is the boat of my dream! But this cold railing is no dream . . . .

Last night, while sleeping I dreamed that I looked across a bay, or perhaps it was a wide river, and I saw a large yacht, a streamlined boat with perhaps eight portholes along its side, and in my hands I held a miniature replica of the same boat. It was about a foot long. Somebody said, "It's the *Daymoon*."

The Opera Singer's Vacation

On her vacations the famous opera singer lived alone in a cottage on a small island where she practiced to her heart's delight, and she could be heard at all hours like a faraway bird by wild animals on the most distant shores of the Canadian lake, which lay at the bottom of an uninhabited valley.

The silence at the center of a becalmed lake is for her the most beautiful sound in the world.

The Arsonist at the Zoo

The poisonous orange salamander of Peru in its glass cage at the Staten Island Zoo attracted the gaze of the arsonist (wearing blue sneakers and carrying a rope in his belt), who had broken in at midnight to start a fire, but had become distracted from his insane design by the liveliness of the nocturnal animals; not that they were wild or especially noisy—they were merely awake and alert. The great cats were playing with their cubs, the raccoons were chasing each other, the primates played quiet games, and the place was alive with moving reptiles. After an hour he left without having started a fire, and he never returned to that scene of what could have been his greatest crime.

And he never set another fire, but he became a drunk, closing the bars each night and staggering home at dawn.

There is something about us, we who are nocturnal, that nobody can ever understand.

A Lady of London

That seer upstairs at her seances who got those ghosts going with their shrieks and moans and grisly sighs until it was hard for a body to think, and at all times of the night, and such early morning hours she kept with her blasted meetings, the little old lady of London! Thank god she's gone.

Coat of Arms

Once upon a time there was a coat of arms ... an extraordinary garment constructed by a tailor-lady out of old coats customers had left at her shop and never called for—the coat had twelve arms altogether, gathered in a circle at the top, so that when worn, five limp sleeves hung down in front like elephant trunks, and five hung down in back like a crazy cape.

The coat had no opening in front, it was slipped on like a sweater, and indeed it had no front, for the wearer could turn it whichever way he pleased, this time choosing the velvet sleeves, or the next time perhaps thrusting his arms into the tweed, or the black plaid.

The Flabbergasted Reader

The flabbergasted reader closed the book but held it in his hands, turning the book this way and that, studying the edges of the pages almost as if he were reading the title on the binding, all the while musing, pursing his lips, shifting his weight from one foot to the other, full of thoughts, he touched his forehead, and outside the summer-evening silence began to shimmer with the sweetly insistent sound of giant raindrops.

The Tornado of Snow

The brilliant white funnel of the tornado of snow dances atop an iceberg, vividly undulating against a sky that is black and yellow and brown, while below in the bay a blue whale suddenly surfaces beneath a giant waterspout. The boat is bobbing so, I can hardly write . . . . I think it's my turn to row.

The Orchid Grower

The orchid grower looked like his plants. Strange purples and browns blotched his complexion on livid wattles, flesh suspended like ear lobes from his forehead and cheeks, sprinkled with light white moles. He lived in his greenhouse, a rather large complex of buildings, a veritable labyrinth of glass roofs and walls where for years he had conducted a successful business in tulips and dahlias — but his pride was his orchids.

The Celestial Sirens

Riding, being carried, lifted by a high wind a thousand feet in the air, 10,000 katydids silently swarm on the wings of a great ascending glider, and suddenly, as the silent ship enters the white heart of a cumulus cloud, 10,000 katydids, as one, burst into their joyous song resounding as sirens here where shadows swim in fog.

Cape Cod

Atop a sand dune at Cape Cod a girl in a red and brown dress waves a yellow scarf. A crow and a seagull for a moment hover over her. Thunderclouds boil above them – they part, the seagull and the crow, and the clouds, and the sands are flooded with sunlight. At the foot of the dune stands a young Indian chief, and he raises his longbow in a graceful greeting. Taking great jumps, she rushes down the dune into his arms. At that very moment, on that very August afternoon, Lao Tzu was born, but there it was midnight, and there was a New Moon.

Dishes

The obese puppeteer washed the dishes in the dark.

The Sacred Cow

The sacred cow stumbled in the mud, blinded by tropical rain, lurched forward onto the ooze, twisting its neck awry as it fell; and one of its long curved horns slipped between the roots of a tree, like a key in a lock, so that when it lumbered to its feet its horn was held fast and its snout pressed down into the mud; for five minutes it struggled and the next morning was found, a great white beast drowned in a puddle.

The Sunken Subway

On Thanksgiving Day the subway sank and the holiday riders stood in water up to their chests and then – single file – they all managed to escape up a ladder through a manhole that let them out at Herald Square into the midst of the Holiday Parade.

The Fans of van Gogh

I saw all the fans of van Gogh, all past and future ones, all the millions fluttering about in the air, making the sky black in back of him, all trying to get a peek over his shoulder as he sits there, very hungry, and looking not unlike a scarecrow in the sunshine in the middle of a wheat field, painting the crows.

I Thought You Were Writing

"I was afraid to say anything to you because I thought you were writing." It was his muse who spoke.

What Happens Next?

None of us could get out of the way.

There was nothing we could do.

Those ten seconds when we saw it coming toward us seemed an endless time.

There was no transition, no pain. Suddenly we were no longer there. We were here . . . listening to your story. But I don't mean to interrupt . . . you were telling us a story . . . what happens next?

The Ghost Town

About two hundred houses roasted in wreck under a Western sun.

Only wild cactus grew in the gardens.

The fence boards fell off and lay in their places, the gables were gray, and whole houses were weathering away. Not a speck of paint was visible.

Dust reigned.

Things with thorns flew through the hot air, and balls of tumbleweed raced through the empty streets.

Cucumbers

Cucumbers by the billion bombarded Paris, dropped from the skies by angry French peasants; they had hired a horde of Piper Cubs to fight a price war with their government; the cucumbers fell down chimneys, fell into children's sand piles, landed on lovers in the park, hit thieves while at their second-story work, covered the lawn of the British embassy, pummeled tennis players, dropped into the poorhouse . . . .

A Very Ancient Dwarf

He parted his beard in the middle, and tied the ends to his two big toes, but this only a very ancient dwarf can do.

An Imaginary Biography

"I should like to write a short biography of Poe pointing out that the heartbreaking miseries of his life were a hoax perpetrated by his publishers, and that he actually led a happily proper life, wintering in Samoa, playing in amateur theatricals in Paris, with a cook from Peking to placate his Epicurean appetite, he was a collector of objects made of mother-of-pearl, and danced too much, his wife said, with her maids when he returned home from his famous binges with young Baudelaire."

The Listening Reader

The old-fashioned key was as big as a pistol and weighed three-and-a-half pounds.

His bedroom was circular and it had no door.

The man had a dagger tattooed on his nose, and he slipped into bed without any clothes, donning earphones and spectacles, he adjusted his ashtray, got his book in hand and twirled the dial to "distress" on his short-wave radio, while beginning to read.

It is the lighthouse keeper of St. Lisle.

The Stamp Collectors

The brown stamp on the envelope was carefully removed by a jet of steam from a teakettle by the eight-year-old collector in Venezuela who had just received the letter from Pennsylvania, from an older collector who lived in a tiny house in the woods, who had been snowbound for three weeks, who had been a sailor since his youth and had become familiar with the oceans, for forty years the lookout in the crows'-nest of a clipper ship, come home old to his birthplace to die in comfort, whiling away the time, doting on his stamp book, cared for by two orphan girls; and with a fine Spencerian hand he kept up a constant correspondence with those living in many foreign lands—for he had a wife in Borneo, Alaska, Australia, Norway, India, Malta, and in China, as well as Venezuela.

All his grandchildren collected stamps.

What About *That?*

What about that? A broken arm, a black eye, amnesia . . . found raving drunk in a cheap dive with your pockets full of diamonds.

Attic Animals

Walking up the narrow stairs, dark and dirty, to the brightly illuminated attic, afternoon sun ablaze through three windows, I saw a mole running in circles in a square of sunshine on the attic floor.

I had a feeling there was someone else in the room. I whirled around, and there sitting in a chair which had been covered with a sheet sat Beelzebub, my friend's cat, staring at the mole.

The attic was filled with the sound of buzzing flies.

Four Snow Leopards

Four snow leopards in transit by train to the Cincinnati zoo were by accident loosed from their cage, and unbeknownst to their sleeping keeper, they leaped from the slowly moving boxcar at sunset, together disappearing into a Kansas field burgeoning with wheat that stretched as far as the eye could see. It was not until midnight, when the train pulled into the Chicago station, that their absence was discovered.

A small forest rose like an island in the sea of wheat. The leopards made for the trees. In a month there will be snow.

My Dentist Story

"The book that glitters with mischief
The writing most sparkling with glee
The pages that jump at my touch—
Your teeth—that is the book for me!"

. . . sang the mad dentist, dancing a jig on a tilted dental chair, shooting Novocain into the air; he made a leap for the ether and smashed it . . . to which all the dentists and nurses and attendants at the Northern Dispensary Clinic who had rushed to the scene, succumbed. He stood on the dental chair and stared in wonder and triumph at the dozen unconscious forms around him. As his co-workers slept their deep sleep, before he left them forever, to vanish into the labyrinth of the non-dental world, there to become a respectable old sculptor—he pulled all their teeth.

The Saloon
Where doppelgangers meet . . . that's the kind of saloon it was;

A Jumpy One
The evening was a jumpy one, the mosquitoes were insufferable, the distant drums were wild, their pet monkey spit in the soup, and so it was no wonder, what with the piano out-of-tune, their servant in tears, her best dress torn by a thorn, that the wife of the escaped convict was fed up.

The Fish and the Hermit
The verandah overlooked a canyon, the canyon held a thrashing stream, and in the stream there was a luminous fish, visible from above on dark nights, for which in his loneliness the hermit fished with a net on the end of a long, strong string.

The only shining object in the dilapidated shack was a large empty fish tank filled with water and illuminated by a deep-purple bulb. Indeed, it was the way the fish imagined heaven, much spookier and quieter than nature.

How they yearned for each other, these two, on such different levels.

The fish tried to imagine how the devil he could climb the string.

The Porcelain Figurine
The porcelain figurine grew waxen, her eyes grew glassy, shining as if alive, and with a sudden movement her arm dropped to her side, and timidly she turned her head to look around in wonderment. For years she had had her place upon the mantelpiece and now she tip toed to its edge and gazed into the abyss of my living room—and then she turned to me and in a tiny voice she said, "You . . . you must be Hans Christian Andersen!"

"No, I am not," I answered.

"Oh!" she sort of sadly said, and slowly retraced her steps to that place where she had stood, assumed her familiar pose, and has retained it to this day.

Where Is That Part of Me?

Where is that part of me that writes long elaborate stories, writes line after line? No doubt that "personality" thinks that it deserves a vacation in the Caribbean and has departed, leaving me here for a while. Or perhaps it is in Canada, eating bacon and eggs by candlelight while the Eskimos patiently wait for him and impatient huskies howl. Yet does he loll perhaps in India, collecting prayer wheels and certain satins, green gauzes and yellow scarves ordinarily only treasured by primitive maidens and monks; now in some Himalayan hideaway he drinks dark tea surrounded by chests of ebony in which he keeps his collection of marbles, shining spheres of immortality; and does he not, though I be distant as in some dream, does he not ever think of me?

A Peculiar Greeting

"It is I, the rotten apple in the barrel, whose turn it is to fly and, smash and splatter, thrown like a meteorite from the hand of a master—ah ! I have caught your eye—I greet you!"

Blue

Three violet flowers nod in the breeze, busying bees, ballooning their violent color in an ultraviolet fog around their pistils, tapering to cobalt.

A turquoise insect appears on a twig.

It vanishes into the blue sky.

"Would you like an orange?"

Bloody Indigo

The clouds at sunset scream bloody indigo, and the fox pisses on the pumpkin. In the orchard there is a thief in every tree. The black cat loves the scarecrow more than you or I might imagine. For them every night is Halloween.

The Bloodthirsty Macaw
The bloodthirsty macaw that killed raccoons spoke Dutch.

The Sky Darkened With Greenery
The plants began to move, first withdrawing their roots from the soil, they began to writhe on the ground, pounding the earth with their leaves, bucking and jumping, and finally waving, like wings, their leaves, they flew, fluttering but a few feet at first, but soon the brown ground was bare, and the sky darkened with greenery.

The Hangman
The hangman turned and shot the prisoner whom he had been about to hang, and then he hanged himself.

A Kitchen in Time
Grinding of grain, hour before dawn, room full of red light flickering, jumping shadows of oven light, the clang of cast iron, the cook speaks Chinese to his helpers who have pigtails, great frying pans hang from the ceiling, a jar of huge spoons stands on the table, through the hush of night a distant gong beats three times, franz, franz, franz ... one senses this scene is occurring in a different century, that these words are being translated from a foreign language ... perhaps from the German, around 1920 possibly in Prague, in a crowded tiny restaurant with checkered tablecloths a bank clerk is scribbling this on his lunch hour.

The What-you-might-call Madness
The what-you-might-call madness of a man who survived ten days without food at the bottom of an abandoned well was that from then on he developed a passion for climbing trees.

Michigan Highway Mirage
A Michigan highway ...
Tired of walking, clothing full of sweat, handkerchief sopping wet, shoes dusty, and thirsty, thirsty—yearning for a true *mirage.*

Yearning for palm trees, a vivid lake that will vanish, or the sea that really recedes, even as we approach it.

Up ahead a gas station comes into view, and I hope the Coca-Cola will be cold . . . but what are those, moving into the driveway?

Camels . . . .

Sky-blue Shadows

The speck of white that is a sailboat and the one that is a gull . . . .

The speck of black that is the vulture and one on the waves way out there . . . a porpoise, perhaps, leading a parade underwater . . . .

It is 8 a.m.

A gibbous moon rests quietly, goes almost unnoticed, in the cloudless sky. The shadows of the mountains on the moon are sky blue.

Freedom

"*Freedom* is spelled with seven letters," noticed the wise man, fondling his beard with his finger, thumbing its curls, while with his other hand he turned the pages of the Bhagavad Gita, and at that same moment that he said it, he opened the Book of Splendor, while with his other hand he made a note in pencil of a paragraph in the New Testament, while his other hand held up the Confucian Analects, and his other riffled the Koran, his other two hands are holding this book. He frowns.

"Bring me more light! Bring me my glasses!" he exclaims. "I have only two eyes, and I can hardly believe what I see here!"

A Saltwater Fish Tank

In the saloon in a great yacht, in an illuminated saltwater fishtank over the bar, there were fifty tropical fish, three scarlet squid, eight golden shrimp, and 48 snails.

In a furious storm, in which the ship floundered for five days, in the heart of the Pacific, it sank, a thousand miles from land, and it is said, and in a way it is true, in a sense, that there are no survivors.

Fire

Walking across the lawn in bare feet, otherwise rather nicely dressed for dinner, to turn around and see the building in flames, and to realize immediately that it is but a vision, understanding you must quickly leave this place you put on your shoes – and now to go in and face them all, old friends: to look into each face as if you had never seen it before, drunkenly making your adieus, probably we would think you weird, you who could receive the sign of our imminent doom.

Clouds of Orange

Clouds of orange dust rose into the air, and lightning shattered the sphere of summer silence with its thunder, smashing at the instant of the flame that tongued its way down the chimney filling the room with blazing death, utterly destroying the famous Oriental collection at the small museum deep in the suburbs of Chicago; and the fire would not be quenched by the downpour nor by Chicago firemen, but went on burning in the drizzle, so all that was standing was the ancient chimney – still smoking – when the Dalai Lama arrived.

Tell Us What the Tiger Fans Did *Then!*

"Tell us again, Grandpa ... !" The retired baseball umpire sat deeper in his leather chair. The young boy continued, "How with the bases loaded in the ninth inning in the World Series the batter hit a line drive toward second base where you were standing and the ball hit you right between your arm and your chest and stuck there, and how your other hand just automatically reached over and plucked it from your armpit – "

King Midas

Her body flashes many bodies at me – lignum vitae, mercury, meerschaum, ice, jellyfish jade, banana-yellow cigarette smoke; she whispers hoarsely, "Think! – What would have happened had King Midas attained enlightenment? – Would that turn him into an ordinary human being?

"Or would the Universe turn into gold?"

Gumball

If you've never swallowed a gumball you won't know what I mean.

The Shoemaker

To be a shoemaker in a land where the people go predominantly barefoot is an art.

In Color

On moonless nights he walks over the oozy bog in snowshoes taking time exposures in color of luminous mushrooms. It is the police chief's son.

Recognition

He found a folded up foreign newspaper on the subway. He studied the front page trying to determine what language it was, but it was written in an unfamiliar alphabet. He was struck by the resemblance of someone pictured there to himself.

Memento

In a New England mansion after midnight, the great living room was lit by a few candles. Aware of distant voices, now alone in the room, now drunk, I sat on the floor clutching my glass.

As if having a race, a gang of baby Galápagos tortoises came galloping across the floor toward me; each was as big as a hatbox, and bore in blazing letters branded on its carapace the word "Memento."

The Sauce

The sauce was solid yellow ice, the fireplace was splattered, the cave cold, icicles hung from stalactites. A Neanderthal baby lay frozen in the arms of its mother, sprawled like a dancer since the days of the glaciers. Flashlights crisscrossed over the perfectly preserved bodies.

Lemon

He cut the lemon in half and found a hard-boiled egg inside.

Warts

A hook-and-ladder truck screeched a warning horn, and the horse-drawn wagon of apples and watermelon barely escaped collision. In pulling sharply to a halt, the wagon had swerved and a half-a-dozen apples fell onto the pavement right at the feet of a young boy who held a rope that was attached by a loop around the neck of a goat. The goat immediately began to eat one of the apples. The driver of the horse-and-wagon turned and stared at the goat eating the apple, and at the apples on the ground, and to the young boy he said thoughtfully, "I suppose it doesn't really matter, seeing as we're just characters in a story."

The boy said, "Imagine all my freckles turned into warts."

The Collector of Cymbals

He built his house over the elevator shaft of an abandoned salt mine, and in his house there was a small room whose only window was a trap door in the floor. He was a collector of cymbals, and whenever he got hold of a cymbal he would drop it down the shaft, and listen to it echo as it fell. He was a writer, like me.

Objects of Mu

Objects of Mu, pearls of Ur in turquoise pools repose, while bold ghouls, six bald heads whose doctorates were on the dead, archeologists, gaze fondly down on them, their "discovery" (six grins above the blue bowl) untouched beneath the temple for six thousand years, each still perfection of pale purity. On being popped into a felt cloth the finest pearl reflects—"How different were the smiles of the ancient kings."

Five Hundred Yellow Cabs

The intersection filled with yellow cabs.

The garage of the cab company was on fire and the news had flitted from taxi radio to radio and cabs came from all over the city out of curiosity and, like bewildered insects whose nest had been destroyed, they gathered and moved around the huge burning building, blocking the way of fire trucks, some vehicles abandoned in the middle of the street as drivers got out and gathered in groups to chat where they could get a better view, and as two floors collapsed with a tremendous crash and fire filled the windows with renewed fury and the black smoke of grease and gasoline put a plume into the stratosphere, the drivers began to blow their horns as cab drivers under stress have a wont to do, and that mourning music, such vibrant brass, of five hundred taxi drivers blowing their horns could be heard across the river.

On the New

Winging past floods down into Ethiopia, the stork disappeared over the horizon, while far below by a pyramid a Nile sparrow sang for a dying Pharaoh.

His tents were like flames on the desert sand.

Tethered white horses flashed in the sunlight.

Far below in the inner folds of the cloth palace a cricket hailed the sparrow by his own song, and together they sang.

The wind joined them, playing the palms of the oasis, and the tent posts creaked, shifting from foot to foot as if tents thought of dancing this morning.

The new pyramid had already begun to practice its silence.

The Lovers

Once upon a time a forest boy fell flat on his face.

The boy was a wild thing, lost by his parents in the Amazon maze of animal paths and rivers which border the million islands of mystery, those places where man has never touched his foot, unexplored places where dangers or treasures lurk, or nothing.

Where only animals roam, and exceptions, explorers, occasionally.

His parents had not been exceptions. They were missionaries and had stuck to the rivers, to their canoes with their Indians who were taking them to a distant village inside Brazil where there was civilization of a sort, but no Christians. A village of mud huts where ignorance reigned, where rituals took the place of medicine, and on Saturday nights hallucinations from a green plant took the place of movies.

The boy, who was five then, climbed on a log in the night and pushed it into the river and floated away.

He was scared.

He looked up—and there was the man in the moon smiling down at him. He smiled back, and waved.

The many-forked river swallowed him in its mystery, and the search for him was fruitless.

They assumed he was dead. He was having a wonderful time! He had stolen a knife from one of the Indians, and he cut fruit from overhanging trees as he glided past, and lunched on the abundance of the jungle.

With his parents he'd been terrified.

But away from them, free, he felt no terror of anything. He scampered about petting pythons, black panthers, playing with hairy spiders, sporting bravery as other children wear lead police badges over their hearts, with nonchalance and happiness at the glitter of it in the sunshine.

He swam in alligator pools and his absence of fear, coupled with coincidence, time after time protected him.

He loved everything and everything loved him back — and amused him, and fed him, and was a pillow and his blanket that, unspeaking, cared for him.

He wandered, and swung on the vines from the trees, and swam, and made spears, all for the fun of it, until he was sixteen, until the day at that time, he fell flat on his face.

He fell in love.

He was flying through the air on a vine, wrapped in a skin he'd cut from an old jaguar corpse he'd found, as he crashed into a parrot flying.

They both fell.

The parrot had broken its wing, and was skwaaaking and running in circles hysterically. The boy chased it and caught it in his arms.

The parrot bit him.

The boy carried him at arm's length until he reached a rude hut he'd built. He blocked the door and let him go.

But instead of trying to escape, the parrot collapsed.

The boy wondered what to do, so he went over and began to stroke him, and he laid him in a bed of leaves, and sprinkled water on him.

The parrot was breathing. He went for food.

He climbed a clakatee tree and gathered white nuts which hung from long strings, which he knew parrots liked the best, for these trees were filled with them every morning. On mornings past he had watched the parrots cover the tree with their rainbow bodies, skwaaaking excitedly as the sun rose, devouring the nuts.

He laid the food beside the parrot and sat watching.

He straightened his feathers and petted him some more.

The next day the parrot revived a little and ate a little and hobbled across the hut into a dark corner.

He stayed there all the while his wing was healing; the boy fed him, and brought him water; the parrot got well, that is, he lived, but lost the use of his wing.

He loved this parrot as he would have loved a girl, had there been a girl in the jungle.

The parrot also fell in love in the only way a parrot can — he allowed himself to be tamed.

They lived together.

They traveled together—the boy flying through the trees, swinging from vine to vine through the air, while the parrot ran like a mad chicken on the ground.

He taught the bird to talk, to laugh, to cry, to say hello—good-bye, to use the language he had almost forgotten from lack of use, due to his separateness from human beings.

Some years they lived together—until, indeed, the boy became a man of twenty-five. He had grown short, his body was blackened by exposure to the wind and sun, his hair hung in beautiful bleached golden snarls down to his waist, and his eyes flashed like an animal's with gentleness.

He wore a leather thong tied tightly around his waist, through which was stuck the dagger he'd stolen years ago, the only possession he valued.

And the only thing he valued more was his love. They always slept together, the parrot perched on a stick, over the man, as if guarding him. Every night the man would say—Happy dreams.

And the parrot would repeat in his skwaaaking voice—Happy dreams.

When he walked, the parrot would often sit on his shoulder repeating phrases like a broken record.

He still knew no danger, never felt fear, was friendly with all the animals. He was gentle as a dandelion.

His wanderings over the jungle were aimless and one day he saw smoke over a hill from a trading post. He approached curiously, but suddenly stopped. Dead still.

There was a thrashing sound in the undergrowth ahead and he heard a woman's voice say—Tie my boot, dear. It keeps coming undone. Here. Let me hold your gun . . . .

The first human voice he'd heard in twenty years stabbed, like an ice pick, his stomach, stirred memories, and he dropped to the ground behind a big bush.

That voice.

Impossible.

It sounded like his mother.

Was it really his mother?

Were they still looking for him?

The parrot, not knowing all people were not like his master, scrambled through the foliage at the voice.

The woman screamed.

Bang!

The parrot shrieked.

He dashed through the brush and caught the parrot's last words—Happy dreams!

He turned to the woman holding the smoking rifle, and the man at her side.

His eyes were like forest fires.

He leaped at the woman, but the man grabbed his gun, and it smoked, and he fell with a pain and hole in his stomach.

Confused, his stomach burning, he stared at them. They stared back, just as amazed.

He jumped again—at the man—and took a bite from his throat.

Then he raced through the jungle, through the trees, clutching vines, jumping, falling from branch to branch. Away ! Away ! He must get away and he went, scrambling and howling like the animal which he was, until for a moment he shuddered, and died—and that night was devoured by laughing hyenas under a large yellow moon; the moon was watched also by the young couple, for lovers they were.

They stood in the moonlight on the trading post porch. She kissed the white bandage on his throat. He stared into the blackness of the jungle and murmured—I wonder if I killed him?

She murmured—I wonder who he was?

She looked up.

The moon was smiling at them.

Marriage of the Dingo

A jovial fellow with a big brown moustache, big as a cat-tail, got it infested with dog-fleas in Australia.

He had almost perished in the desert there, came actually crawling into a camp of aborigines, who saved him. He traveled with them a month, sleeping without shelter under the cold desert wind. He became especially fond of their dog, a dingo, who returned his affection; and the dog curled up beside him every night, snuggling warmth. At the border of civilization he cashed a traveler's check and bought the animal. It was an obscure exchange that he never quite understood. He had given a certain amount of money to the man at the trading store, and the natives had gotten provisions, and the American had gotten the dog—however, it had been done in a weird way. "These people make a ceremony out of everything," the trader had explained to him. "Just do as you're told . . . and you'll get the dog." They all sat in a circle, and it took about an hour. They played drums. Some sang. And they acted out little skits, wearing only elaborate make-up as costumes, in which the provisions and the trader, and he and the dog, all had their parts—some ancient pantomime, conducted entirely in a language of gestures; but the awkward man in the European clothes was not forced to lose any dignity; indeed, it was the solemnity of the whole silent thing that bothered him.

The dog didn't bark once.

The dog walked placidly beside him across the circle to where the priest-chief sat, and perhaps at a signal from that old magician, the dog suddenly stood up on its hind legs, putting its paw demurely in the hand of the American, while the chief made numerous magical signs.

Another Impostor

Once upon a time a millionaire playboy burned his face off in an automobile accident.

After that he became a recluse, he stopped seeing all his friends, and he lived up in his big stone house on large grounds which he never left.

Wild rumors ran about him, about the splendor of his life, about rare wines he drank, and women, women were there, it was whispered, and they said he had great collections of things like art and books and drums and daggers, and they said he kept live smooth fish in his secret swimming pool someplace deep within the walls of his impenetrable house.

His theater was on the roof, and he'd hire whole Broadway casts to play for him there, and stars of the ballet and concert stage to come and perform for him.

He never spoke to any of the stars who came into his house, but they would see him occasionally over the footlights with a black covering over his face, languidly lounging in his comfortable chair, the only chair in the theater, smoking a cigar or, perhaps, with a purple drink.

The millionaire spoke to no one.

His go-between with the world was his butler, who paid his bills, arranged his entertainments, and was interviewed by the press, and who, because of his peculiar relationship to the millionaire, also became famous.

One day an actor who was feeling very depressed because he had no work was sitting in the Waldorf Cafeteria reading a newspaper.

He happened to read a story about the eccentric millionaire and he realized — he was about the same height and build as this millionaire, and he was about the same age — and he realized that if he could somehow kill the millionaire and take his place, why, it would be easy to impersonate this man who spoke to no one and wore a black covering over his face.

He was afraid of the butler, though.

So he studied, from newspaper files and things, the habits and characteristics of the butler and the millionaire.

One dark night he sneaked onto the grounds and by luck ran into the millionaire, who was looking down an old well at the back of the house.

And so he hit the millionaire over the head and killed him.

It was dark by the well. He hurriedly got into the millionaire's clothes and put the black covering over his face and dumped the millionaire's body into the well, and he noticed at the time that the body didn't make a splash.

So dressed, the impostor walked into the house, and into a life of ease and luxury.

And he found it was a cinch!

Because this butler was—a perfect butler.

He never had to give an order. The butler just knew what to do. The butler would bring him his breakfast, would run his bath, he arranged for him to have women, furnished him with cigarettes of hashish, ran the household, and planned all his fabulous entertainments.

His living was effortless.

And after a while he realized—no one could ever discover his identity. The scheme was perfect.

And he was right.

No one would ever discover his identity.

But this man's weakness was his conceit. You see, it never occurred to him that someone else might get the same idea he got. It never occurred to him that the man he killed was not the millionaire at all, but was an impostor, like himself, and that in a couple of months another impostor would come along and kill him, and that as a matter of fact, during the last few years there had been quite a few impostors, each with the same weakness, that same conceit.

No, no one ever knew of this—except the butler, of course—but he never told, because he likes his job.

Finders Keepers

THE neatly dressed immigrant family who died in five days of different diseases from picking through piles at the city dump for the bag
of cash that had gotten into the garbage—I'll never forget the indus-
triousness of that family, for while they searched through bags of filth
for their life savings, I came to watch them. I am their garbage man.

The first day I came, I brought the cash.

But allow me to explain: I work with two other men on a garbage
truck. One is the driver, and the other, like me, empties the cans into
the rear of the truck. On this particular day, as I threw out the
contents of a can, I noticed a brown paper bag that had money in
it. My partner was across the street, so I stuffed the bag inside my
shirt and didn't say anything. I was at home by noon that day and
discovered thirty-eight thousand dollars was what I had.

That evening, the newspapers were full of it. The man had wanted
to purchase a house for cash and had taken every cent out of his
savings account. The man had nine children. There were photographs of him weeping. Somehow the money had gotten thrown out
with the garbage, and it wasn't discovered until after the truck had
been unloaded. The driver knew exactly where he had dumped his
load, but the trouble was that two other trucks had discharged the
day's refuse in the same place, on top of the load that should have
had the money in it. It was a mess.

The police cordoned off the area where they thought the money
might be with bright-blue rope. And that night a city fire truck
illuminated the scene with powerful lights, so that the family could
search through the day's refuse of a city. Throngs of spectators,
informed through the radio and press of the family's plight, came to
watch. Many, many offered to help. But the distraught man who had
lost his money indignantly, you might say hysterically, refused all
help, and he pleaded with the police to keep the crowd outside the
blue rope. He would allow no one except his family to search for the
money, and a thoughtful police captain, after surveying the scene and
after a consultation with the mayor, decided to allow the man his
way, and indeed to help him in what ways they could in his search

for the money. Television crews added their lights to the ghastly scene which they reported on the morning news; and the next day the whole city was waiting for the money to be found.

I report here that I didn't sleep well that night.

Earlier I had been interviewed several times by the police, and by my supervisor, and without question they believed me, for I have worked for the sanitation department for ten years.

I am still amazed at how easily I lied about it, but then no one from the beginning ever suspected me. They dismissed my words as being the truth, and turned their attention to the monstrous mound of garbage. Ordinarily the garbage would have been plowed and treated with chemicals, but now they let it lie there untreated, and soon a noxious odor flooded the vicinity. I don't see how all those people could stand it. It was a strange crowd, those who came to watch, and there were several scuffles with the police that night with irate citizens who insisted it was their Right to search for the money. They argued that if the money had been thrown into the garbage and the garbage delivered to the city dump—that it was now public property, and that it was everybody's right to search for it, and that whoever found it should be allowed to keep it.

You might think I would agree with that logic, but the truth is I didn't. If the man had thrown away the money, it would have been a different story, but he had merely by accident misplaced it, and the money was obviously still his.

As I regularly do, I went to work quite early in the morning the next day, and on returning home, having taken a shower and had a hot soak, as I always do after work, I sat and watched the noon news while having a bite to eat. I remember I was eating a tuna fish sandwich.

There I saw the noon wrap-up of the night's garbage scene.

I saw the three people whom the police had arrested being hauled away in police vans. There was a garrulous, wild old woman who shrieked at the cameras, and a strange, prissy college student who threw himself on the garbage heap and went rigid so that it took three plainclothesmen to carry him off, and another, a middle-aged man who looked dangerous, like a huge rat, like a man who obviously belonged in jail, who regularly drank too much, was handcuffed and hustled into a patrol car.

These were those who passionately believed in finders-keepers.

I decided to return the money. I put the package of money in my lunch bucket, and took the bus to the end of the line, where the city dump was located, where there must have been two hundred people milling around.

It was easy to find the family. They had set up two tents just inside the blue rope where they took turns napping, while the others searched.

And there they were, that neatly dressed family, kids of all sizes, on the garbage heap.

I had been picking up their garbage for five years, three times a week, and the whole family had become quite familiar to me. I had noticed how the children grew, and occasionally, though not often, I had had brief conversations with them, giving them information about our pick-up schedules. Indeed, among all those strangers they seemed like old friends, and I went directly to the man, who was inside the blue rope, to give him his money. He saw me approaching, but I could see he didn't recognize me. He rose to his feet and frowned oddly at me, thrusting his jaw out at the same time.

Then, incredibly, he twisted his body into a strange posture like a dancer and his leg shot out like a fist and his heel hit my stomach, so that I fell back outside the blue rope, doubled up with pain. He shook his fist at the crowd around me, and then bent again to search through the garbage.

It was several minutes before I could speak, and then some stranger helped me to my feet. Shakily I stumbled back toward the bus stop, away from the mob of onlookers who had witnessed the encounter. As I fled, I heard someone shout, "Hey buddy! Is this your lunch bucket?" I thanked the stranger.

The Three

Three sisters each sang bass.

Their father was famous for his excellent boys' choir and for these marvelous daughters and was himself responsible for their musical training.

On the concert stage the pretty young women harmonized with scintillating skill with a feminine manner that belied their deep voices — and their performance of "Old Man River" always brought the house down, and would cause ladies to groan and grown men to weep at the poignancy of that rendition, in purity of tone and pure power rivaling Chaliapin, Paul Robeson and Samuel Ramey, claimed critics from the *Times*, the *Telegraph* and the *Sun*.

"Almost indescribably fascinating," said the one from the *Sun*. "They are violet dancers in a yellow world."

Dream of the Bobbers

The bobsled team were fat women, absolutely obese, over five hundred pounds each. Together the four of them weighed a ton.

They had a special Swiss sled.

They called themselves the Bobwhites, and each wore a sledding costume composed of russet, white, and black feathers someone terribly clever had fitted together to form a surface like that of a wing of a bird. Bobwhites are raised commercially in several counties in New York State, and so actual feathers of the bird were readily available in the huge quantity needed to cover the surfaces of these vast spherical bodies with four skintight sledsuits. If you touched one of them, it was like touching the body of a bird. The suits gave superior protection against the freezing wind.

The driver was a daredevil and daydreamed of being a dancer.

Another's daydream was to know that thrill of the pole vaulter thrusting herself toward the sky at that moment when she senses that—without touching it—she has cleared the horizontal stick.

Another daydreamed of getting the great view of the Grand Canyon, flying its length by hang glider.

A recurring dream of the braker who sat at the rear of the sled was that she was in a spotlight flying through the air catching a trapeze.

The bobbers in their most secret thoughts dreamed of being balloons, weightless, flying in the wind—and *here!* at least, the dream is true—for down the twisting icy track as they careened they positively flew with the greatest of ease.

On Demons

Is my soul so simple?
Can a soul be draped?
In this fashion can I cloak
Your cold? By splendid images?

In olden days of the Arabian Nights a fisherman threw his raggle-taggle net into the Mediterranean. He pulled, and pulled, and pulled the net onto the shore, and he discovered nothing in it except an old ivory jar. He lifted a piece of seaweed off the jar, and saw that it was ancient and intricately carved with a procession of people and beasts winding spirally around it, so that whichever way he turned it, three lines of people appeared. At the top was a stopper. It was made of lead. On it was impressed the Seal of Solomon.

The fisherman opened the jar and smoke began to come out of it, began to pour out of it, making a rushing sound, and the smoke gathered into a huge cloud, and the cloud became the body of a demon, or jinn, or genie, or genius . . . or call it whatever you want.

The demon put the fisherman in the palm of his hand, and gave him a choice of a number of hideous deaths.

"But I was the one who freed you!" protested the fisherman.

"Listen," said the demon, "I've been in that jar for 50,000 years. For the first five thousand years I joyfully planned how I would reward the man who freed me . . . . I would turn him into an emperor! Give him palaces, the whole world for his dominion . . . . But ten thousand years passed, and I began to be a little depressed, and I lost some of my enthusiasm, yet I said to myself: whoever frees me, I'll give him a comfortable princedom, a good castle, servants, so he'll be set for life . . . . But more years passed, and after 15,000 years I became so disgusted, so disgruntled, that I decided I wouldn't give any reward to the fool who chanced to free me . . . . But as more time passed I began to hate humanity, they who ignored me . . . . And I began to devise methods of murder, of torture . . . . Oh! The things I've thought these 35,000 years . . . . I have daydreamed of this day, and of the way I should kill you. I have thought up thirteen horrendous ways for you to die. These are the ways: listen carefully, for I shall give you your choice."

"You can obviously do whatever you want with me," said the fisherman. "You can kill me on the spot. But nevertheless, the truth is the truth, and you're a liar."

"What?!" said the demon.

"You couldn't have been in this ivory jar. Look how small this jar is, and look at yourself, you're as big as a mountain. Any child could see that you aren't telling the truth. You're a liar. Kill me if you want, but don't expect me to believe your fairy tales, don't make me laugh. Kill me if you want, but don't expect me to believe that you spent centuries in this little jar. Don't be ridiculous. Kill me if you want, but don't expect me to believe such an obvious fable."

"What!?" said the demon. "I'll show you!"

Whereupon his body began to dissolve into a huge cloud of smoke, which began to twirl like a tornado, and the smoke condensed and entered the ivory jar, and the fisherman quickly replaced the stopper, and it has remained there until this very day.

While demons wait, my soul languishes.

I test words on them. I begin sentences, trying to jar them, but they hardly listen, so my sentences languish . . . .

Language is their lunch, their vital element, and lunacy, their play; and love, they say, is succulent.

Ah . . . dessert!

JELL-O!

(But O! This work . . . I must carve this essay carefully as an ivory jar.)

JELL-O!

I can see it quite clearly; I am having a vision: it is the elegant view:

A long banquet table.

Above its center hangs a crystal chandelier with 216 ivory candles gleaming while below, the silver beams — but the table's a mess, for tuxedoed guests have risen from the middle of dinner and are out on the balcony watching the fireworks, a mock atom bomb, for permanent peace is come; servants lean out the kitchen windows admiring the famous holiday display; a moment before this penthouse room was filled with the great, now it's quiet as the museum's antique room was last New Year's Eve; alone, and utterly untouched, in the center of the grand table sits a giant, cut-glass serving bowl of Jell-O.

Two smoking people appear as if by magic standing near the Jell-O. One of them I can't make out . . . I can't quite focus on the person . . . is it a man or a woman? Or what? But I *can* see quite plainly that the other one is you, my reader; and, pardon me for laughing, but you look very out of place in this fine dining room, almost like a thief, or an actor, or a character in a dream, for you are dressed in exactly the same clothes as you have on now. That other person at your side, who I know is really responsible for your being here, is your listener.

You hand the listener two straws and your listener plunges them into the Jell-O, and . . . Oh! That is interesting: . . . The listener is sipping color out of the Jell-O.

The Jell-O is becoming clearly colorless, now glass-clear.

Now what is that listener doing? Hovering over the bowl . . . and staring intently into it as if it were a crystal ball . . . .

Hmmm. The surface of the Jell-O is smooth as glass except for the two tiny punctures which the straws made, and it has become a mirror. All the objects in the room can be seen, but it can also be seen that this is no ordinary mirror, my reader . . . . It is the only mirror in which a vampire can see his reflection. A vampire cannot imagine what he himself looks like (he does not even cast a shadow) except from a glimpse in this Jell-O mirror. And conversely, ordinary people, such as yourselves, for instance, are utterly invisible in this mirror.

You cannot see yourself in this mirror.

Try it. Bend over the table, look into the bowl . . . . It is a little scientific demonstration.

You see? You are invisible. You have no reflection here. That is what a vampire sees in ordinary mirrors. He can see everything except himself. That is why vampires are vain.

That is enough, reader, come away from the mirror.

Reader! Come away from the mirror!

I know you cannot see yourself.

What is so fascinating? To see for a moment what a vampire sees? It is curious, isn't it?

Yes, interesting.

But that is enough of that. Come away, reader!

What do you see? . . . Oh! . . . Ah. . . . Of course, directly above you is the chandelier . . . .

But look at the spots!! The lace tablecloth! Look at the surface of the mirror—They are dripping ivory, ivory drip, drip-of-ivory, ivory drippings, drips ivory drips, ivory of drips, of ivory drips, dripping drips drip (they've each begun dripping on you, as if by your staring at them in a mirror, you had turned each candle upside down), drips-ips ivory of, drippings of ivory, ivory of drippings of, ivory drips of dripping of, ivoring dripory . . . .

UMBRELLA!

(But O! This work . . . . I must carve this essay carefully as an ivory jar.)

UMBRELLA!

I can see it quite plainly; I am having a vision: it is the elegant beast.

Of all beasts that have elegance, "The Final Machine" is most welcome#

　　　　　#

　　#An umbrella opens up to become a sundial#

　　　　　　　　　　#

　　　　　　　　　　#A porcupine with clockhands instead of quills.

Each quill in her body is a different kind of clock hand.

Hands from ten thousand clocks.

Her tail is the big hand from the grammar school clock.

Her teeth are the golden hands of watches, set in perpendicular rows, meant to mesh when gnashed.

Her tongue, fragile and flat, is a fabulous hand hand-made by magical moors, a singular silver mobile filigree.

She walks along well-padded paths through monstrous moss jungles, unaccompanied by insectsong.

For she is the only animal on earth—she and her relatives—her race, who wholly web the surface of the planet with their paths through plants and snow which casually they drink and feed on, en route, waddling on and on and on; perhaps now needing an ever-lasting savor, she nuzzles earth each noon for her narcotic, gnashing (this is what her teeth were made for) noisily (like two hundred ticking-fine chronometers) and spearing the white hairs that spring out on certain roots . . . . I must invisibly bend down (as a newsreel cameraman, for you) and look into the eyes of this animal.

Look! The eyes are between baby blue and deep purple.

Giddycolor.

Dim dazzle.

Ignore luster and focus finer . . . .Those are not flecks but figures in a circle, gloomy numerals from the face of a clock, miniaturely etched on each iris.

One set is perfectly ordinary.

But the other set of numerals is reversed, that is, what a clock could see if it would study its face in a mirror. What now . . . ?

I see her destiny.

This young porcupine walks into the house.

Her nest is a hemisphere and she sits in the middle on a mound.

There are many, many such spheres, and wandering porcupines may enter any sphere and sit a bit on the mound floor; its inside wall is just like a planetarium—the circular ceiling is scattered with ten thousand luminous numerals each differing in size and kind as do the stars, or as would numbers from as many clocks.

Each quill points at its own star.

That is, each clockhand, by its style, matches a number on the ceiling at which it strains up toward.

The small and boldly modern hand points at a slight and boldly modeled number; the long thin gold hand is raised elegantly to the golden roman numeral; and so with all the rest, each hand rises on tiptoe from her skin.

Those numerous lights on the ceiling of the porcupine nest do not change like the lights in the planetarium.

They never change position.

Even every nest shows the same sky.

Even so, every burning numeral in the sky of the nest is changing—in value, so ten becomes eleven, eleven becomes twelve, twelve becomes one, one becomes two, as time goes by.

One tells the time in China, one is measuring the time in Berlin, but there's a different time entirely in Syracuse. The "orbits," so to speak, of these stars are all from one to twelve; numbers at which large hands point travel through their "orbit" of numbers once an hour, while a number of a small hand will take a dozen times that time.

But there are figures from stranger clocks up there—one is from a clock measuring the age of the universe, another clocks the life of

the porcupine's mother, one clocks the season for the flower seeds, another clocks the last time she ate, and as she sits on the mound the hands pull her skin outward in every direction toward those times, and she swoons (you can tell by her eyes) in a sort of ecstasy of awareness, full of pinpoint knowledge of the rhythms and cycles of existence.

And as all these animals do, she attains the final state of perfect contemplation.

This is what perfect contemplation is: it is to be aware of all the times that share this moment: say a seer breaks an egg into a frying pan—as she does so, she is aware of the cycle of the egg she interrupted; she is aware of the evolutionary chains of circumstance in which a chicken appears; she is aware of the pleni-temporal changes in the fire, the momentary molecules in fractions flaming; she senses the gaseous beginning of the cold metal handle which she holds and the warm thing it is becoming and how it all (sensing it) ends; she is aware of the speed her heart beats, and the silent rats, and the silent rate the paint is peeling off the walls, and that the universe collapses—all at once: she is aware of all the times.

Simply, she perceives a fourth dimension.

Such a sage would consider me as senseless as Einstein's shadow on a sphere.

For these are the last animals on earth—this is the superior species which survives.

Every member of the race leads the life of a sage, and they are so few they do not overcrowd their earth, and each spends much time simply ambling among the ancient paths, each still alive with curiosity.

Curiosity.

And so, as invisibly as I bent to see her destiny (at least I was invisible as a shadow), perhaps your shadow at this moment bends intricately about your chair to get a better view of you, and can see yours, your destiny#

#

#*The schooner sank. About it were the broad blue waters of the tropical sea in a cloudless noon, and the horizon formed a perfect circle around the unmarked place*#

#

#I do not find such attentions

inappropriate at any moment to my object, for by studying the manner these two-dimensional creatures (my shadow and my reflection) deal with me, why, I can learn a great deal about "them" who wander in the fourth dimension, waddling down ancient paths, the gods.

By exactly such studies as these I am able to get this "look" for you (as if I were a newsreel cameraman), and it is a very special view of "them."

In the silent language of wild, exaggerated gesture a shadow plays on children's fright — and in the same silence, but with super slowness, so precisely, does my mirror over the years communicate certain things to me —

Is that my fancy changing shape?

I notice now neither my reflection nor my shadow has ever heard a single word, nor song, nor any sound. Thus composers, who attach their soul to sound, cannot be seen in mirrors. To the extent that a composer believes he sees himself in a mirror, exactly to just that extent is he not a composer, for the "reflection fellow" is deaf and dumb, and as silent as a mirror is believed, realities plunge in silence by.

A great composer would not see himself in a mirror. That is why great composers are not vain.

The scientific people are a special strain. They have reflections but they cannot face them. They cast shadows, but like black cats, each is afraid of his own — arching back; for instance, I once saw a scientist up on the edge of an airport platform suddenly spotlit by a searchlight below, and the unexpected enlightenment permanently blinded him, for he had stood with his back to the beam, and had viewed his shadow rushing into space, huge as the demon in the Arabian nights. It's because they get views of themselves like this that scientists are not vain.

Vanity is death in the fourth dimension.

This is death in the fourth dimension: all their life the porcupines have a constant knowledge of their own mortality, and can accurately gauge the moment coming, and each in his age begins to build his tomb, a hemisphere of numinous numerals, and inside the careful work of years he digs his own grave, and at the last moment he climbs down into it and with the last movement of his limbs, with

the last gesture of his life, he covers himself, leaving a neat mound, a nice nest, and for some unknown future porcupine a perfect couch for contemplation of the gift of his ancestors—his enormous present.

However, back to the story.

The young female porcupine cannot imagine what I saw in her eyes.

I remember distinctly I saw an image of the face of the clock, and I also saw a mirror image of the same clock.

Do you understand? Not one numeral metamorphosing into another numeral.

I saw the whole shebang!

I saw all twelve numbers at the same time arranged in a regular circle!

I saw her destiny.

She is to see the world as I see it.

For these animals cannot imagine the clock as we know it (they think of the clockhand as being part of themselves); if they were to imagine twelve numerals in a circle, they would automatically assume there were twelve clockhands each pointing toward its own number, and that every hand was telling the correct time.

However, she shall see all twelve numbers at the same time—in a vision.

She shall see a phantom clockface, and beside it, its mirror image—just as I saw it in her eyes. Each will be slowly spinning in an opposite direction, the reflection turning clockwise, the phantom will turn counterclockwise, and the two will have only one single moment to know each other, to touch forever, now.

She will see the past developing into the future receding into the past.

I know you must notice that this hasn't happened yet. But it shall happen, inevitably, in a few minutes, perhaps, or it may take a few days, I don't know, but you know perfectly well I cannot write a story, as I'm obviously doing, about this porcupine if nothing extraordinary is ever going to happen to her—so it is necessary that what I say be true.

And I'm not going to pad this essay with a lot of fantasy while I'm waiting, though let me assure you I have the imagination and skill to do so.

What I'm going to do is simply tell you what's going to happen to her, and you'll have to take my word for it.

This is how fate is written:

When it happens, I do not think it will be a matter of ecstasy, or anything like that.

At the moment of her sudden vision she shall with justice simply shudder, rattling her scales.

Each clockhand, sharp as arrow shot by archer, will shoot from her skin and pierce its numeral on the ceiling.

At that moment there will be ten thousand bull's-eyes.

The nest will flutter down in dust.

The now spineless porcupine will know that she is here.

She will know now that there is only one correct time.

One place, one time.

Here and now.

Full of her knowledge of this oneness, she will stand erect upon a sphere and raise two paws in awe to a brilliant sky and name the oneness, and naïvely she will pronounce the name of the one god, and by that unique recognition gain an immortal soul.

She will die of exposure.

It is a shame.

Without a quill, in prayer perched upon a sphere, she will die of sunburn.

GARBAGE!

(But O! This work . . . . I must carve this essay carefully as an ivory jar.)

GARBAGE!

I can see it quite fully; I am having a vision of all beasts that exist.

Of all beasts that eat garbage, the vulture is most welcome.

On the last day I spent in a certain tiny village on the coast of Yucatán, I got up from my hammock and walked sleepily into the blazing sunshine of my yard and discovered fifty vultures hobbling about, milling around, flapping up, like chickens in their salivary excitements, but as always, so silently, so silently as in slow motion coffins move about, changing places under the tombstones in the cemetery.

It is impossible to regard the vulture as anything but an omen.

However, soaring motionlessly high, high as the reaches of vision, they are sublime as they range, roaming among the clouds, floating and sucking on invisible drafts of hot, rare air, they are but black punctuation marks up there, so solitary, one among the cumulus like a lonely witch among tropical blackening storm clouds of war.

Vultures are farsighted.

The idle mind in Mexico turns on the vultures.

They are an emblematic species—like the eagle, and the dove; memories of the vulture are stamped and cartooned.

Circling, soaring motionlessly high as vision reaches, they inspire; as they fight over the bones of a rat, the corpse of a dog, or a bunch of fish heads (as those in my yard were) glistening stickily on the ground, we are kept from vomiting only by a thought that they eat vomit . . . .

In New York City, at the Museum of Natural History on 79th Street, on the third floor, in the permanent exhibition of the objects of the olden days of Chinese civilization, there are some whistles.

Flutes or whistles?

I've never heard them, but I imagine them to sound Chinese and flutelike; they were made to be fastened on the backs of tame garden birds, doves, so that as a bird flies a note sounds in the air, the note changing as the wind changes, the tone shading to the curves of flight.

Nowadays it would be impossible because they don't make whistles like that anymore, but in my imagination I ordered ten thousand such flutes from the fifteenth-century store and would tie them onto the backs of the vultures, so that, as an animal was dying, and as one by one the vultures gather, circling overhead as they do, there would be music.

And suddenly I see an Indian hut, and an Indian woman turns her head up from the three stones of the timeless cooking fire, and says, "Listen. Something is dying."

As more and more vultures gather, it would become absolutely symphonic.

Then, quite suddenly, as the birds come to rest, the music would stop.

Real Magic

The magician on the stage dropped his glove. Yet he still held a glove in each hand. The elderly performer turned slightly, and as if by accident the glove in his left hand fluttered to the floor—yet he still held a glove in each hand. He looks at the gloves as if wondering where to put them down, and then puts them down on the table in full view, but at the next instant two new gloves appear in his hands. He puts these immediately down on the table on top of the first pair and flashes his hands empty so all can see with a gesture that would indicate that he is finished with the gloves, yet at that instant two new gloves appear in his hands. He takes both gloves in his right hand and places them over the back of an empty chair, and lo! there they are—and his right hand is empty, but two new gloves have appeared in his left hand. He takes the gloves into his right hand and flings them into the audience. In his hand outstretched from throwing the gloves, two new gloves appear. He also throws these to the audience, yet a new pair of gloves appears in his hand. He puts the right glove on—and invites a young member of the audience to touch one of his fingers as he spreads the fingers of his right hand wide. The girl touches his little finger. Without taking his other fingers or thumb out of the glove, he takes his little finger out, so that the little finger of the glove hangs limp. He takes a pair of scissors and cuts the little finger off the glove. He now pushes his little finger out of the hole so everyone can see. He then begins picking up all the gloves, and as he does so he shows the audience that each glove has only a thumb and three fingers; each glove has had the little finger cut off.

Members of the audience can be heard to murmur as they examine the gloves which he has thrown out to them, for these too have had the little finger cut off, although one person can be heard loudly protesting that when he caught the glove he had examined it, and that it had been whole.

The magician regained the center of the stage, and concluded with these words: "During the First World War, I served overseas as many men my age did and I saw a couple of battles. In one of them I was wounded, and at first I thought it was a calamity, for I had been left with a deformity which I thought to be grotesque and evident to everyone I met, one which was especially repulsive and tragic for a man of my profession, for I was then already a master of card magic, though I'd not yet begun to perform professionally. I then made a discovery which to me to this day seems truly magical – a discovery I shall share with you this evening, and if any of you are ever afflicted by a blemish or a sudden deformity I command you to remember immediately the message of my performance tonight – that message is this: that when you work with people, they really don't see your deformities.

"If you could have told me in my twenties that my deformity was going to be invisible I would have scoffed bitter disbelief; indeed I would have found it incredible that one day I should with a certain pride display – as if I were doing a magic trick – the fact that long ago on a battlefield in France I lost the little finger of my left hand!"

He thrust out his left hand and held it steady so that all could see.

What the old man says is true.

And then as those old showmen could, with his left hand he waved them a gracious "Good evening!"

The Santa Claus Murderer

Once upon a time there was a person who ended wars forever by murdering 42 Santa Clauses.

It all began ten days before Christmas when a Salvation Army Santa Claus was murdered midtown.

A morning newspaper carried the story, but the next day five more Santa Clauses were murdered and it hit the headlines of every paper in the country.

Four of them were killed collecting money for the Salvation Army, and the fifth was stabbed in the toy department of Gimbel's.

And people were outraged! They were indignant! They thought, what a monster, what a ghoul this guy must be, I mean, to spoil the children's Christmas by murdering Santa Claus.

They weren't concerned over the actual lives of the men murdered; it was just what effect it would have on the children that upset everyone.

So the next day the town was filled with city and state police, FBI men, and even some Naval Intelligence officers, Treasury agents, and Department of Justice officials, all of whom found excuses to get in on the case—and ten more Santa Clauses were murdered, and the elusive killer wasn't caught.

So that night all the working Santa Clauses held a secret meeting to decide what to do.

They realized their responsibilities toward the children, but on the other hand it seemed sort of foolish to go out and just get popped off by this maniac.

And so one man, who was a brave man, and who had no dependents, volunteered to go out the next day in costume under heavily armed guard.

But his throat was slashed in his bed that night.

And so the next day there were no Santa Clauses in the city.

And people were all sort of irritable and jumpy, and kids were crying, and it just didn't seem like Christmas without the Santa Clauses.

But the next day some daffy Hollywood chick, some actress who wanted some publicity, came out dressed in a Mrs. Santa Claus costume.

And people and kids flocked around her, being the nearest thing to Santa Claus on the streets, and she got a lot of publicity, and she wasn't killed.

So the next day several more prominent women came out, all dressed up like Mrs. Santa Claus with white powdered hair and red skirts and pillows in their stomachs and Santa Claus hats, and they weren't killed either.

They decided maybe this maniac had stopped, so they sent out one Mr. Santa Claus as a test, but within an hour his body was being taken to Bellevue in an ambulance. There were three bullets in him.

And so Christmas that year was spent with Mrs. Santa Clauses.

And the next year the same thing started to happen all over again, so they sent the women out immediately.

The next year the same thing happened; and the next, and the next — and year after year this patient and elusive maniac would kill any male dressed as Mr. Santa Claus, until finally, in the newspapers, in advertisements, and in people's minds, Santa Claus sort of dropped into the background and Mrs. Santa Claus became the central figure.

I mean Santa Claus was still there. He made the toys up at the North Pole and he was in charge of the elves, but it was Mrs. Santa Claus who rode the sleigh with the reindeer and slid down the chimney and gave away the presents and led the Christmas parade each year.

And the funny part of it was: women really seemed to enjoy being Mrs. Santa Claus. No one had to pay them, and it got to be such a fad that the streets around Christmastime were jammed with Mrs. Santa Clauses. And as time went by, they began making little alterations in the traditional costume, first changing the shade of red, and then experimenting with entirely different colors, so finally each costume was unique and fantastic, beautifully colored, gorgeous.

It became a real honor to lead the Christmas parade.

And the kids loved it!

Christmas had never been like this before, with all these Mrs. Santa Clauses, and all the excitement, and gee!

But these kids, this new generation of children who grew up *believing* in Mrs. Santa Claus, were sort of different.

Because, you see, Santa Claus to very young children is — a god.

And about the time they stop believing in Santa Claus they start going to Sunday school and learning about a new God. And this new God doesn't just give them presents. He's sort of rough.

But all their lives they yearn for their old childhood god, their Santa Claus god.

Like witness their prayers, their saying—give me what I want.

But this new generation of kids, who grew up believing in Mrs. Santa Claus, seemed to have a different attitude toward women.

They began electing women to Congress and they elected a woman president and women mayors until pretty soon the country was entirely run by women.

They were mainly concerned with things like food, and there was much debate in Congress about various diets, and pretty soon even the poorest people had a lot to eat; and they were interested in houses, and soon there was no housing shortage.

But there was one thing they wouldn't stand for.

They just weren't going to do it.

I mean what possible political reason could make these women send their guys out to get killed! It was ridiculous!

So with their political power and their financial power and the prestige of the United States, they forced and encouraged other countries to let women run things.

So war was ended forever.

Men went on doing just what they'd always done. They worked in factories, and studied higher mathematics, and gambled on horses, and delivered the ice, and argued about philosophy.

But these arguments about philosophy didn't cause people to starve and kill each other.

And pretty soon all over the world, why—no one was hungry—everyone had nice houses—there was no more war—people began to be happy.

You know when you stop to think about it, a world revolution had taken place.

And gee, 42 Santa Clauses, that's not many people killed for a world revolution.

But the murderer, or really, the saint to whom humanity owed so much, who planned and carried out this almost bloodless revolution, was never caught and crucified.

Just went on living.

No, no one ever discovered the identity of this saint that is—ahh—except me.

I know who the saint is.

Oh, I have no proof, but, you see, that's exactly why I'm so sure I know.

Because there is only one person capable of this, there is only one person with the genius, the daring, the imagination, the courage, the love of people, the blood lust, and patience required to carry out this greatest of all deeds.

That person is my little sister.

The Blond Bat

Once upon a time a big blond bat sat down next to a bartender.

The bat had the most beautiful eyes the bartender had ever seen.

As they flew forty miles an hour on the Independent Subway, the bartender wondered if those baby blue eyes would glow in the dark like dull purple flames, like the blue light bulbs on the ends of the subway platforms.

Her costume was made of black velvet with silk black wings and satin gloves; she wore a curious mask which revealed more of her face than it hid; her shoes were high-heeled and furry, and he noticed her feet were delicate, and he wondered whether she was barefoot underneath those shoes, or whether she wore stockings, and he bet she had beautiful toes.

This bartender was falling in love.

That was an odd performance, now—a bartender falling in love with a strange beautiful girl wearing a bat's costume on a subway!

Most subway loves get off at 34th Street to go into a railway station and thence to Saskatchewan—but it doesn't have to be that way.

For instance, in this story the bartender will not only have the courage to speak to this girl—they will even fall in love.

What! you say. You're a little indignant. You accuse me of sadism. To allow my character, the fat red-faced bartender, to fall in love with the young girl. She will soon tire of him, you say, throw him off for a younger, more suitable man, for by the grandness and good taste of her costume and the dignity and grace of her features it's obvious she comes from a good family. How unhappy you're going to make the bartender! you say to me.

Fiddlesticks! I'm not going to make the bartender unhappy.

To be sure, though, the bartender will have many months of horror after this night of love and many years of sadness after that, but this is not unhappiness, for he will commit many kindnesses out of thankfulness to the world for allowing him his magic night.

No, unhappiness is something else; unhappiness is to be without the courage.

But back to the story: The train roared into the Delancey Street station, and the bartender's eyes popped out of his head because hundreds of people in costume were dancing and singing and blowing horns and running and shouting and whoopeeing on the subway platform.

The girl got up.

The bartender also rose, and with eyes averted and distracted, he followed her out onto the subway platform and it was there he spoke to her.

She looked at him, startled; she looked him up and down; then she laughed, but she wasn't laughing at him, he could tell—it was a laugh of glee he was to remember.

She ran.

He chased her!

She ran through the crowd, she was slippery, she seemed to glide between these mad gesticulating revelers while he had to fight for every foot, and in his passionate pursuit he stepped on Napoleon's toe, knocked over a shrieking fat witch, hit a clown in the stomach, sat a surprised gorilla down, tripped the queen of England, and on and on she ran, out of the subway down Delancey Street toward the river until finally he caught her and she rested quietly in his arms while she caught her breath, giggling occasionally with glee.

She was so soft he kissed her, and then they walked, arm-in-arm, watching the fireworks and the crowds, stopping, now and then, for a beer.

The whole town was having a party!

Everyone had a costume, everyone had a mask, and there were searchlights, confetti, and fireworks everywhere just like a marvelous Mardi Gras or something, and the bartender felt a little out of place with his drab street clothes and without even a mask.

But the girl said he was dressed fine.

And he asked her what all this celebrating was about—he hadn't heard of any celebration—but she just giggled and kissed him, and that was that.

And so they struggled happily through the crowds and the night, stopping occasionally to dance to slow strange music in the taverns or the fiery jazz played on almost every corner.

She pointed at a big clock on a building. It was eleven o'clock.

She hurried him over to a long line that was walking slowly before a judges' stand, and when their turn came the judges made a big fuss over them, and one judge kept fingering the bartender's bright necktie admiringly, and so they won the contest, and both of them got big loving cups.

The judges ushered them up to a giant love seat built way up above the cheering crowd, a tremendous couch it was, bigger than a mattress.

This was their throne! They were king and queen of the night! They had won the costume contest.

Then the bartender heard a tremendous gonging.

The crowds began to shriek and scream.

He heard a siren long and low.

Delancey Street was mad.

His girl took off her mask, and he held his breath. She was so beautiful as she pointed at the big clock on the building—she whispered to him, and soft with passion, lovingly she said—"It's midnight! Take off your mask!"

The Blazing Blue Footprint

A footprint in blue ink from a birth certificate was blown up to the size of a football field, and projected in sections one night onto the White Cliffs of Dover by pranksters from Amsterdam, young artists. Ships in the Channel saw it, the bright blue footprint, reported it, and refused to enter the port when they could get no explanation of it on their radios. A squadron of RAF fighters swarmed around it. Three large naval vessels hovered offshore, and many men studied it through field glasses from the bridge, a blazing blue footprint. Finally landing parties were sent from ships in small boats, battling a choppy sea. Submarines surfaced and turned toward it, torpedoes ready, aimed at—"A blue footprint!" Helicopters swarmed down around it, and at first they didn't see the projectors, which the kids had taken elaborate pains to conceal, and the nearby town panicked—thousands left Dover that night on every available conveyance.

"Before I send you to jail," said the Dover judge to the dozen Dutch youths gathered in front of the bench, "have you any explanation as to why you caused all this commotion?"

"Your Honor," said the youngest looking of them, "I traded my white bicycle for this document because I thought it was a grand thing to have, sort of a collector's item, you know."

He handed the document up to the judge.

"You see the footprint on that paper . . . a bunch of us were sitting around one night, studying it in a sort of admiring way, looking at it through a magnifying glass, and standing off and squinting at it from a distance, and I got the idea—it was my idea," he confessed, "I said wouldn't this footprint look wonderful—big as a battleship—flashing luminous on the White Cliffs of Dover. And everyone thought it was a beautiful idea, and so we did it."

"What is this!?" exclaimed the judge.

"It's a real copy of Winston Churchill's birth certificate."

"Do you mean that the cause of all this was Sir Winston's footprint from the day of his birth?" exclaimed the judge.

"Yes, we thought he'd rather like the idea, if he were alive, and that it would make him laugh—"

The judge looked out over his spectacles at the London newsmen rushing out to the telephones.

"I shall have to give this case further consideration," said the judge. "This trial is postponed until after the weekend."

But the trial was postponed again, and later it was moved to London, and postponed again. The youths in London were invited to many parties and were soon in the swim of artistic society, several of them married English girls, some got studios and settled down to work, the youngest one formed a successful musical group—and the trial never did occur, although neither were the charges formally dropped, for to just forget is Justice when crimes are dreams.

Doubletalk French

Once upon a time there was a man who was . . . . It's hard to explain.

I don't know what he was.

There is no word for what he was.

He began life ordinarily in the Midwest. When he finished high school, he decided he wanted to become a painter, an artist.

Well, he wants to be a painter, so his parents ship him off to an art school in New York City. You want to be an artist—you go to an art school—that idea.

When he arrived in New York City, he made a discovery. It was 1950, and he discovered something he'd never seen before in his life in the Midwest. What he discovered were the foreign movies—Italian movies, French movies, Japanese movies, and at that time movies were never dubbed, but always had English titles, so that one could actually hear the actors speaking—always in a foreign language, of course.

He became a regular foreign film fan.

He developed a peculiar talent, if such a thing can be called talent.

He learned to imitate the voices he heard in the movies.

He used this talent in two ways:

Par example: when someone would insert a French phrase into a conversation—which he didn't understand, of course—he would say something like, "*Je roi métre, anon? Carance nous toin tarque se vous . . . .*"

And the person would always look a little embarrassed, and answer, "Well, I only studied French in college three years. . . ."

Or they'd look a little anxious, and explain, "I only spent a few months in Paris . . . ."

And then he would always tell them that he really didn't speak French, that he was just imitating the sound, that it was just doubletalk . . . nonsense.

But he'd had his little triumph.

But his grand triumphs—they came at night, when he would walk through the streets daydreaming.

All the characters in his daydreams spoke this doubletalk French.

Sometimes he'd be a great politician, and with great gestures, proclaim, "*Je quoi rien aitre!*" ... well, there's no point in my imitating the other characters in his daydreams. They are easily imaginable. Anyway, these were his grand triumphs.

All art students must study in Paris, and so, when he got into his early twenties he, too, went to Paris.

The trouble began as soon as he got on the boat.

It was a French line. He went into the bar. The bar was empty.

The bartender was polishing glasses, as they do, and the American sat down, and said, "*Je bourai – ah – un pernod!*"

And the bartender said, "Oui, monsieur," and began to pour a drink.

"I'd like a beer, please," said the American.

The bartender frowned and said, "But monsieur, you just ordered a Pernod."

"What!" said the American. "You mean I was actually saying something!" And then the American explained that he really didn't speak French, that it was just doubletalk, nonsense, and that it was just coincidence that he had sounded as if he were actually saying something.

The bartender looked at him a little funnily.

"Well, as long as you have the drink poured, let me try it – *Pernod*, you call this."

He took a sip of the drink, and – Uggggh!

It was sweet.

It tasted awful. He asked for a glass of water, and paid for the drink, and walked out on deck; and as he walked out onto the deck, he was thinking that it was rather peculiar his blurting out that doubletalk French, because he really hadn't intended to, when suddenly – he blurted out some more!

He looked around to see whether anyone had heard him.

Someone would think he was crazy just talking to himself, and particularly if they understood French and knew he was talking nonsense.

Luckily, no one heard him.

For, as a matter of fact, he had just been speaking excellent French, and he'd made a very vulgar, nasty comment on the morals of one of France's leading ingenues.

When he arrived in Paris, he continued to blurt out phrases and whole sentences in perfect French, and this "ability" somehow kept him from learning the language.

He meets a girl. They fall in love.

The girl speaks both French and English, and sometimes she tries to translate these things that he's saying, but they never seem to relate to anything that's actually happening. They're like sentences out of the air, from nowhere.

The girl tries to get him to see a psychiatrist, someone she knows, who speaks both French and English.

The American realizes—well, that obviously there is something a little peculiar happening, but he keeps putting off the visit to the doctor.

One afternoon they're walking along the *Rue Charant-Sant* (that's the theater section of Paris) when the girl suddenly points up at a theater marquee. "Hey!" she says. "Here's my favorite actor playing in a show!"

(Some matinee-idol type; she is one of his fans.)

She says, "I'd like to see this show! You won't understand what's happening because it'll be in French, but maybe sitting in the dark and hearing the voices—maybe it'll calm you down a little."

For the last five minutes the man has been speaking in *both* French and English about how he really should see that psychiatrist. "Maybe tomorrow I'll go."

They buy tickets. The show is just about to begin. They take their seats.

The American stops talking, but she can tell he's tense.

They wait.

And they wait.

And they wait . . . and nothing happens.

The whole audience begins to get restless, and they begin stomping their feet, and whistling, shouting for the show.

Finally the American says, "Let's go! Let's go see that doctor. Right now!"

They get up and leave the theater, and just as they are leaving, a man comes out from between the curtains and announces that the famous actor has taken ill and won't appear this afternoon anyway, so they haven't missed anything.

They take a taxi to the psychiatrist's office—his office is just his apartment, which he uses as his office during the day. There is a pretty secretary dressed in a nurse's uniform, and she tells them, "Please sit down. The doctor's busy right now with a patient, but he'll be with you in a few minutes."

The man says, "Aaaah . . . is there a men's room?"

The secretary says, "Well, yes, that door there—but there's someone in there now."

But the man doesn't seem to hear.

He walks over and opens the bathroom door, goes in, and the door closes behind him, and—no one comes out.

The secretary frowns because the other person in the bathroom had also seemed to be in a rather disturbed state. She decides she better get the doctor.

The doctor comes out with raised eyebrows at having his session with his patient interrupted, and goes over and opens the bathroom door.

There, sitting on the bathtub, is a nude man.

There are two piles of clothing, one on either side of him.

The doctor looks around the bathroom. There's no window. There is no way anyone could have gotten out of the room. The doctor turns to the secretary and demands, "I thought you said there were *two men* in here!"

"But there are!" says the secretary.

The doctor stares at her suspiciously, and then turns to the man, and says, in French, "Well, monsieur, what are you doing sitting on my bathtub with no clothing on? *What is the meaning of this?*"

The man explains, in French, that . . . well, of course . . . he is none other than the famous actor whom the young couple had gone to see that afternoon. "Just before the performance today it got to be too much. I have to talk to somebody about it! For the last several months I've been blurting out sentences in perfect English . . . a language I don't speak ! *American* I'm talking! *American*!!! I don't speak American."

And then the man—the same man—begins to speak English.

He explains that he is an art student from the States, and that for the last several months he has been blurting out sentences in perfect French, a language he doesn't speak—"Just like I did just now!" he exclaims. "The things I say don't make sense. They never relate to anything that's actually happening."

Then the man—the same man—begins to speak French again, "You see what I mean when I talk the English!? The things I say never make sense; like voices out of the air, they never relate to anything that's actually happening! And I can't control it! I just blurt the words out! I never know what I'm saying!"

Then the man began to speak English again, "You see what I mean, doctor, like just now when I spoke that French. I can't control it. I just blurt things out. And I haven't the least idea what I just said."

"Well," says the doctor, "Get some clothes on. Come outside . . . and we'll talk about it."

The doctor goes out and speaks to the young girl, who had accompanied the American to the office, and to the actor's manager, who had accompanied *him* to the office.

He returns to the bathroom and finds that the "*man*" is having difficulty getting dressed. There are two piles of clothing on the floor. First he starts to put on one pair of trousers, and then, obviously confused, reaches for the trousers on the other pile.

With the doctor's help he gets dressed.

When he finally comes out, he's dressed pretty weirdly.

He has on one blue sock and one red one, one brown shoe and one black one. He's wearing a coat from this pile and trousers from that one.

"Listen!" says the doctor, "This is impossible! This cannot have happened. Two People who were leading separate lives suddenly have only one body. [I mean, Reader, as if your mind and my mind suddenly discovered ourselves in one body—you might like asparagus—*I hate it.*] It is not a medical case. It is simply impossible. This cannot have happened! Look! Why don't we all go downstairs to the café and get a *drink*."

While they are winding down the narrow Parisian staircase to the café below, I'd like to glance for a moment at the positions of the others:

Par example: There's the actor's manager. You can see he's worried. Here he has a matinee idol, a star—well, I mean a dummy, a puppet, a jerk, someone who would do anything he was told to do ... for money, for fame, or whatever reason, and through clever handling the manager had managed him into a million-dollar proposition. And the manager senses that from now on the actor isn't going to be as easily handleable as before, if handleable at all.

And there's the poor girl. Here the innocent, naïve American art student, whom she loves, has suddenly become her daydream hero, the figure of her most private fantasies, and one can imagine that the actor in actuality isn't at all what she's imagined him to be.

Well, they get down to the café, they sit down, and a waiter takes their orders, but when he gets to the *"man"* he says, *"Je maître suare—un pernod!"* And then he adds, "Aaaah ... gimmee a beer."

"But monsieur," says the waiter, and then he adds uncertainly, "Sir ... *What do you want?"*

"He wants a beer," says the young girl.

"He *ordered* a Pernod," says the actor's manager.

The waiter turns to the man and says, "But monsieur, *you must decide.* What do you want?"

I cannot help noticing that there are two ways this little problem of the drink could be solved. There are in fact two ways in which the grander problems this *"man"* must meet can be resolved. There are, as a matter of fact, two possible endings for this story.

For instance: they can look down the menu and find some drink which they both like. They can compromise. The Frenchman can learn English, and the American can learn French. They can help each other out, learn to tolerate each other's prejudices. They can become friends. Until eventually, though inevitably it must take some time, they can become almost like one person again, and perhaps a more complete person than either of them had been previously.

But there is another way this story could end: They can each be stubborn. They can each insist on having his own way. They can begin to irritate each other, and annoy each other. They can embarrass each other, and play little practical jokes on each other, until eventually they grow to hate each other. And when two people hate each other in this situation—from such hatred—inevitably—Oh! I made a mistake . . . pardon me, my Reader, but I am wrong. I said before that there were two possible endings to this story, but I'm wrong . . . for to any story whatsoever, inevitably . . . .

There can be but one conclusion.

The Prime Minister's Grandfather

A walrus swallowed a candle, grimaced, made a little face at the taste and decided it was a mackerel, and then dove to the bottom of the Bering Sea, nosing about among cold boulders where the best lobster live. He chose to glide about a foot above a seaweed meadow over beside a new Canadian submarine being shown off by the Canadian Secretary of the Navy, who was playing host to several members of Parliament, and the Prime Minister, himself, on an inspection tour.

"Mr. Prime Minister," said the captain eagerly, "you asked whether we might see some underwater life, and I think this meadow might be a good place."

And he gave crisp orders that powerful lights located on the outside of the submarine be switched on, so that when the periscope was dropped beneath the surface of the water, it was possible to view the bed of waving weeds for several hundred yards in any direction, such is the clarity there of those northern waters, such the penetrating power of modern submarine lights.

"This was an expensive ship," mused the head of state, and as if to test its mettle he rapped the wall three times with his cane.

On the other side of the two-inch steel-plate wall was the walrus who was worrying a steel loop that swung loosely on a hinge, used to secure the submarine with cable when the boat was at a dock.

Mimicking the Minister's knock with mammalian fidelity, the walrus knocked the steel loop against the ship's hull three times.

"That noise came from outside," said the captain.

The Prime Minister rapped twice against the wall with his cane, and the walrus, obviously enjoying the game, rapped back—twice.

"Who is out there?" asked the Prime Minister.

"It's odd. I don't see a living thing out there," said the captain, turning the periscope this way and that. Fish were often curious about the submarine, but today the presence of the walrus had caused them all to flee, and the walrus at the moment was swimming about directly above the periscope, his attention attracted by its turning, but he was out of view.

"May I look?" inquired the Prime Minister, and he put his eye to the glass, and at that moment the walrus swam down so that his face filled the field of the periscope's view.

"May I look?" inquired the Prime Minister, and he put his eye to the glass, and at that moment the walrus swam down so that his face filled the field of the periscope's view.

"Good Christ, it's my grandfather!" whispered the Prime Minister, aghast and visibly shaken. As a boy of nine he had attended his grandfather's funeral in Toronto, and lately the old man had appeared several times in his dreams, admonishing him to conduct the affairs of state in a proper fashion. "*You protect the wild animals . . . ,*" his grandfather had said to him in his dream only last night. The old man had wagged his finger at him and in his dream he had felt like a child. "*The walrus, the musk ox, the caribou, the polar bear, the white fox . . .*" The Prime Minister had awoken in a cold sweat and had clutched his heart with a pang of guilt.

On disembarking from the submarine at the naval base, the Prime Minister got on the phone to the Canadian capital, instructing aides and different legislators on his position in regard to the new wildlife protection laws which were to be enacted by Parliament soon.

"Now Mr. Prime Minister," inquired the leader of the Opposition Party, whom he had gotten out of bed at an early hour, "the law as it is being written affects the musk ox, the caribou, the polar bear . . . but what about the walrus?"

"What?"

"What about the walrus?" repeated the lawmaker.

The Prime Minister's mind worked furiously. A walrus! Could that have been the face he had seen through the periscope?

"Yes! The walrus!" exclaimed the great man happily. "By all means—include the walrus!"

Fear of Firecrackers
& 6 untitled paragraphs

Rain filled the flat plate which inadvertently had been left all night in the yard, and in the early morning sunlight it was visited by birds, by a robin, some purple finches and starlings. On the previous evening a hole had been dug there as a grave for the cat who had been seventeen years old on the Fourth of July. The cat had been born on that holiday and had carried with him a lifelong fear of firecrackers and had retreated under the porch to die on his birthday.

*

A tramp steamer carried a full load of used rubber tires from South Asia to Puget Sound. The ship was permeated with the odor of used tires. Even the ice cubes from the refrigerator in the galley smelled like rubber. In the middle of the placid Pacific the long churning wake of the ship smelled like a busy highway.

*

At the summit of a mountain in Chile a luminous gnat landed at night near the center of the giant lens of the largest telescope in the world, laid its luminous eggs there, and then vanished into the heavens.

*

He held a newspaper over his head in the sudden downpour, and yet it soon was sopping wet, and disintegrated in his hands, leaving a word from a large headline plastered on his bald spot.

*

Looking like a piece of the moon, a giant clinker from an abandoned coal furnace is found by a five-year-old with his nine-year-old brother, who are playing among the ruined buildings of the old factory down by the river. The only intact structure on the grounds is a brick chimney four stories high. Goldenrod grows between the railroad tracks.

*

Conversation was difficult but irrepressible among the dozen patients in the doctor's waiting room, who were all ages and from all walks of life, there alike to be treated for severe hiccups.

*

It is his lifework to meticulously draw with a diamond-tipped pencil great arrays of streaming raindrops on panes of perfect glass.

A Rare Yellow Emerald

Redheaded woodpeckers travel in bands on the Pampas in Argentina.
Flocks appear in numbers at some unappointed place and move
as a great band for a few weeks or months until at some unknown
signal from nature they disperse into identical flocks to settle on a
"territory" from which they will not wander—until the strange phenomenon which scientists have labeled "wanderlust" moves them
again to gather, to soar again together over the plains 10,000 strong.
"The Robe of the Pope" is the farmers' name for the phenomenon.
When the scarlet, hungry cloud is seen approaching an orchard or
vineyard or cornfield, the children shout for joy, "The Pope is bless-
ing us!", for it will mean a good season, the crops entirely free from
the blights of insects, all of which the birds gobble up.

A yellow emerald was found.

The red birds had come to a happy vineyard at the feet of the
Andes, and school was let out so that the children could see them;
and younger ones were allowed to wander among the birds, and to
stroke them, for the birds were very tame at such times, seemingly
knowing that the farmers welcomed them.

A child of three stormed a flock on a vine with her giggles,
shrieking with glee as she stared at them. One of the birds flew over
onto her shoulder, and she turned stone-still, ecstatically terrified.
The bird had a yellow stone in its beak, which it dropped as it flew
off into the sky. The little girl picked it up and carried it home. It
was her treasure. She put it in a box with her other things.

The stone would be worth $50,000 in the right hands.

But the girl will keep it, and when she grows up she'll call it a
"good luck piece." She'll keep it with her cheap jewels and crosses.
After her death the stone will be lost again, thrown away by another
child, who will not know its value.

The White Mirror

A silent swamp aswim with worms all up to the surface in the shade, wriggling blades, little purple flat things, pink-mouthed, white-toothed carnivores.

The swamp is connected to the Amazon by a single slow stream, up which men come rowing furiously in a scarlet canoe, tossing off it like ballasts hunks of jaguar meat and flesh of fowl.

They are luring a school of piranha into the plantation of the worms.

The swamp trees are filled with Indian children and women waiting, legs dangling above the water, to watch the most barbaric spectacle of blood devised by man to honor the Deity.

The children have brought chicken legs which they drop to watch the worms crowd, while they wait for the men to come in their sacred craft with the flashing, half-mile tail of splashing water agleam with teeth—as a dragon is feathered.

As the canoe enters the swamp, a roar is heard as the two races meet.

It takes about an hour. It's always the same.

Fish eat worms.

The massacre is for miles.

The blood of the worms is white, and oozy, and covers the whole surface of the swamp as silver does a mirror.

The piranha leave quickly and quietly under the reflection.

The Indians have never seen snow, such whiteness.

It is the most perfect mirror they know.

By moonlight they ride from vine to vine around the swamp into the dawn.

Chess

Once upon a time there was a demonstration of Russian courtesy.

There is a fair-sized city in Russia, the center of a great gray barren region.

In this town there is a chess club, and anyone in the whole area at all seriously interested in chess belongs to this club.

For a number of years, there had been two old men who were head and shoulders above all the rest of the club members. They weren't masters, but in this area they were the chief players, and for years the club members had been attempting to decide which of them was the better; each year there was a contest, and each year these two tied. First one would win, then the other, and then they would draw, or stalemate. The club was divided: half the members thought one was superior, half the other.

The club members wanted to have one champion.

So they decided this year to hold a different sort of contest. They decided to bring in an inferior player, an utterly unknown person from outside the area, and each of the candidates would play him a game, and they simply assumed each of the candidates would win against the mediocre player, so there was no question of winning or losing; but rather they decided to vote afterward, after studying and discussing each of the candidates' games, and award the championship to him who played with better style.

The tournament evening arrived, and the first candidate played with the inferior player—until the inferior player finally shrugged his shoulders and said, "I concede. You obviously win." Whereupon the first candidate leaned over and turned the chessboard around, himself taking the position the inferior player had given up, and said, "Continue." They played longer until finally the inferior player was checkmated.

Then the second candidate played the inferior player until finally the outsider threw up his hands and said, "I concede." And the second candidate, exactly as the first candidate had done, turned the board around, and said, "Continue."

They played for a while until the harassed inferior player, looking blank, leaned back and shrugged his shoulders and said, "I don't know what to do. I don't know where to move. What should I do?"

The second candidate twisted his head around to get more of his opponent's view of the board, and then said tentatively, "Well, why don't you move that piece there." The outsider stared at the board uncomprehendingly, and finally shrugged his shoulders as if to say, "Well, it can't do any harm, and after all, what does it matter, as I know I'm going to lose anyway." With that gesture he moved the piece *there*.

The master frowned and pondered the board for several minutes before moving.

His frown deepened.

The corners of his mouth turned down.

His eyes hardened; he turned a sullen, stony, defiant stare at his audience for a moment before whispering in a choked voice all could hear, "I concede!"

He leaped up from his chair, raised his gold-headed cane quickly into the air, smashed it down onto the ebony and ivory chessboard, and split it in half.

He rushed from the room muttering loudly a long, strong string of profanities that were marvelous to hear.

He was, of course, awarded the club championship, and had, I think, incidentally demonstrated the proper way to lose a game.

The Monroe Street Monster

Once upon a time a monster moved into 91 Monroe Street.

That's a tenement block, full of Puerto Ricans and Italians, Jews and blacks, Irish and some Chinese, many first-generation immigrants, a lot of artists and bohemians; all these people wear costumes.

But this monster was very strange looking.

He was short and ugly and had bright carrot-red hair and was forty years old. He wore a long green cape which completely covered him; it dragged along the ground a little bit when he walked, so you couldn't see his legs.

This made him strange looking, but the thing which made people call him a monster was the peculiar way he walked—or rather, moved.

Because he didn't walk like ordinary people do.

He sort of glided.

It was like someone was pushing him on roller skates, or he was riding a one-wheeled bicycle, and some said he really sat cross-legged in the middle of the air, floating.

Some thought he was an angel, others thought he was a devil, but everyone, old ladies, young gangsters, and children alike, felt the same fear when they saw him coming, gliding.

People would rush inside to watch him from doorways and through windows, peeking at him from behind curtains, as he glided grimly down the vacated street.

It went on for about two weeks.

He had very regular hours. He went out early in the morning and returned early in the evening, and nobody ever knew where he went or what he did when he got into his apartment.

One evening as he turned down the block, and as the block emptied, a bum fell out of the bar at the other corner.

The bum began to stagger up the street toward the monster, and he was so drunk, swearing and lurching and talking to himself, he didn't notice the silence, or the emptiness, or the green-caped redhead moving quickly toward him.

But all of Monroe Street was watching.

They met.

The bum looked — and he saw the monster — and he reached in his pocket and brought out a cigarette (the cigarette was broken) and he said, "Hey, buddy! You got a light?"

The monster fiddled around underneath his cape and brought out a match and lit the bum's cigarette.

It was at this point that the bum, who was so drunk, collapsed, and in falling, fell on top of the monster, knocking him down, knocking him into the middle of the street, and in the process, he grabbed onto the monster's cape and pulled it off.

The monster was completely exposed!

And the people rushed out and they formed a big circle around the monster and they just stared — !

And then someone said in a sort of disappointed voice, "Aww, he's only got three legs."

Then someone else said, "Yeah, he's no devil. He's no angel — hah! He's just got three legs. That's why he walks like that!"

Then they began to get angry with him, shouting at him belligerently for frightening them.

And the poor monster, there were tears rolling down his cheeks, as he tried to tell them that he didn't really mean to frighten them, it was just that he was ashamed of his deformity — that's why he wore the long cape.

Finally a guy stepped out of the crowd and helped the monster to his feet, and said, "Say, buddy, what you need's a drink!"

So the monster, cape over his arm, glided down to the bar at the corner, and a crowd of men followed him in.

His hands were shaking as he took his drink, so the other men pretended not to notice. One of them said, "You think the Yankees'll win tomorrow?"

Another said, "Well, I got two bucks they will!"

The monster turned, pointing a steady finger at the man, shouting, "I'll take that bet!"

Because, you see, he was a Dodgers fan.

That's really the end of the story.

But I can't help noticing that the monster and the people have completely forgotten the bum.

While they sit drinking and talking about baseball, the bum is unconscious in the gutter, and he'll never even know of this great deed he committed.

Kids are careful not to step on his body as they run back and forth chasing each other, but that's about the only attention he gets.

But—as the author—I have a certain power.

And so I'd like to express that gratitude which my characters failed to show. You see, this bum is going to die in a couple of months anyway of tuberculosis, but I'm going to have him picked up by the police on an alcoholic charge and they'll take him to Bellevue, and they'll discover his TB there, and they'll send him to a state sanitarium to die.

They'll take care of him.

The Green Gardenia

Green green Gardenia covered with dew, sunlit, planted in a flower-pot, struggling for its existence . . . .

Little white marbles had been tossed in the pot to make it prettier.

And the Gardenia thought they were its bones, and shuddered in the breeze, in horror of viewing them, so bare, so bare.

If the Gardenia could speak, it would shriek.

But its soul was mute.

In a distant corner of the city, in the corner of a church, an organist's fingers practiced caresses on the ghost teeth of his instrument, and the chords he fingertipped filled the church like a warm liquid, softening its dark red walls like rubber, and the man, more like a squid, breathed the water as if it were the fragrance of our green Gardenia.

The man loved music, and his passion led him to stray churches, like this one, where it was quiet, lost in the suburbs.

In a gray way he was a genius. But the man scratched a livelihood from funerals.

Flames tossed about in the air like oriental angels hula-hulaing on the tips of the white candles, pale, in the colored sunlight shooting through the monstrous windows, through the bodies of some painted saints, a lamb, and a goat.

An eternally tired golden Virgin Mary stared down at him.

She was on the ceiling.

Between two arches she clung to her plaster; as he played, as he was alone, he let his head fall back to stare at her, and there seemed to be a glitter around her; through heavy eyelids little violet flashes fell around him from her, through an air of darting swirling dots; and he wondered what the color of her eyes was.

The lamb and the goat became dim, and the hula-hula dancers were demanding more attention, and a cleaning woman came bustling down the aisle talking to herself.

So he stopped, and went down to the corner for a beer, and a bus.

He fingered his coin nervously as he waited on the corner, and was amazed at the loud clang it made as he pushed it in the slot of the automatic fare-taker, and the sounds of the people in the bus rushed over him like a gust of overheated air, making him dizzy for a moment.

He sat down and gave himself to the jiggling of the bus, and stared at his dark reflection on the window, and tried not to listen to a fat woman screaming about something to a skinny woman, who was knitting, and nodding.

He lay awake till dawn. He slept for an hour, and dreamed of a green Gardenia.

"Cantaloupe."

"Cantaloupe?"

He nodded and picked up his napkin.

"Coffee."

"Coffee?"

He stared at the waitress, wondering whether to be annoyed, and he decided she was probably tired too, and occupied himself with thoughts of his dreams, like a child trying to reach his boat with a stick, but the boat was stranded a little too far out in the pond, so he could barely touch, tickle the end of it, and it was very exasperating.

All he remembered was a green Gardenia.

The funeral was at ten.

Somehow he enjoyed his work, the flowers, the weeping women, and the brave men; how many hundreds of funerals had he watched in a little mirror set on the organ, where he watched for signals from his boss? Where were his glasses? Ah! He felt them in his pocket.

The weepers and criers he had classified into gentle amusing types, for to take them seriously was impossible, and would make his job, his life, impossible—pain was too frequent an experience in the world, he had decided long ago, and laughter was his protection; he wasn't contemptuous of them actually, except when they bored him, as one or two would do occasionally—seeking sympathy, a pseudo-father, or what? Sometimes he couldn't tell, and rarely cared.

The children, though, the confused, sad creatures, he always flirted with, with gentle eyes and tender smiles, to distract them from the sordidness of their relatives and parents—poor children, surrounded by cracking shells, and platitudes, and fear shrinking them in the sweet heavy suds in the metal washtub of a funeral parlor.

That green Gardenia!

It kept haunting him, his vision of it, and it kept bobbing and popping into his consciousness as a woman would have, had he been in love.

That green Gardenia!

So soft. Its petals had touched him like the face of a child.

The breakfast clatter in the kitchen, trays and forks and plates, shrill screeching laughter, a businessman belching for a joke, all hit his ears like boxing gloves, and he rushed from the restaurant as fast as he could pay his check.

He walked in the sun.

Past bright, painted wooden houses with iron fences, made of metal tubing, edging the crisp lawns, he strolled, like a well-oiled machine.

Morning!

At the end of the lawned block was a square stone building reaching out toward the sidewalk with an awning and a neon sign.

Mort's Mortuary.

The black hearse always waited like the Egyptian cat, full of patience, for its daily child; on receiving its bundle each day it would purr away as only a Cadillac can; and like a cat it would always reappear each morning, empty and greedy; and what care it got: this sleek aristocratic cat, worshipped like an idol.

He played and did his job as usual; the dead person was a fat man, and the mourners were usual—nothing strange about the early day.

As he walked outside, the hearse was pulling away, full of flowers and the fat man—a flower fell into the street from it—it was the green Gardenia of his dream.

He walked into the street and picked it up; it was exactly the same. He touched it to his cheek. It even felt the same.

He carried it home in the palm of his hand. He dropped it in a bowl of water, and sat and watched it on the table.

The Gardenia was dying.

It was dry, and he sprinkled drops of water on it.

He examined it closely with his eyes, and straightened a bent petal.

He blew on it, as if to blow some life to it.

But the Gardenia was dying.

It had been cut, taken from its pot, and sold that morning, and it had ceased to struggle. It no longer wanted to shriek, it no longer felt that terror of the pot, for death had taken half of it already.

All day the man sat there staring at it softly, like a madman, I suppose, staring with soft eyes at the dying thing, and yet it did not die.

Through the night he watched it, and yet it did not die; if anything, it seemed to have grown brighter, greener, fuller in the gloom, under the little white light, under his soft gaze, his tender mad affection.

Once near morning he walked away to get a blanket to throw around his shoulders, and when he returned the Gardenia seemed paler, and then to revive again as he blew on it once more.

The funeral was at ten.

But he did not go this morning.

Still wrapped in the blanket, he sat watching the flower, and sun streamed in, and noises came in, and a cleaning woman came in, but he waved her impatiently away and told her to come back later, and still he sat, with big red eyes.

The thing seemed dead.

He picked it from the bowl and held it to his mouth and felt currents fill his head and roam around his body as he inhaled death's perfume and he pressed the blossom to his lips and from these lips came a shriek which brought the neighbors whom he easily convinced that he was sane, and safe.

A Gardenia had spoken, and was dead.

The Purple Bird

Fluttering down of a purple bird to the plaza near the place where I sat in the sun each afternoon outside my hotel in Yucatán occasioned remarks in Spanish which I could not understand. The bird was as big as a robin, and was purple except for a white spot on its forehead and a baby blue breast. Six wind-worn umbrellas fluttered their tatters over tables in a way that in a cornfield might have frightened off birds, but this purple bird landed on a table one day and the waiter shouted something to his wife in the kitchen. She came outside with three plates in her hands and stared at the bird for a moment and immediately returned to her work, but from inside she shouted out, "Mi chinaca tompata que!" And the bird flew away.

On another afternoon the bird landed on the peak of an umbrella, and a nine-year-old boy, all dressed in white without shoes, sang out a song at the sight of the bird:

Chinampala talpo!
Se coro mular . . . .
Chinaca tompata!
Me cora mular . . . .

Or at least, that's what it sounded like he said to me, but I couldn't understand the words, and his Spanish sounded softly like Chinese as does the Maya language. The boy had oriental eyes, was pure Indian with the classic Maya profile, and he shouted out excitedly in Maya when he saw his parents coming, obviously telling them about the bird, and the bird vanished.

The next day, as I sat there, I spotted his flash of color up in a nearby palm tree, and I pointed it out to the waiter, saying the Spanish words for "The bird . . . ," but the waiter didn't seem to understand me, and he stared a moment at the treetop obviously puzzled. The beautiful bird had hopped behind a frond out of view. After consulting with his wife, he returned a few minutes later, and waving to me, walked over to the tree at which I had pointed and, patting its trunk, repeated a Spanish word three times, obviously the name of the tree. I nodded smiling, saying, "Thank you . . . thank you. . . ," in English. A little later I glanced up at the tree and the bird was still there, moving around among the branches, but I didn't want to engage the waiter in another conversation. I left him a largish tip, for he was obviously being friendly, and had tried to help me.

"Simpala te quilá!'"

"Orozocar tamin . . . ."

"Poche quinar?"

I had half-dozed in the sun at my usual table, and these voices mixed themselves with dreams. Only half-awake, I opened my eyes and beheld the purple bird perched on my knee. Without moving a muscle, I was instantly awake. The bird made a small odd sound and flew off to the tree. I stood up, and there must have been thirty people standing around me in a wide circle, all staring at me seriously.

I immediately went into the hotel. That evening, when I came downstairs, there was a flurry of excitement as I entered the small lobby to inquire after mail. Half a dozen people crowded a door that led to the kitchen, all of them staring at me with wonder in their eyes. A small girl tried to smile at me, but she dropped her eyes in embarrassment and stared at the floor. As I walked outside for an evening stroll, several customers of the restaurant rose from their table at the sight of me, and gawked.

Wherever I went that night, people were friendly. Strangers bought me drinks at the bar.

An old woman selling flowers fastened a perfect beauty in my buttonhole and laughingly refused to allow me to pay for it, chattering away in Spanish saying the Lord knows what.

Continuing my stroll, I passed a group of young women outside a church who giggled friendlily and also stared at me.

I cut down a side-street as I usually did every evening on my walk, but tonight as I passed, people came out on their porches, and several waved a friendly greeting to me, and I waved back, smiling for a moment.

I had become famous in an afternoon.

I left the village the next morning and went into a different state to complete my stay in Mexico, because it's no good being famous . . . when people don't understand.

Paint

He put his foot in the gallon of paint.

He put his other foot in the can of varnish.

He opened a new can of bright orange and a pint of blue and stuck a fist in each, raised his arms up into the air so that the paint ran down his sleeves, and started off to the masquerade, to which he was late.

He stepped out into the street at the corner to hail a cab, and five cars screeched to a halt at the sight of him. One of the five was a cab.

It sounded like somebody was moving the garbage cans as he clattered awkwardly to the cab. "To the American Academy!" he cried, tears streaming down his face, "And Institute of Arts and Letters!"

He patted a shoulder holster with the orange tin still stuck on his fist.

And he began to mumble that he was going to *get* those fashionable artists, all of them.

Every true artist, at one time or another, carries such a fare in his cab.

The Cat Who Owned
an Apartment

Once upon a time a man sat listening to music.

His fingers hung limply over the arm of his chair, his eyes drooped, and his feet rested on a sheepskin-covered ottoman. He breathed shallowly.

An expensive phonograph was twirling in the corner; a booming symphony filled the room, and filled the universe as far as he was concerned, so passionate was his attention. Each note he heard, each quiver of the harp strings, bang of the cymbals, nuance of the violin, snore of the tuba, plink of the piano.

The man loved music. He was a connoisseur.

His Siamese cat sat on the table.

The cat heard the music.

But the cat heard other things too. It heard the honking of automobiles, the sound of the refrigerator, leaves stirring in the wind, a dog barking down the street, someone shout.

The man heard none of this. He was completely absorbed in the music.

Then the cat heard the sound of the window being slowly opened and the floor creaking as a man in a leather jacket, wearing tennis shoes, stepped through.

But the man listening to music heard none of this.

The cat heard the sound of the man's tennis shoes as he tiptoed across the room, and the sound of a knife being drawn from the leather jacket.

The cat yawned and listened to the sound of the knife as it sank into his master's throat, his master's gasp, and to the sound of the man who was listening to music as he rolled down to the floor – dead.

The cat listened to the murderer as he walked back toward the open window, and heard him climb out onto the fire escape.

Then there was the sound of footsteps in the alleyway three stories below.

The light from the open window shone on the murderer. He jumped off the fire escape onto a wooden ledge which ran along the building.

The cat heard all this. But the cat heard the ledge creak as well. The murderer listened intently to the footsteps.

And the cat heard the ledge creaking and creaking and finally breaking, and heard the scream of the murderer as he fell to his death on the pavement below, and the shriek of the child who'd been passing.

Then the cat heard a funny little scratching noise behind the refrigerator.

A mouse poked his head out, pricked his ears, sniffed, and scampered across the room.

The cat leaped.

He landed on the mouse, and bit.

The mouse was dead. The cat looked around. They were all dead. It was his apartment now.

Wishing

Once upon a time there was a man who was always wishing for things.

He'd wish for things like there'd be no more wars, or people everywhere wouldn't starve anymore, and then sometimes he'd wish he had a million dollars or magical powers, so he could change all the misery around.

But he didn't do anything except wish for things.

He was a bum.

One day a bartender asked him, he said, "Look here, why do you make all these fantastic wishes? I mean if you want to end wars, why don't you go into politics and do something about it! Or if you want a million dollars, why, man, go out and earn it! Or at least, if you have to wish for things, why don't you wish for something you can possibly get? You know these fantastic wishes are never going to come true."

And the bum explained himself this way, he said, "Look here, a man goes through life wishing for many things, and some of our wishes come true, and some don't—but no man lives his whole life without ever having a wish come true. I mean God must grant every man at least one wish during his lifetime. But you ordinary people! You make so many petty wishes. You wish you had five dollars to buy this or that, or you wish you had this girl or that one, why, it's easy for God to grant one of your wishes. But look at me on the other hand. I have never made an ordinary wish!

"Do you understand?

"When God gets around to answering one of my wishes, he's going to have some trouble. You're going to see a lot of changes around here when God gets around to answering one of my wishes, because do you understand? *I have never made an ordinary wish!*"

Well.

The bum grew older, forty, fifty, and sickly and skinny because of the way he was living, and still none of his fantastic wishes had come true.

One day he happened to wander into the zoo.

And he began watching the giraffes, which were in a large cage by themselves near the edge of the zoo, so they had a lot of room.

He watched them galloping around swinging their big necks to and fro like ponderous dancing.

He realized that this was the most beautiful thing he'd ever seen.

But something was wrong.

He couldn't figure out what it was. At first he thought it was the fact that the animals were caged that somehow spoiled this almost perfect scene, but the cage was landscaped just like a regular jungle scene with rocks and little trees and things, so he decided this couldn't be it.

Then it hit him!

It was the fact that the giraffes were so big, they were out of proportion to everything else.

They seemed out of place.

He noticed some flowers growing in the cage, and he thought—wouldn't it be great if the flowers were giant. He wished that the flowers were tall.

Then he got dizzy, and he put his hand over his eyes, and the dizziness went away, and then he looked and—

There they were!

The flowers were tremendous—eighteen feet tall!—and the giraffes were running around among them, batting the big flowers with their necks, sticking their noses into the morning-glories, and the perfume! the perfume filled the air; and colors! the great green stalks, purples, reds, and oranges of the blossoms sprung among the brown and yellow spotted careening giants, stunned him; and then all the giraffes began to lick the flowers from which they seemed to get some substance, their tongues flickering like pink fish, and he watched them one by one drop to the ground, their eyes drooping, and closing, until finally all lay asleep.

It was even more beautiful than he'd imagined.

His wish had been answered.

His wish had been answered!

And—I mean—well—the giraffes and the flowers were nice, they were really very pretty, but—this was nothing like no more war, or people everywhere never having to starve anymore, or Christ! he didn't even get a million dollars.

And he wondered what to do now. He'd never learned a trade or made any real friends, and he realized there was nothing he could do. His life had no meaning now.

He was drinking a bottle of orange pop, and he broke it against the bars of the cage like he'd seen someone do in a Hollywood movie, and very methodically he cut his wrists.

And then for some reason he kneeled down and slashed his ankles and lay down on the grass with his arms stretched out like a man on a cross, to die.

As he lay there dying, he reflected that God had been rather mean. Here he'd been so faithful to his belief, never wished for food when he was starving, or a lover when he was lonely—and he'd been so lonely. He felt cheated, as if God had taken advantage of him. He felt somehow that God hadn't been a very good sport.

But a few minutes before he died he happened to glance back at the rest of the zoo, at the rest of the world.

He leaped to his feet, shocked at what he saw.

For he saw that God hadn't answered his wish at all.

And he realized that had he not taken his own life, God would have granted one of his great wishes, because He hadn't made the flowers giant. He'd merely made the cage, the giraffes—and the man, very small.

A Chocolate Reptile
& 3 untitled paragraphs

The deep-brown carnivorous mushroom with a cap shaped like a doughnut swallowed through the hole a tiny green chameleon tail first, and the last of it to disappear was the pink revealed by its extended jaws emitting an ultrasonic scream as it vibrated a forked carnelian tongue. No human could have heard that scream—one hundred million years ago—yet it was immediately heard by a mother, by an eighty-five-foot-long green chameleon, who twisted her neck around to that place on the ground where the murderous mushroom grew, and she bit off its bitter cap, letting the foul fungus fall to the forest floor, and from the wound the chocolate-colored baby reptile scampered free.

*

The sacred, flowery orange ceremonial robe of the Dowager Empress was sold in London at auction at Christie's to a dirty old man for cash. But he was not a filthy-rich American; he was an Australian impostor, the money counterfeit—and the old varmint vanished. The robe turned up two years later in the boudoir of a murdered English actress in Brisbane. Although the garment is undamaged, she had had it altered.

*

The orchid opened like a firecracker, all at once—with a silent explosion of odor that struck like a gong in the jungle gloom, with a stench so strong it seared the nostrils of mammals of every size and species, from jungle mouse to jaguar that were within twenty yards of the gaping blossom, inducing in all of them symptoms of extreme seasickness. It is the only flower fertilized by snakes.

*

The old French king had his dentist construct for his aging mistress a set of false teeth with thirty-six real pearls, perfectly matched, put in place of the teeth. Although her bite was perfect, pearls are fragile, and the only time she used them to eat was when she ate oysters. When she wore her pearls in public, she couldn't help but smile.

IV

10,000 Reflections

A hundred feet up in the air, the great crystal chandelier was flashing with the light of five hundred candles nestled in its glass.

Five hundred flames tossing, reflected ten thousand times.

The rude guests were aghast at the glittering giant—for the hall below was filled with peasants—it is 1789, it is July 14, the French Revolution is on!

This is the great dining hall of the Duke, his dinner guests have been stabbed in their chairs, and while their corpses sit still at their table, the peasants eat—grabbing fistfuls of cake—gobbling it.

As the dining hall filled with the riffraff, ravenous, as it became chock-full with hysterical murderers—all waving blades and clubs and shrieking with freedom and passion—the great chandelier began to tinkle.

Now it is an awesome sound to hear ten thousand finely cut pieces of crystal begin to rub shoulders, and the acoustics in the room were good.

It was as if someone had begun to ring a million glass bells all at once.

The tinkle cut through every shriek.

The sweating throng grew quiet.

All eyes fastened themselves in wonder on the thing, all faces were turned up, aghast at the trembling splendor, and to a man—terror struck.

It was almost imperceptible at first—the sound of deep sighs in the silence around the tinkling; just as imperceptibly the chandelier had begun—this way and that, back and forth, on the cast-iron chain on which it hung—the chandelier began to swing.

The room became filled with the sounds of sighs as they all saw it moving in the arc of the pendulum.

Then the sighs ceased.

The pendulum swung—it swung faster now, each time its arc grew wider, its five hundred flames were bent flat, first this way, then that, as it raced through the air, increasing its speed.

The nature of the tinkle changed: in gaining momentum the tinkling grow᷄ silent as the chandelier plunges on its path, but on the end of each swing the tinkle returns, a crescendo of glass, a hundred times louder!

But in the silence of the swing a tiny voice can now be heard.

It is the tiny sound of sobbing, of wanton weeping, it is the tiny voice of grief.

It is the voice of an angel, and it seems to come from the very center of the air above their heads.

Every member of the mob is a statue, face upturned, eyes closed, breathing deeply in perfect time with the swinging light, hypnotized.

Here is a perfect example of mass hypnosis. They are all unconscious, deeply asleep.

They'll stand here like this until the sunlight wakens them at dawn, but their memories will be all confused, and they'll never have any idea what was happening on this night; they hear no tears, nor how the childish shriek of grief turns into the rage of revenge in each crescendo.

The pendulum swings faster.

The room suddenly darkens as most of the candles blow out, and on the next swing the room was plunged into a pitch blackness, utterly lightless, and at that moment the five-year-old daughter of the Duke lost her grip on the cast-iron chain of the chandelier, which feverishly she had been pumping as yesterday she had her playground swing, and her grief-shaken body flew through the air, from the dead light was flung, through the blackness, pitched over their heads.

The Weir of Hermiston

Characters in the following story were first drawn by the pen of Robert Louis Stevenson in his long romance, "The Weir of Hermiston," which lay unfinished at his death. Sensing that Stevenson desperately wanted the romance to be finished, the raging tensions in its plot to be resolved – I have done so – if too briefly, surely resolutely. The words of my first paragraph were the last words Stevenson ever wrote:

He took the poor girl in his arms, and she nestled to his breast as to a mother's, and clasped him in hands that were strong like vises. He felt her whole body shaken by the throes of distress, and had pity on her beyond speech. Pity, and at the same time a bewildered fear of this explosive engine in his arms, whose works he did not understand, and yet had been tampering with. There arose from before him the curtains of boyhood, and he saw for the first time the ambiguous face of woman as she is. In vain he looked over the interview; he saw not where he had offended. It seemed unprovoked, a willful convulsion of brute nature. (R.L.S.)

"I'll tell the town I saw you two!" shouted a familiar voice from behind a blasted oak. It was Frank Innes.

The startled pair sprang apart.

"Ye canna doot!" pleaded Archie Hermiston timidly.

This Innes now is chinning himself on a branch of the oak, as if to demonstrate his superior muscular strength.

Kirstie, the girl, stands by, hands on her hips, and a black look on her face, grave as a siren can be, she was silent as their graves are now.

She stared from one to the other, and thought of everyone else she knew and how they'd be laughing at her name. She stared first at the weakling Hermiston, and then to the strong man, but never once did she stare to the sky for help, for she was not that kind of a girl to start praying at what she saw to be her own funeral, so to speak.

"Laddies," said she, perhaps to them both, but she spoke as if delivering a judgment for herself to hear, "Ye're nae good! Ye'd be the livin' death o' me! Ye'd make o' ma name a morsel for the fat and skinny to chew. Ye're city boys, fresh as the dresses in the Glasgow shops, so smart ye appear to be with your English words, but can ye no' hear a country girl's heart when it thumps ye the message and calls your souls by name?"

"Kirstie, be quiet," says young Hermiston.

"Young lady," mocked Frank Innes, "Did ye call ma soul by name? I dinna ken."

The pretty young girl lifted two fistie rocks, and spat viciously on the naked spots where the rocks had lain, and then she replaced the stones, each in the other's place.

She said. "I jest drownit two white worms that nae fishie will iver eat fer his good supper. Did ye ken ma two stringies? Did ye see they was your virrey selves? Lookit!"

And again she lifted the two rocks from their places, held up two "things" (the Lord knows what they were!) in the fast falling twilight for them to see. "The white worms ha' turnit BLACK. These are your virrey souls ye see in ma hands here. LOOKIT!!"

Frank Innes lowered himself to the ground from the branch of the oak tree where he'd been holding on so spryly, but let out a yelp as he landed the wrong way on his foot, twisting it.

Young Hermiston had been holding on to a branch of the same tree, but more for support, as his impotent rage had made him dizzy, and his helplessness in the face of the stronger man's taunts had at one moment nearly caused him to faint; but now his hand tightened around the branch, and with an easy movement, snapped it off the tree, and his eyes gleamed in hatred. He stripped the branch of its twigs to make a clean club. He exulted in an easy strength he knew to be his own, but which he'd never known—until this moment.

While Frank Innes quailed, and felt fear, his stomach quivering like an apple jelly, and he recognized his fright to be his own, that he'd always carried it beneath his belt he'd always pulled so tight, terror that he'd hidden, as if it were his treasure, beneath the bravado.

Hermiston lashed out with the club and broke Frank Innes' left arm.

Kirstie reached under her apron for a knife and rushed it to the trembling right hand of Frank Innes.

"Go it, Laddies!" she whispered hotly.

Frank Innes lunged like a girl with the knife, yet he stuck it straight in Hermiston's stomach, and withdrew it from the flesh in a flash of blood. Hermiston stood there grinning, bleeding, standing over Frank Innes, and says, "Ye think a wee bloody blade can stop a man whose destiny is to kill you?"

Innes backed away into the bushes, his teeth loudly chattering, shrill whimpering his only answer until suddenly he began to emit a staccato of squeals, becoming bloodcurdling screams, for he had crawled backward into a large field of thorns, and Hermiston laughed and followed him into the dark forest of thorns, driving him backward over the land of a million spikes, and though Hermiston, too, was torn by thorns, he only laughed, and grinned, and chuckled weirdly, wildly.

Through the night they fought until all hours.

Cottagers whose land bordered that forest were woken by their screams, and knew they were ghosts that so ranted through their woods in such wild rage; and they bolted their shutters and cowered inside, a whole family around a candle through the night, even after the shrieks had ceased, until the sigh of dawn, when they began to search the copse, finding many bloody trails that crisscrossed; and finally they found two black corpses, and there was difficulty telling which was which, almost unrecognizable they were, so eaten were they already by white worms.

The Scotch Story

An ugly man from Alabama moved to Scotland where his strange accent and foreign ways took the fancy of a highborn beauty of the Highlands, and though he was quite poor and she quite rich, they married.

She would not hear of him working and what was he to do? The judge in Alabama who had sent him to the workhouse had called him a loafer, but that wasn't exactly so, for he'd been making moonshine up in the mountains since the time he was twelve, in his own backwoods still.

But he played quite the gentleman in Scotland and with some success, and he was well liked, and by his many nephews and nieces he was adored; he played croquet well, and he got good at golf; he was a jovial drinker, a jewel of a host, and his wife was a generous soul and their lovely parties were at the heart of the good times that were had in that land.

With a Southern simplicity he was devoted to his wife like a hound dog to a beautiful master.

In the latter part of the Nineteenth Century there was a decade of unusually severe winters and a Great Depression enveloped Europe, and Scotland was devastated by crop failures and business failures; great families fell and many men were broken, and in the Highlands the poverty was appalling, and people stopped playing golf and going to parties.

Several years passed as the misery deepened.

One night the dour Lairds of the county of Glenlivet met in the home of the Alabama boy, grown much older in these few years, yet his wife, though pale and thinner, tubercular (she was doomed to die of it in two years, and her husband with Southern simplicity a week later died of sorrow), his wife retained her glow of beauty through this winter that was polar.

"We must do *something*," said one of those around the table.

"We must *do* something!" said another, his frown deepening and deepening.

"We *must* do something!" exclaimed another, almost weeping.

"*We* must do something!" said another, hopeless.

"Kin ah give ya'll a li'l drink," said their host gently, pouring a generous portion into each glass.

They sipped their drinks awhile and sighed, and perhaps it was the liquor, but their sighs grew not so hopeless. Then one got argumentative, and he said angrily, "How can you afford expensive liquor like this in times like these?"

And the man from Alabama explained in his affable and drawling manner that he hadn't bought any liquor in four years, but that it was something he'd cooked up himself.

The men looked at him in disbelief.

They lifted their glasses to their noses, and smiled, and shook their heads in disbelief.

Each took a tiny tasting sip, and rolled the liquor round his mouth, and one laughed and said, "You made *this*?"

Another laughed louder in a more mocking way, and asked, "You *made* this?"

Another chortled almost madly as he doubled up with laughter at a thought so outrageous: "YOU MADE THIS?" he screamed, rolling on the floor.

"Yes sir, in Alabam' we calls it moonshine."

Where did he make it? they asked. And he explained that he had a little still up aways in the hills, tucked away sort of cozy, where none of them could ever find it. And now it was his turn to chuckle as he thought to himself how he hid it. "You could never find it!" he laughed, as he suddenly imagined them all looking for it.

But how did he make it? they all wanted to know, and he explained that *that* was a mountain secret, and if it was anything he'd learned growing up in Alabama, it was never to betray to a foreigner the secret of making moonshine. Foreigners being anyone not born and raised in those mountains, and the term included all city-folk, and especially folks from Montgomery, the capital of that state, and where the tax collectors came from. He explained to them: "I promised my grandpappy on the day he died that I'd never teach a foreigner how to make moonshine." He shook his head seriously and said, "And I never will."

"Of course," he said, "it doesn't taste exactly the way it should because I had to make do with whatever I could get around here, and it's got a strange smoky taste from the peat that I couldn't do anything about, and of course in Alabama we mostly use corn, but they mean something different by corn in Alabama."

But then his eyes lit merrily and he added, "But it's a pretty good taste, hain't it?"

And the men began to point out to him that if only he'd show them how to do it, why, they'd start a business, the whole bunch of them there were ready to back him up because in this dreadful winter what the whole world needed was a drink like this, and that if they could start producing it, why, people would be driving sleds from London to buy the brew, and each sled would bring a bag of money into the county, and he'd be the savior of them all.

"I could not tell the secret, and break my oath to my grandpappy," he told them.

"In these times, lad," said the oldest and the loudest of the Lairds standing on a chair, "it is the duty of every Scotsman to come to the aid of his country. *Are you not a Scot?*" the old man asked him.

"Me . . . Scotch?" he said thoughtfully, obviously struck by the idea that had never occurred to him before. "But I was born in Alabama," he protested.

"Is this your house we're sitting in?"

"Certainly," he answered.

"And does the land your house is on belong to someone else?"

"Certainly not," he answered, looking over at his wife uneasily.

"This is our land," said his wife to him.

"Well if that's *your* wife, and this is *your* land . . . then you're a Scot!"

"You mean I'm Scotch?" he asked amazed.

"You're Scottish!" they shouted at him. "Are you not one of us?" they asked.

"Well, if I'm Scotch. . . and y'all are mountain men . . . then . . . then . . . then you aren't foreigners!"

They cheered.

"You are my true friends," he said, "and I'll share the Secret with you."

"Perhaps you'll be the savior of the county," grinned his wife. "And I'm very proud to be your wife," she added.

"But what'll we name the new drink? How about *The Glory of Alabama!*"

"How about *Alabama Moonlight?*" suggested another.

"What about *Alabam' Moonbeam! Alabam' Moonbeam!* That sounds wonderful!"

"No . . . no . . . my friends . . . as I'm the one with the secret, I get to name it. My friends, I've lived a life in Scotland that would never have been possible in Alabama, and I would like the name to express my gratitude, and I will be most gratified if it's called . . . simply . . . *Scotch!*"

And so it has been, has it not?

And the Alabama boy need not have feared the anger of the ghost of his grandpappy, for that mountain secret has been well kept in the Highlands.

Miss Lady

Once upon a time a sad little girl walked along a summer road.

She was about three years old, and she was crying because her brother was walking so fast she couldn't keep up, and then she stumbled, in a cloud of dust.

Her brother heard her cry but he kept on walking faster and faster and faster.

She was alone.

She looked over and saw a cottage and there was a man watching her from a window, peeping at her from behind a thick curtain, so she waved.

The face disappeared.

She walked to the back of the house, and there was another face, at another window, peeping out. She waved again.

And that face disappeared.

She climbed up on the back porch and knocked on the screen door, and after a few minutes the door opened a little. She walked in.

There were some men, and they gave her a Coca-Cola, and she talked with them, explaining about her sunburn, about her brother, and something about a trip to Canada her mother and father were going to take, and the men listened to her earnestly.

She hit one of them!

He picked her up and swung her through the air and she screamed! Then he perched her on his shoulder and she held his head tightly afraid of falling, but then she lost her fear and just sat there, and they all laughed at her.

So she asked for another Coca-Cola.

One of the men got it for her and she insisted on drinking it out of the bottle; she sat on one of the guys' laps and listened, while the men talked of other things taking great slugs of Coca-Cola occasionally.

Then she began prattling again and the men all stopped to listen to her. She asked one of them to fix her dirty stringy hair ribbon.

She played quite the lady and the men spoke to her with exaggerated English accents and this was wonderful!

Then she pulled one of them down on the floor and got up on his back and rode him like a horse, shouting gidiyap! gidiyap! gidiyap!

The little girl asked if she could come and live with them, and the men said sure!

So the men and the little girl got into a car and drove to Florida. You see, these men were bank robbers.

The little girl loved it! She lived with them for eight months. She played on the beach with them, swam in the ocean, ate in big restaurants, lived in the best hotels, even drank champagne once! And she had a pretty maid who did nothing but wait on her and help her buy white dresses and orange bathing suits and all the toys little girls need.

They were always buying her presents and she loved them very much, but one day she got homesick and began crying for her brother and her mother and her father.

The gangsters were very unhappy but they bought her a ticket to her little hometown and they saw her off on the train. The conductor assured them she would arrive safely, which she did.

The police searched Florida for the bank robbers but they had flown to far corners of the globe.

The little girl continued her life with her family in the little town. She went to school. Much later she went to college; as a matter of fact, she attended Vassar.

2

Now she is a prostitute in Buenos Aires.

She is lying on a couch and her eyes are red from marijuana. Her clothes are lying on a chair. A sailor heavy-footedly leaves her room. She is so sad. Look! There is a tear on her cheek. Smoke is in her eye. What a rare tear.

She is so pretty!

I can't help liking her. Because I know her secret, her quest, and why she lives this way.

I know she's looking for them.

A Following

A little girl walks behind her brother on the way to school.

As they pass a huge red house a little girl dressed beautifully in blue starched bows appears from behind a bush and joins her, falling in step behind him.

From a yellow brick house down the driveway comes running another tot, whose elegant dress is as gray as the clouds that over-hang the luminous country this morning.

Down the block they are joined by two more girls, each popping out from behind a fence or tree after he had passed, and as he does not glance back at his sister once, each of them is, by him, unseen.

Now another jumps out and joins them.

They are each seven years old. He is eleven.

He takes from his pocket a ball, and begins to bounce it as he walks.

They each do the same.

They are quiet as mice. Each bounces a ball, each walks like he walks.

For no reason he leaps, as if leaping over a stream.

The six little girls do the same.

By them, *unseen*, but playing their game, behind them all comes another, a foreigner, a fifty-year-old bouncing a tennis ball, whose face is as gray as the tennis ball, to whom the day is not luminous, but flat, dreary, dank and dark, who sees in their homes naught but vulgar opulence, who has seen war, famine and the horror in the camps, who is sought even now by Israeli secret police, who limps slightly — Oh! if that story were told.

Now like the leader, for no reason, he leaps.

It is the eccentric new truant officer.

Ghosts

Five children peered inside, their chins above the windowledge, their noses pressed against the windowpane. All five of them wore glasses.

Finally, and quite suddenly, the singing of the frogs and crickets ceased.

Silence ensued.

And now the only sound is the clicking of the children's glasses against the windowpane.

There is no one within to hear these sounds, nor to contemplate the silence. The haunted house is empty.

They are waiting our arrival, for the show to begin.

The One Come

Encrusted with colonnades and bright steeples, the little Southwestern town looked from the mountain as if it were an Early American engraving.

Sheet lightning flickered in the sunset.

There was a chimney below from which red smoke poured, and another loosed a long black line which curved over the valley; the orange forge glimmered in the twilight.

It was as if a churchbell should ring.

All the birds were quiet.

The dark pool offered an unmoving reflection of still twigs, and later, of a million stars among the black somber hunks of trees.

All the fireflies were quiet.

This pool was as if a suicide had stayed in its sludge, its skull a nest of salamanders.

It was as if some haunting were going on.

In the town there was a cheery brightness from each window and the light absolutely streamed out of them, illuminating the shrubs and silent squares of lawn; as one would move on down into the squalid sections where the children were still out playing in the streets, the lighting changed, the windows were grimier, narrower, the shades more frequently drawn, and the streetlamps were without frosted glass, but bulbly glared, casting ghastily a blacker shade.

Along an unlit lane at last at the farthest edge, not too distant from the city dump (on one's right might be a deep ditch) there would be the odor floating in the darkness of garbage cans in the tall grass, of wild daisies, dandelions, and marvelous weeds, and of grease . . . .

Old stars are the only light, and they aren't much help. The stars were great as guides on grander journeys over oceans to discover continents, but when one's problem is immediately not to trip in ruts of uncared-for roads . . . .

A giant cloud begins to cross the sky.

Now there is no light . . . whatsoever.

A moment's light!

Lightning.

There was a turn ahead and if that flashing moment's image were correct, one should begin right here the veer, and the ground should begin right here—ah . . . yes it does! to rise as I round the corner.

Flash!

The thunder threw my senses into a keener pitch, and memories of a mad music and the sunlight of that Monday morning, and the memory of her mood, and the mangle of her muscles twisting in the pool.

Crash!

A tree burst into flames in back of me, and there is the ozone smell of the fiery fork which missed me by a hundred yards back there, but the sharp CRACK! which seemed to explode almost inside my head moves me forward now in a faster race, and all obstacles vanish underfoot, and there's no question of falling to caution my motion, for I move in a miraculous balance.

I blink like a banshee in the blast of water, like the banshee—I am, in the great gush I grin, and just as whirling rain turns rut to mush, I begin.

I am the one come to avenge suicides.

The Hunger of the Magicians

A stone lamp at an altar was lit by a flaming wand.

It was two thousand five hundred years ago to this very moment, in Greece.

It was a hot gray morning.

Overhead stormclouds are streaming by, but for months there's been no rain. Soon they will hear distant thunder, but still there'll be no rain, and very soon thirst and famine will finish them.

Out of saintly stubbornness they will starve to death, for they would not leave this place, this stronghold on Mount Olympus.

But now look! The lamp illuminates the lighter's face.

He wears a pointed hat.

Perceive the hat: it is two heads high, a cone, precisely wrapped by a single piece superbly cut—of gray stuff—heavy and rough, a giant swatch of undyed wool which falls from his cone to his toes, leaving a place for his face and hands to be free, forming a complete cloak.

It is the dress of a magician.

The master has a gray beard.

In his hands the light burns brightly. Look! There are fifty-two gray beards. The room is full of pointed hats. Their heads are bowed. All hats point to the lamp. It is a den of magicians!

In unison the masters groan in monotone the various vowels.

They wear no garment between their skin and their grotesque gray hats. Between their skin and their bones there is no flesh.

Here are the greatest magicians in the world, this is the Golden Age of Greece, these are the men behind that scene—but drought and famine have hit the countryside. The thrashing streams of Mount Olympus are dried up.

Nobody brought them any water or food.

And it made them mad.

Indeed, it was less than five minutes ago that the lighter of the lamp, the Young One, spoke up with a sublime assurance to his elders. This is what he said to them five minutes ago:

"The world is not going to forget this.

"I place the memory of this outrage inside the altar lamp.

"The sight of our miserable state shall rest here in the lamp until five hundred years has passed five times, until that veritable moment – and then it shall flutter free of the lamp and enter the head of a writer whom it'll madden for an evening, for he shall see us all here, and write it, and perpetuate this scene in the Literature of his language; and whatever language he writes, all the shining Literature of that language shall be transformed at that instant into lamps of rock more durable than this stone lamp, for that tongue shall survive to become the only language spoken on earth; at the moment when the vision flies, fifty-two writers of that chosen language shall become aware of the *hunger of the magicians*; they shall come as close to death as we are now; they shall witness vanity in horror and forget themselves; then Greek gods will be reborn; in them our light shall shine again; they shall refashion that language: new letters shall be added to its alphabet, and, as pigeon, it shall flutter between Hebrew and Chinese, and crystals of grammar in silver syntax shall be worked with ornaments from ancient tongues to transform it – they will make that language ready to write the history of the world; in their dreams they'll see what has duration in a language, and each in writing shall see a secret of perpetuity.

"I plunge my wand into the water, and . . . ah! I have speared a fish!

"Let us eat! Let us savor this moment of time.

"I plunge my wand into the fire. How quickly it catches!

"I destroy my wand to do this deed. This vision of us is our property, our land forever, and to sign the deed we must light the lamp.

"Magicians, great scholars, seers, if . . . it is your will?

"How brightly the tip of my wand flames.

"They shall see us everywhere, our quiet stare, in every line they write – a haughty mien, our silver smile of mercurial weight.

"For noon has come, and doubt is gone. There are no shadows anywhere.

"Now at last remorse surrounds the sources of our memory like purple light, the Godhead is bowed in blight . . . all our thoughtful frowns are snaked, our dragons are drowned, our lions are suffocated, our eagles are grounded . . . .

"And if, when tomorrow comes with bells, Sorrow slaves at many works—then jonquils will be carried by canaries to this bright yellow spot, and sports will be performed by plants running on their roots ... like a merry-go-round the great oak spins ... and when, to a trembling touch, stone faces bend ... petal-thin flesh shadows we can lift from the ground ... bluejay's flash of sound ....

"The sound of the seer is heard like a bluejay's shriek in the inner ear as it cuts crude consciousness away.

"Those fifty-two writers shall witness vanity in horror and forget themselves."

The stone lamp at the altar is lit.

Prose for Dancing

For Nannette Domingos

To have a good cat is a good beginning.
My typewriter is a *Meower*.

*

Beauty mused, as if to herself, "When I agreed to be in this piece
it was understood that there was to be a fresh typewriter ribbon."

*

The flies are chasing the mosquitoes, so the unanswering centuries
I address are not entirely silent.

*

The bubbling Babylonian tablet came clean in the bath of acid.

*

He was a trader in tourmaline, emerald, and ruby in the back bush;
and he wore baggy trousers, each leg of which had twenty pockets;
and each pocket had a button, and each held a gem.
He had his legs memorized.

*

The shadow of a maple tree encroached upon the cat, whose pupils
widen . . . .
The breeze dealt him a shadow blow; he turns one ear.
A butterfly distracted him, and he turns his head to follow its flight.
But now a garter snake skims over the grass, and when it arrives at a
point about two feet in front of the cat, the snake stops, and raises its
head until its eyes are level with the cat's. It sways gently to and fro, and
its forked tongue shoots in and out. It is as if the forces of evolution had
all conspired to create the snake to act just so in order to astonish a
curious cat.
But in confronting all of the forces of nature incarnate in the
moving body of the snake, a black cat can have recourse to the occult.

With an expressive smile the black cat crossed his legs and took off his white socks.

*

His job was to take the gum from the bottom of the seats at the movie theater.
She was an usherette.

*

The hatch hung open, and the waves washed in, putting a blanket of sand on the bottom of the boat.

*

An orange flag swirling in a stiff breeze ballooned out and engulfed the figure of the general, who, in trying to untangle himself, fell off the reviewing stand at the parade of the paratroopers.

*

He was the Emperor of Antarctica.
He was the dominant male in the colony of emperor penguins that meet to breed on the Ross Ice Shelf.
He was the Emperor of emperors.

*

The Jostlers are an ugly club whose sole activity is to create confusion in crowds, riots at rock concerts, and mass hysteria and mayhem at sporting events.

*

The nimble nincompoop would adroitly climb up any streetlamp in the park and stand on his head atop the globe, bathed in light.

*

When I grumble, only the volcano listens. When the volcano grumbles, everybody listens.

People would be crazy not to listen to a volcano. A man who talks to a volcano is crazy.

*

The ibex stretched its neck upward while standing on the rims of its hoofs.
The ibis stretched its neck upward while standing on the tips of its toes on one foot.
Why should there be such an art as the one I practice?

*

A piece of English rag, a tube of French maroon, a sable brush . . . do you get the picture?

*

I filled my boots with marbles and ran home barefoot through a thundershower.

*

I found a ladies' wristwatch in my tuna fish sandwich.

*

He stole a blanket from a polo pony and raced diagonally across the playing field.

*

I am stuck in this chair in front of my typewriter like a fly on flypaper.

*

I'm beginning to see the light that's coming in through the back of my head, since recently I started getting bald.

*

The choirboys sneezed in unison when the assistant conductor raised his baton.

*

She coughed into her sandwich, and a piece of lettuce from it fell into the goldfish pond.

*

The yellow flame rose into the air like a yellow rose about a yard wide.

*

She walked on stilts through the field of sunflowers.

*

A silhouette of a white cat appeared on the window ledge beside the black geranium.

*

He manufactured horses for merry-go-rounds, and spent his paycheck each Sunday at the racetrack.

*

The ceiling of the cellar dripped slime.
The floor was covered with broken slate.
The only door in the room opened into the bottom of a well. A ladder of iron spikes protruding from the well wall allowed a climber easy access.
All that was needed was a fire in the grate to make it a cozy place.

*

She had twenty thousand pairs of green galoshes all the same size, which she bought off a boat from Hong Kong because they just fit.

*

LOT BOTANY
A Picture Book of Weeds,
Including Certain Wildflowers and Small Trees
Commonly Found in City Vacant Lots
Or Growing beside Fences of Gas Stations and Parking Lots,
Which Spring Up, Survive, Thrive and Spread
Unattended by Man.

*

"Miniature flamingos live upon our bayou, and now at sunset will skim the surface feasting on the schools of singing flying fish. Would you like to take a walk to the end of the pier!"

"Not especially."

The Mirror Story

Once upon a time there was a poet who wanted to turn his brains into money.

He was a good poet.

He was devoted to his profession, to the craft of his field, with his whole being.

He was well educated, or at least, well read; and he had a fine imagination, and could be eloquent—when writing—but he didn't know how to talk to people; he was shy, and he always had the feeling that people were relating their words to something that he didn't understand.

As he was a real poet, it of course means that he must work at menial jobs—restaurant work, clerk jobs, messenger jobs.

There is no way a true poet can earn money by his work.

One day he looked around—and he saw all these morons, these vulgar, criminal, immoral, stupid, dull, all these idiots—all of whom can earn a living!

And he figured there must be some way a person of his intelligence could figure out so as not to have to work at these ridiculous jobs.

So he borrowed a black leotard from a dancer friend, and got a heavy black piece of cloth which he put over his head like a monk's cowl, and he got an oval piece of glass, just a little larger than a face, which he put in front of his face under the cowl; but it was not regular glass, it was what's called one-way glass; that is, it was the kind of glass that when you look through it one way it's clear, transparent glass, but when you look at the other side it's a mirror; he put this glass in front of his face so that he could see out, but anyone who looked at him saw only his own reflection.

He went to a Greenwich Village nightclub and got a job as an oracle.

A fortuneteller.

He had a little table in the nightclub, and he'd sit there, and people would come and ask him questions of the sort one asks an oracle, about the future, and he'd just say anything that came into his head. He'd make up nonsense, speak gibberish, quote lines of other people's poetry, and he had a good imagination so he'd make up little fantasies, stories, and people seemed to like it.

He discovered that when he had his mirror on he lost his shyness. He could talk to people easily.

Some people even took him seriously, but he just laughed at them, and never pretended to be anything other than an entertainer.

After a while, he found he was earning a good living at the nightclub.

There was a girl, a striptease dancer, who also worked at the nightclub.

She worked under black light.

Ultraviolet light.

But only her costume was luminous, she wasn't, and as there was no other light, as she did her dance, as one by one her clothes dropped off, she disappeared.

Only her clothes were luminous, so when the last bra or panty dropped, she was invisible, and the stage was left littered with luminous blotches of clothing.

That was her act.

They fall in love.

But the poet when he doesn't have his mirror on is still his same old shy self. He doesn't know how to approach the girl, and doesn't know that she's also interested in him.

One evening (it's the middle of the week, business is slow) he sees the girl walking across the empty dance floor toward him, and she's holding something behind her back, so he can't see what it is.

She sits down at his table, and . . . .

Wow! Here she is!

And he has his costume on, his mirror on, so suddenly he can talk!

He's just about to express himself, to express his love—when the girl says, "Look! I don't want my fortune told. I don't want to know about myself. I want to know about you!"

And at that point she took from behind her back an oval mirror from her dressing table, just a little larger than a face, and she held it up in front of his face-mirror, and said, "What do you see?"

Excuse me, my reader, but I must digress a moment to explain what he would see: You know when you stand between two mirrors, or when you sit in a barber chair, there seems to be a passageway in the mirrors; but if you ever stop to notice, you'll observe that, though you can see perhaps six or seven levels in, you can never see to the end of the passageway; always your own first reflection gets in the way, and if you try to bend out of the way the whole passage bends out of the mirror frame.

But in this case he would see out of the glass and see a mirror, but the mirror would "see," so to speak, only a mirror, which would in turn see a mirror, et cetera.

There would be nothing in between the mirrors to block the view so he would see the passageway going straight out to infinity.

So to recap the situation: The girl whom he loves is sitting in front of him, and he has his mirror on, so he can speak, and he is just about to express his love when the striptease dancer says, "What do you see?" And at that moment the girl vanishes, the nightclub vanishes, and the man sees a passage to infinity.

He doesn't say anything.

The girl takes the mirror away, and says, "Say something!"

But the man doesn't say a word.

She tugs at his sleeve, and says, "Don't just sit there, say *something.*"

But he doesn't move.

And for seventeen years he hasn't moved.

He still sits, exactly in that same position, a catatonic in a mental hospital—he's fed through a tube, and is incontinent, and has completely lost contact with the outside world.

But the doctors and nurses can tell—from changes in his facial expression, and from the words he mutters just inaudibly, so that they can never quite make our what he's saying—they can tell that he's leading an active life in his mind, in a dreamworld he is having experiences . . . .

And in this world of his dreams, in the life he leads inside his head—all the rest of the people are wearing mirrors over their faces, and only he doesn't have one.

He feels very much like an outsider because of this, and he tries to find out, he questions people—why doesn't he have a mirror over his face like the rest of them?

But people either give him very phony answers and try to con him, or they pretend they don't know what he's talking about.

And because of this he finds he has to get very menial jobs, like dishwashing jobs, clerk jobs, or messenger jobs.

As this "whole world" is, after all, just his imagination, as it's just his dream—why—anything can happen.

I mean there are any number of ways this story might end.

Anything can happen in a dream.

For instance: After working all week at some awful job, he takes his whole paycheck and goes to the drug addicts' den.

(No real drug, of course, just what he imagines a drug addicts' den is, for in a dream whatever you might think a drug addicts' den is like—that's the way it *really* is.)

But the other people at the drug addicts' den, when they got high, oh! they danced, and sang, and laughed, and had a wonderful time; but he never did, he would find a comfortable chair and just sit.

And as the years went by, he became adjusted to his world. Actually, he forced out of his consciousness the knowledge which he has, that he is actually different from the rest of them, that he doesn't have a mirror over his face. Whenever anyone made any allusion to this fact, he would pretend not to hear, or he would pretend that they were talking about something else. And as the years go by, he grows to think of himself as "normal." You know, everyone's a little neurotic, everybody has problems. But he grew to think of himself as just another ordinary human being—although there are times when he does suspect, there are times when he does think that it's just a little peculiar that a person would go out and spend his whole paycheck at the drug addicts' den, I mean—just to sit.

But there is another way this story might end, for instance: He meets a girl, and the girl also doesn't have a mirror over her face, and of course they recognize each other immediately—that is, that neither of them have mirrors in front of their faces.

And she tells him (she's been in "this world" longer than he) that he doesn't have to work at these awful jobs, and that she can show him how to get by . . . .

"Come to my house," she says. (Their relationship from the first becomes like a brother-and-sister relationship, rather than a sexual one.)

And so they walk out of town down to the edge of the ocean, and they walk down the beach for maybe a mile to a very isolated spot where there are no people; there's a very pleasant grove of palm trees, and in the center of the grove there is a small tent.

"See!" she says, "I live here. I don't have to pay any rent. I go swimming every morning. It's healthy living in the sun. It's wonderful."

"Well, yes," says the man, "It's great—but how do you eat?"

"I'm just about to fix lunch now. Why don't you stay and have lunch with me."

And so she spreads a blanket out on the sand, and gets two tin pie plates, and goes down to the edge of the ocean, and he watches her down there, gathering things from the surf and placing them in the pie tins.

She returns and puts the plates down on the blanket and they sit down cross-legged on the sand and she begins to eat.

He looks down at his plate and there in the center is a little pile of pebbles, little pebbles worn round and smooth by the ocean.

He picked one up and examined it—it was really just a stone.

He put one of them in his mouth, and made a little face, gulped—and swallowed it.

She said, "It's a little difficult at first, but you get used to it after a while."

There is another way this story could end, but that ending's pornographic, and I don't write those kinds of things.

Pornography has no place whatsoever in literature.

Fingernails

When the Paris police surgeon operated on the dead woman, he discovered her stomach filled with a cup of fingernails.

The apelike expression on the dead face, its ugly grin, set in gangrene, was photographed in color. The grotesque head, gross, horribly demonic, sporting bleached hair, had been attached unnaturally to the body of a teenager. And the ghastly surgery had been successful, for the older woman's head had lived two years on the youthful body.

In such operations the cortolon balance is invariably upset. (Cortolon is a substance which controls the growth of fingernails and toenails.) Either a patient's nails disappear entirely or, as in this case, nail growth frequently is speeded up to several inches a day.

She could have been immortal if she hadn't bitten her fingernails.

True Confessions Story

Once upon a time there was a real Henry James tea party.

It was a regular English weekend at the turn of the century. There was the great green lawn, and the terrace of white Italian marble onto which figured French doors opened revealing oaken gleans of furniture polish.

There on the lawn were a few mannered children quietly fingering their hoops and solemnly petting terriers, and their elders were scattered about chatting, grouped mostly on the marble.

But above the general chatter-level one voice was continuously recognizable by its queer, clear, cultivated pitch, and a certain forcefulness of tone. This dominant voice was punctuated by phrases from the Continent, and a twang ghostily edged it, cutting the surrounding buzzing.

This voice belonged to an American.

She was a society woman about seventy years old.

She was a mildly famous old woman of letters who had come to Europe at eighteen, and such were its enchantments and her successes, she had stayed. Years ago she'd published slim volumes entitled "LETTERS," which by chance had been written prophetically to the right people who by sterner work were to create a literary world of that age.

She'd ridden their wave.

Suddenly, and with a sort of squeak, the voice stopped.

This sudden ceasing signaled a slowly mounting silence which enveloped even the children on the lawn who turned, curiously suspended toward the portico . . . the old lady walked stiffly toward the French doors, but with a trembling, and behind her on the white marble trailed a yellow stream of water.

As she reached the doorways one of the terriers began to bark shriekily.

The old lady turned on the still astounded groups.

"What do you mean embarrassing me like this!" she demanded. "I'm an old lady! I have bladder trouble! What do you mean by this vulgar show of silence! How dare you! I've never in all my life witnessed such vile taste!"

And she stomped angrily and disappeared into the mansion, and she decided then, right there, to go home.

After a decent interval ordering her affairs fanfarelessly, she left Europe for good . . . for the Upper Peninsula of Michigan.

She was a different person when she arrived at the little town of her childhood.

She had taken off her girdles, her dresses darkened, and her hair was now snow-white, and instead of the perfectly groomed society woman, she appeared there the perfect picture of a nice old lady. She had come home to die.

The family home (it was always referred to as "the house") had been closed for years; the others in her family had died long ago; she was a sole survivor.

She decided it would be fun to fix the place up as it used to be, as it had been in her childhood.

So she hired carpenters.

And within a month she moved in, out of the town to the estate in the woods.

In the Upper Peninsula there exists a group of Indians who, since the Seminoles in Florida recently signed a treaty, are the only tribe that have never signed a peace treaty with the United States.

They live in poverty. Now, their national sport is croquet (this is true, incidentally).

There was a small settlement of these Indians living in shacks off the road between her house and the town. In the little village a baby was born to an unmarried Indian woman who died in childbirth.

The old lady offered to care for the child, and on a happy autumn afternoon the baby girl was brought to her by the Indians.

The old lady adored the child.

She would get right down on the floor, too, and play with her; and she was particularly lax about toilet training so that the child was four or five years old before she learned to use an ordinary bathroom.

And at first the old lady had many daydreams. She thought how wonderful it was going to be to educate her, to turn her to great books, to the great paintings, and the mass of music, to the wonders of civilization.

For herself it would be to renew many old acquaintances.

However, after a while the old lady realized that her daydreams were never to be realized. For the child was a . . . well, there's nothing wrong with it, it's actually a very common occurrence even among the best families, it was just that the child was a . . . moron.

She didn't love the child any the less because of it; she showered the growing child with attention and affection.

And the old lady just didn't die. She lived another twenty years until she was ninety. Then finally she did die.

The bulk of her estate she left to museums, for the girl plainly wasn't suited for the responsibilities which wealth entails; she left a small trust fund ensuring the girl's comfort for life, but not so much as to attract trouble to her.

The girl did not weep at the funeral; instead, a frown (and not an unattractive one!) appeared . . . a thoughtful expression began growing over her face; and afterward she took a long walk, a ceremony she would continue throughout her life.

The girl wasn't smart, but she was smart enough to know she wasn't very smart.

She realized that somehow she had been a disappointment to her grandmother. (She always thought of the old lady as her grandmother.) Her grandmother would have liked it better if she had been an artist of some sort, a writer, perhaps. As she recalled her life and her grandmother's love, a pang of pain at her failing throbbed through her. Something. She wanted to do something. Something her grandmother would like, to show her, something that would please her. What gift can be taken to a grave?

She decided she would become a writer.

However, at twenty the poor girl had still never read anything other than comic books and "true confessions" magazines.

Well, she decides she's going to be a writer . . . what that meant to her was that she should write true confessions stories. Only . . . when she read those things she actually believed them, she actually thought they were true, and not just formula stories written by hack writers.

Well, if she's going to write a true confessions story, she has to have something to confess, but she has nothing to write about, so she decides what she needs is some "experience"; so she goes to Chicago and finds a bar that to her looks "evil-looking," picks up a guy, and sure enough, he steals her money, and does her wrong.

So the girl went home and wrote a true confession, telling it exactly as it had occurred.

And as she'd never read anything other than "true confessions" magazines, this was the way her mind worked, and she automatically wrote in their style, so that when an editor read her story, he accepted it, simply assuming the author's name was a pseudonym of a professional.

It never occurred to the editor that what he was reading was actually true. Had he known, of course, he never would have published it. They don't publish "those kinds of things."

So she wrote more stories, and for each story she went out and had an "experience." And, oh, all kinds of things happened to her, for she picked her men carefully for their literary value, seeking always someone sinister for her unhappy romances, and after each she would simply write what happened, the simple truth in a sorry style.

She began to earn quite a good living, and soon discovered she had a lot of money, which, luckily, she turned over to her grandmother's lawyers, who, by chance, were honest, and who saw to it her income tax was properly paid, and her own money put in a solid savings account. She never spent any of this, though, explaining to her lawyers once that "I do not write for money."

She decided she was ready to begin a broader project, a novel. So she came to New York City, and began living with a guy, and every day when he was out she'd work on her novel, simply writing what happened, day by day.

When she finished the novel she left him.

And he was not a little confused at her leaving, for though he'd been living on her money, and in fact, victimizing her, or so he figured, he found he had grown fond of her. Other men were to be similarly startled at her sudden leavings, at discovering themselves alone, and would share this perplexity.

But the novel was a great success.

The critics raved. "What humor! What satire! What ironies! What burlesque!" none of them imagining for a minute that what they read was not written with those intentions at all, but was a simple, serious relating of a world she saw.

The book became a best-seller, a book club bought it, a movie was made of it, a smash hit, and it received Academy Awards.

So she wrote more books. Each had a similar success. And for each she would go out and find some guy, some jerk, and would live with him until her novel was completed.

By chance she had an intelligent publisher who advised her to entirely avoid meeting literary people and literary critics, and so protected her from what would have been fatal interviews; and he explained that she was a shy genius, a delicate and rare recluse; and though she always wrote under her real name, he let it be known to the press that this was a pseudonym; and her own acquaintances, to whom she never claimed to be a writer, and who knew her dullness and simple-minded generosities, couldn't conceive of it; but the publisher himself was a little puzzled at how amenable she was to this plan, although she did once explain to him, "I do not write for fame."

It is said here in America that there is nothing sure except death and taxes.

And to be sure, it was not her literary work that embedded her name in the popular mind, but was rather a prosaic noticing by one of her grandmother's old lawyers that she was a member of that Indian tribe that had never signed a treaty with the government, and so was not required to pay taxes.

She'd had half a dozen best-sellers, and they'd made as many movies from them, and, as she already had an income from her grandmother's trust fund, the millions of dollars she had earned had almost entirely gone for taxes, and the government found itself in the position of having to refund quite literally millions of dollars to her.

One day, she had just finished a novel, and had packed her bags and sent them uptown to a hotel—she had left her man, and she was feeling wonderful. (She always felt exhilarated after finishing a work, she'd once told her publisher.)

It was autumn.

She began to walk, as she liked to do, through the city aimlessly, and discovered herself downtown, near the Brooklyn Bridge. She decided to walk across the bridge.

Just as she stepped onto the bridge, the sky turned yellow, and the wind began to blow, and she looked above and saw the clouds moving fast across the sky, and in the afternoon distance there was a flash from lightning.

If, at this moment one could view the bridge from above, you would have seen that, at that moment, all the people walking on the bridge that were on the Manhattan side had suddenly turned back to Manhattan, and those on the Brooklyn side were now hurrying back toward Brooklyn, all rushing to get off the bridge before the storm broke. Finally, only she continued to walk toward the center of the bridge.

She thought it was wonderful. The lightning. The electric air. The booming foghorns and the thunder. "How great!" she laughed. "A storm!"

So that finally, when she got to the very center of the Brooklyn Bridge, she was the only person on it.

She looked out over the city and saw a huge gray curtain moving slowly toward her ... it was the rain she saw, of course, dissolving the city as it approached her.

The very opposite of running from it, she held up her arms to the coming rain, welcoming it, and said, "Ah! What a *grand* thing it is to be an artist!"

Frenzy of Barbarians
& 7 untitled paragraphs

Where grass grows nine feet tall and tablecloths of beige moss spread out on every boulder, and utensils, delicately carved by doodling nature from the bones of vultures, lie exposed on the brown rocks to dry out noon after noon undisturbed on the impenetrable plain; for the great grass grows densely about each boulder, and the bending blades that gently dip are razor sharp, and in the gales of autumn can cut birds in half as they wildly thrash, in that wondrous wind like a Paris of Fencers with sabers delirious, all slashing—then like a Frenzy of Barbarians—annually they cut each other down.

*

When Lincoln fell, how the Arabians wept. On the White House steps a clump of women wailed—in the conventional way—behind pastel veils. A saffron coach stood darkly by, its four black stallions, such startling beasts in beauty, trembled impatiently and were calmed by strange words from turbaned, stately servants, while for hours the women kept the vigil. With a curving four-foot blade in each hand, twin giants in pantaloons stood guarding them, arms akimbo. The curious sensed that they did not speak English, and no one questioned them.

*

He sold his seal hole and his igloo to the bank for quite a sizable sum, indeed, for oil had been discovered offshore. And so the old Eskimo hunter went to Florida to live out his remaining years. He loved the weather, and practically lived on the beach, and could be found there on every day of the year. Though admittedly, his favorites were those freezing days which Florida experiences every year, days which drive disconsolate tourists indoors, and at these times he had the beach completely to himself. For the one thing about civilization that he could never get used to was being surrounded by crowds of people. He was affable and affluent and soon made many friends, yet

often when they or the crush of the throngs on the beach overwhelmed him, he would take out his kayak and his spear, the only
possessions he had brought South from the Far North, and he would
point his boat toward the horizon. He would be out there several
days, sometimes in the foulest storms.

He would visit uninhabited mangrove keys, and fish.

*

The meadow that stretches among strangely shaped lakes, where
swans are, and buffalo meander among great green boulders—there
is an ordinary giraffe with its family of albinos!—ostriches; slow
armadillos sunning themselves in large groups; large land turtles
abound; although there are many strange snakes, none are dangerous; many kinds of grazing beasts with intricately shaped horns;
elephants. There is another plain on which all the animals are
carnivorous.

*

The sleepwalker strangely snapped his fingers, causing the dog to
bark, startling a burglar who had been about to enter the house, who
changed his mind and left the premises. The dog went back to sleep.
The walker awoke in the morning to find himself in his favorite
comfortable chair.

*

The French milliner and the seamstress were roommates and had
a lifelong association in a shop below their living quarters on the Rue
Armboussent. Their dog was named Renée and their white cat was
named Celine. Both animals were deaf. The animals were thorough-
breds. The dog was a tiny Mexican Hairless Chihuahua, and the cat
was a gorgeous Angora, a long-haired tom with blue eyes.

*

If there is nothing to wrap up, nothing to bring to a close, no
farfetched tales that turn out to be dreams, no light on the hill as a

signal, and if there are nothing but fragments between commas, and if adjectives are not quite right, if hammers are silent though not still ... still, thank god I don't have a tin ear. *(After Virginia Woolf)*

*

(For V.W.) She set out to make herself into a monster with a will with a well-thought-out pill of dried particles of pickled porkfat, gold and sandalwood, rose thorns and crushed thrush beaks, fresh shavings from balsa knots, or sawdust from the core of a living redwood, unused shot from a Puritan's musket, and the tips of trout fins, flaming arbutus roots and dried Scotch whiskey scratched from a varnished desk, ten white warts from a pretzel, ten O!'s from a page in the Iliad, ten tips clipped from French swords, and from an astronomical map — the Pleiades cut apart from each other, half-a-dozen motes captured from the air on a sunny day, one sixteenth of a teaspoon

(more)

On My Great-Grandfather

Dr. George Byron Spencer
Graduate of the University of Vienna Medical College, 1860
Born, 1839, Dublin; Died, 1907 in Weston, Ohio.

He had imported all the way from Vienna two black swans to put in the cemetery pond by the lovers' lane. I wonder how many Ohio lovers pondered the mystery of the black pair, even as I, now when I think of them, wonder why my great-grandfather did it.

*

He buried his face in the grass.

The shovel with which he had turned the sod dangled, balanced in his hand as he trudged, stoopshouldered, an old man, through the moonlit cemetery.

The stroke of dazzle appeared through the maze of trees, the pond in which two black swans swam, scattering countless sleeping polliwogs by their nightly gliding.

"It would be good," he thought, "if there were a stone fence along here, and a path that would wind over there around the great maple . . . ." (The maple was now in a tangle of thorns and poison ivy . . . .) There were many maps in his mind of the cemetery; he had viewed it in many lights in his day; he could see it as it was, when he had first viewed it, almost surrounded by a sort of swamp; he could remember beautiful larvae, even as on the day he had first discovered the name and nature, of the malarial mosquito; he could recall at a glance the tombstones he had once imagined that would fill the places where now solid tombstones lounged erectly; he had cleared that plain, and planted poplars, had drained the swamp, and made a little lake a lovers' lane, transformed a public horror into a pleasant place; he was the doctor.

To be a doctor in a Midwestern town in those days a generation this side of the frontier, sharing that edge with the barbaric . . . what ship, what horse, what spirit in his legs could get a man from Europe there?

This spirit.

On the Truth

For Yvonne Rainer

Over many years, on many occasions, I gathered bits of knowledge, mostly from my father and my family, which gave me in fact a clear impression of my great-grandfather, on whom I wrote an essay. Recently my sister read the essay and noticed that it was not true in some respects, which irritated me considerably.

My great-grandfather was not born in Dublin. Actually, he was born in Columbus, Ohio, and his ancestors immigrated 200 years previously on the second voyage of the Mayflower. He did not study in Vienna, but got his medical degree at Western Reserve in Cleveland, which indicates that Ohio in those days was not too near the frontier.

Were I to change my essay to fit the facts, I would not, in fact, have any essay at all.

I took my predicament to a philologist friend, whose advice is granite, who had previously read and liked the essay.

"Are all the other things you said about your great-grandfather true?" she asked. "Certainly!" I answered. "His hobby was the cemetery. There's a statue of him in Weston. I've seen it with my own eyes, when I was a child. He got people to work on the cemetery by letting them pay off their doctor bills in labor. He was the only doctor then. He drained the swamp, and planted trees, redirected a stream so that it formed a pond. He founded the first newspaper in town, the *Weston Avalanche*, which still exists. My father told me that he remembers when he was a child that my great-grandmother used to bake huge round cookies, and no matter what animal my father named, my great-grandfather could quickly bite the cookie into that shape . . . I mean, though he was not 'a man from Europe,' but rather, just grew up in Ohio, he sounds like he grew up to become a real human being . . . ."

"Were the black swans really from Vienna?" she asked.

"I know that's true," I answered. "I read an old newspaper clipping about it, and it mentioned that the swans were from Vienna."

"Oh," she said, "you read it in the newspaper. Then it must be true."

"Shall I tear up the essay?"

"Of course not. It's a convincing essay. Some other time you can write a more complete account of your great-grandfather, perhaps, but let the essay stand as it is. Philologists are always discovering things like that about old works. The philology is not important to the essay. It is irrelevant.

"Vera!" I laughed, aghast, astonished, and amazed. "What a way to use the word 'philology.' What do you mean? What is philology? The truth?"

The Magician's Daughter

A melon drops from a vine.

It falls a thousand feet through the air and hits a rock, disintegrating harmlessly.

Way up there on a grassy ledge, on an idyllic slope unvisited by man, where the melons grow, where a few wild fruit trees thrive, two condors have their nest.

Below, nothing can grow. Only the tumbleweed roll unhindered for a hundred miles, this way or that only the wind changes. While growing taller than a man on horseback, surrounding this bald wasteland, the two-hundred-mile-deep impenetrable forest of thornbush utterly seals off from mankind that eastern edge of the Andes, which continue rising behind the high, idyllic ledge in sheer, nude rock to an unapproachable, unmelting glacier.

Before the first person set foot on either American Continent, two condors held this loft, and the two in my story are their direct descendants. For fifty thousand years that family tree has held this slope.

Once, one of the condors brought an infant girl there, the daughter of a famous Inca magician. And she grew up there—without learning, without learning a single word. Daily the condors returned to their nest with meat for their young, but these greatest of vultures are not sharers.

Instead, they instilled in the child a lifelong fear of flesh, all pecking sharply at her with gigantic beaks whenever she approached their food. The small stranger was forced to fend for herself. Eating roots and fruit and melons and seeds, she grew into old age, lived on that diet so healthily as to become the world's oldest vegetarian, growing finally to be one hundred and thirty-seven years old ... without ever seeing a human being, caring for the condors, generation after generation, watching them fly off.

At her death the birds did not eat her.

Due to the dry mountain air her body is in a state of perfect preservation ... even as these words are read, like magic so lifelike, she crouches in a crevice.

Yet there is no one to see this small miracle, nor will her body ever be discovered.

In her next incarnation she became a melon.

A true magician should not become famous.

The Giant Egyptian

In a city on the Upper Nile, not too distant from the Blue, a giant Egyptian was brought back from the dead.

He was 40 feet tall, and had a head like a dog. He was a god, of course — Anubis.

They found him almost covered with water, in a stream, as if sleeping. Some country people woke him, and he spoke probably Ancient Egyptian, holding his head as if confused, looking around at them and listening to their talk as if amazed, and there was nothing frightening about him.

He stayed several days with them, as if collecting his thoughts, recollecting, meditating; some saw him in prayer. He would eat nothing.

He communicated with them in a sign language to which they quickly caught on, and answered by gestures he understood.

Some Sudanese government officials in khaki uniforms came in cars to inspect agricultural endeavors in the neighborhood, and the local people became terrified for his safety. He quietly complied with their entreaties and spent the afternoon away wandering in desolate country, taking his huge strides, beyond where any eye could reach. He returned discreetly in the evening after the officials had left, and brought back on his shoulder half-a-dozen trees. Suddenly they had a monstrous bonfire, greater than anyone had ever seen, and he sang for them songs in his Ancient Tongue in a great voice which wild animals in the far distance answered as he sang, as if he were the moon.

Treasure of the Treehouse

The treasure in the treehouse is of course the joy of childhood, toy money and medals for bravery in the face of full-scale attack by the great apes, wielding clubs and torches, gathering in great numbers in the neighboring trees, and in the gathering dusk of twilight their eyes began to shine in those deep shadows – now they are gathering in groups and lighting torches – for these apes can handle fire. For ages they have lived in the caves of the volcano: their skins are resistant to fire, and an ape can put his hand in the flame of a torch and hold it there for a moment and only then break out in uncontrollable bloodcurdling shrieking laughter, which is catching, for as soon as one begins to laugh, others join in, and sometimes you can hear hundreds of apes all laughing at the same time far off in the distance and you know something really awful is happening.

But they have lived surrounded by the heat of the volcano for so long that they cannot bear cold water. If a drop of water touches them, their skin sizzles and shrivels as ours would under a drop of molten lead – we are out of ammunition, but luckily we have these water pistols and a bottle of water, and with these we can hold them off. Their plan is to set fire to our tree, and we must pick them off as they approach.

We are men of water, and they are the fire apes, and battle is inevitable.

There's one on that branch! pssssssst! Got him with my water pistol! See his body down there on the ground. I wonder whether he's really dead or just pretending. There's something about the way he's lying there that doesn't look natural. I'm going to put another shot of water on him to make sure. pssssssst! Look at him writhe and squirm! He wasn't dead before but he sure is now. Look! One threw a torch that stuck up there on that branch. I'm going to climb up and get it. As the boy climbed nimbly up after the torch, a movement in the shadows down below caught his eye. He grasped the blazing brand by its unlit end and threw it like a spear at that place in the shadows, and at the next moment a screaming ape fled from under the tree. The torch had sunk into his eye like an arrow.

They've encircled the tree and are lighting more torches. Each ape holds a torch in each hand, and they swing their arms wildly in the air. They are preparing to rush us, to rush in, and all of them at the same time — fling the flaming missiles into our tree, and our tree in a matter of moments will be an inferno of fire.

But it's starting to rain! We're saved! Those apes can't stand the rain, look at them run!

*

But the pleasure of a treehouse is not only for children. Indeed, I have built a rather elegant treehouse with several bedrooms out in the woods and I would like to invite you all out for the weekend. I'll furnish the transportation for everyone and I'll buy food and liquor so that we'll have martinis tonight in the treetops. I'll pay for everything. But each person, you know, young or old, must furnish his own apes.

Hans Christian Andersen

Once upon a time there was a man who was the greatest of us all. He loved a nightingale.

This nightingale was not an ordinary nightingale because for one thing she had the most beautiful voice ever heard, and secondly, she had no feathers and couldn't fly, and besides, she was a pretty girl and not a nightingale at all, though they called her that.

Her name was Jenny Lind.

His name was Hans Christian Andersen.

He loved her but she didn't love him.

He wanted to be an actor and play passionate parts, give great speeches, talk in all kinds of dialects, make love to queens and princesses, but fooey—he couldn't act.

So in order to live he wrote children's stories.

And in 1875 he died. That's what the tombstone, the monuments, and everybody says.

Oh! if it were only true! If only he could die properly . . . he yearns to.

Hans Christian Andersen today is six inches tall.

He lives.

Today I talked with him here in my kitchen. I had just finished reading two of his fairytales when he popped up out of nowhere.

He stood between the two front legs of my chair.

Gosh, he looked strange.

He wore Kelly green Chinese britches, a blue sailor shirt, ivory sandals with thongs of silver hair—no socks—and on his head he wore a pale red beret.

"Do I frighten you?" he asked.

I tried to speak, but my trembling legs as I stood on top of the refrigerator answered his question, so he said, "Come down. I can't hurt you. I'm Hans Christian Andersen."

This last he said gently, so I obeyed with a bang as I hit the kitchen floor.

"You jump nicely," he said, and smiled, and I blushed, for I like compliments of any sort, even the most ridiculous.

For a moment I was foolish and tried to be sensible.

I asked him to prove who he was. I asked him to make up a great story.

At this he flipped.

That is, he began turning handsprings all over the place, and then cartwheels, somersaults, pirouettes, and then he stood on his head and began walking on his hands on my linoleum floor.

"Stop!" I screamed angrily, for he moved so fast and always in such an unexpected direction that to follow his movements with my eyes made me nervous.

He stopped abruptly.

He turned white.

Wide-eyed.

He fainted.

I rushed over and picked him up. He was cold and breathing shallowly. I held him in my hands trying to warm him, and gently stroked his forehead.

Even his clothes had turned white.

His eyelids fluttered and I apologized as best I could.

His body was clammy from cold sweat, so I wrapped him in a warm wet washcloth, leaving his head exposed so he could breathe, and took him into the bathroom.

I held his limp body in my hands under the bathtub faucet, letting the warm water stream over him, and he loved it!

"Make it hotter," he said.

I adjusted the tap slightly. He squirmed with delight.

"Little hotter," he said.

I laughed.

He answered with a tinkling peal of wild giggling which, so pure in pitch, shattered all the bottles in the medicine cabinet.

"Jörgens blots plisk!" he shouted at me, which I guessed meant he felt better in Danish.

I laid him on a towel and let him escape from the washcloth.

His clothes were wringing wet and were scarlet from sandals to beret, except for the thongs of silvery hair in his shoes which he began to busily brush with a tiny comb while humming a Danish air.

Outside the sun was setting and its rose rays swept through the atmosphere.

Two airplanes purred in the clouds.

The white curtains became restless just as they always do when darkness is approaching in summer, when windows are open, and I could see Japanese lanterns lit across the lake for an Elks Club celebration.

The long blue shadows were covering everything.

Night was inevitably coming.

Soft as gauze.

"Call me Hans," he said, "and let me sit on your lap and whisper to you.

"There, now."

"Do not read any more of my stories," whispered Hans, "for until men and women find my stories boring, senseless, I cannot die.

"When I was young I prayed these stories could be eternal, endure, at least, some centuries, but I was vain.

"It's sad when a thing can't die.

"For to die properly is fine.

"It's bad to clutch a corpse.

"Let me die. Let me die.

"I know what I didn't then. She loved me . . . me . . . . All the time it was me, but she had to wait, as an apple waits on a tree to fall.

"She loved me as an apple loves the autumn.

"She waits in a fairytale forest now where all the limbs are bare and gray, and the leaves are always scarlet on the ground.

"She makes up songs of wanting me to pass the time.

"Oh autumn's come, but for three-quarters of a century I've lived alone in bitter winter here, making rounds to most who read my stories, children mostly, and to each I ask the same—do not read books.

"Let the spring come.

"Let a bright sun melt my footprints in the snow.

"Cover me with flowers."

V

Bullfinch & Goblin

Once upon a time there was a bullfinch.

This bullfinch lived in a marsh and on the edge of the marsh there was a cottage.

In the cottage was a family – a mother, a father and a couple of kids – young children.

The bullfinch loved these children very much. He liked to watch them playing in the yard, running around, chasing each other, and sometimes when they went for walks he'd follow them, but their shouting and screaming frightened him because, you know, bullfinches are shy – so he never came close.

One day they sat under a tree talking quietly.

The bird wondered what they were talking about.

He mustered his courage and flew to a branch of the tree and began to listen.

As a matter of fact they were talking about birds.

One of them said, "I wonder how many different kinds of birds there are?"

The older one answered, "Oh, there are sparrows. They sing cheep cheep cheep."

You know, he tried to imitate a sparrow.

"There are owls. They go whoo . . . whooooooo."

"And crows. Caw . . . ."

"Bluebirds. Tweet – tweet – tweet – tweet – "

"And woodpeckers. Knock! Knock! Knock! Knock!"

Silence.

"And ducks!" cried the younger one. "Wuaaank! Wuaaank! . . . . But aren't there any other kinds of birds?"

"I can't think of any. I guess that's the only kinds of birds there are."

Yi! the bullfinch flew away in a flurry. Here he'd loved these children so much and they didn't even know he existed!

He began to mope around the marsh, and he began to look at himself, and he realized he wasn't very big, and his feathers weren't very bright, but the main thing was he couldn't sing like the other birds.

Moodily he stared into a muddy pool . . . at his own reflection, when up suddenly from the slime oozed a goblin.

Ordinarily the bullfinch would have flown right away, because goblins are little and dirty and ugly and all covered with mud—mud dripping from their outlandish clothes, and, you know, goblins are a little scary—but he was feeling too depressed.

"What's wrong, my friend?" asked the goblin gently. "You seem sad."

He told the goblin all his troubles . . . he wasn't very big . . . and his feathers . . . but the main thing was he couldn't sing like the other birds . . . and gee . . . .

"Well as a matter of fact," said the goblin, "I happen to be a very good voice teacher. I can teach you to sing and your voice will be the most beautiful in the whole marsh. However, I want to warn you I am a very strict teacher. You will have to obey me absolutely. The lessons would take a year."

The bullfinch thought it over and he decided to do it.

They went far off to a lonely place out on the great marsh and began the lessons.

The goblin was a very strict teacher.

He made the bullfinch go on a diet.

He corrected his posture, and taught him how to breathe properly; and in fading light of evening the bullfinch had liked to fly around, high, doing loop the loops, swooping, gliding, doing figure eights for the fun of it; but the goblin said, "None of that nonsense! You have to spend your time at your lessons."

Nights fell quicker.

The bullfinch sang on in the dark.

In the falling whiteness he fasted and shivered: usually he went south at this season.

But the goblin was comfortable cold.

He was covered with dirty icicles which clung at wrong angles to his clothes and fingers and face. He liked to rattle them.

And spring came. Other years at this time the bird had flown out and found a bullfinch hen, built a nest, had baby bullfinches; but the goblin said, "No. You must devote this time to perfecting your art."

The bullfinch continued his lessons restlessly.

The goblin was a great teacher. The voice from the first grew more beautiful, fuller—grander—until finally . . . .

He flew all night over the marsh to the place where the cottage was, and he arrived just at dawn, just as the sun rose.

He flew to the window ledge of the children's bedroom, and he began to sing!

How he sang!

No one had ever heard singing like that before in the marsh.

The children woke, and they looked, and they saw the bullfinch, and they ran into their parents' bedroom shouting.

"Daddy! Mommy!" they shriek – "There's a goblin on the windowsill!"

Tom-tom

Once upon a time a little colored boy was born in the heart of Alabama.

For his third birthday they got him a drum, and gosh! did he play that drum! BAM! BAM! BAM! BAM! all the time.

He drove everybody crazy with it. He'd play it all over the place. In bed at night he'd play it, until they made him stop, and he'd hit it all day in the yard, and one day he marched right up Main Street strutting and pounding as if he led a thousand black sparkling soldiers, and everyone threw pennies at him!

He was a tall kid for thirteen. He would scowl and spit at the mention of school.

On weekend nights he'd crouch outside an old saloon, in back in the shadows, tapping, tapping with his hands and feet to the blaring jazz inside.

Finally he awkwardly introduced himself to the black drummer in the band, and the old man took a liking to him.

The old drummer taught him much.

So when he died, drunk at his drums, one night, the boy, who was seventeen now, got a regular job with the band.

And how he played! how he raged! how he tore at those drums! how he worked! and practiced and practiced, and how deep, deep, deep, was his sleep each night, and two years went by like nothing.

Then the World discovered him.

Gee they made a fuss over him.

Autograph hounds! bobby soxers! jitterbugs! press agents! college students! Gee they made a fuss over him.

After he became the highest paid jazz drummer in history, he learned to read and write.

He studied hard, all sorts of things, but mainly drums.

He looked at ancient drums in museums.

He mastered classical percussion, and went to India to learn its jangly secrets, and studied tom-toms with the Navaho.

He went to Haiti and to China, smoked hashish and opium, and left all this for Harlem cocktail parties and performances.

Serious musicians wrote music for him; he gave solo concerts at Town Hall and starred with symphonies at the stadium; he toured Europe and became its idol, and in England played a command performance for the king and queen, at which the princess clapped uncontrollably.

At forty-five he had retired from public life, except for occasional benefit concerts. He lived in a mansion in Maine. He kept blooded horses. The great weekended with him. There was a movie of his life.

Then he made the mistake of going to Africa.

An anthropologist, one weekend, had told him rumors of a tribe who worshipped drums; he flew over the ocean and took a safari to find them; he looked on deserts and into jungles, into the mountains, everywhere, desperately at last.

The other members of his safari were weary, and without warning, one day they vanished.

He was alone in the wilderness.

On a log he floated across a big slow river; he waded in mud; he walked in dust across a wasteland; he killed a snake and a panther.

One day he stood on a mountaintop and looked at the world.

Bare white rock surrounded him for several hundred yards.

No animal, no plant, no thing would dare come up here. Only a man would come here to watch the sunset and the stars come out.

He looked way out about him at the miles of greenness full of snakes and dangers and mosquitoes, and all the other irritations of a life, and wondered, why couldn't he stay right here?

Darkly, he stood stark on the white mountaintop in the blue sky, clutching a strange red fruit.

He'd forgotten he had it.

He'd picked it from a pretty tree on the mountainside. It was curious and soft. He bit it. It was delicious!

A bubbling spring babbled over the warm rocks, and he walked with it, followed it downward into the jungleful of sadness, frowning, wondering why he had to go.

Over a crag and under a branch and through the grass he went, and then he heard an explosion of drums.

A parade!

A fantastic procession! There must have been a thousand of them, marching over the yellow plain-grass, warriors, their bodies painted and oiled, glimmering in the sun.

Drummers led them!

The rain of drumsound drenched his body; he looked around and saw trees trembling, saw monkeys standing, watching; he saw the river shimmer; the ground glowed; the flowers looked at him, and butterflies sped around him like racing flames—every leaf a lamp reflecting sunlight at him.

He followed the sound.

Their village was vast, each hut and temple had some shady trees around it, and the streets were sandy and warm.

Naked women stared at him from porches as he walked toward the center of town. A group of men followed him.

He was led to a straw castle where he met the leader of the tribe, a woman, about forty.

"Welcome, white man," she said in a dialect he'd learned—for they were pure black in color and he was a light brown.

She explained to him they were in the midst of a five-day celebration of war.

They never fought anyone, so they celebrated this every year, for they loved parades!

They played war games and did dances, covered with paint, their speartips and bracelets flashing in the firelight and moonlight, they whirled, they stalked, they lunged and threw daggers, jumped from trees, and friends fought in the dust over who buys the drinks.

"We needn't fight," she said.

She offered him a drink.

He accepted it; it was a yellow drink in a tall bowl; a tiger lily floated on the surface of it, and she said it was made every day of willow leaves gathered on rafts from drooping branches, from the soft walls of the river.

She told him that each woman in the village owned a house. Men lived by hunting. Or they became priests—that is, drummers, for drums were sacred, and only the priests played them.

She explained that any man could enter the priesthood.

Each year after the war festival any man could go with a class and old teachers to a lonely place, to learn the mysteries of the drums. They studied there a year, and then a contest was held; she pointed out the open doorway at an ornate tom-tom standing like a statue at the center of the town; each took a turn playing the great drum, and the ones who passed became priests and were feted for a week.

The ones who failed were caged for five days, then burned alive.

He told her he wanted to go. He wanted to learn how to play as they did.

She said all right, but she warned him that if he failed he would suffer as her own son or brother would, he would die.

He went.

They went through narrow paths that twisted; green walls became ceiling too, shutting out the sun, covering them with blackness he found not bad at all, but which they dreaded . . . shivered under like frightened zebra; somebody's hand gripped his shoulder, his hand clutched the man's shoulder in front, and on and on the line in the dark like a cartoon caterpillar, falling apart now and then, here and there, stumbling, squealing, tripping, cursing strange names on the nightmare march.

Food would be passed back from he knew not where.

What leader led the way? He knew not, nor cared. He trusted them. This was their country.

Occasionally they would sleep.

He lost all sense of time.

The ground trembled.

An earthquake.

Trees fell noisily, invisibly in the darkness.

One hit him, and he cried out! But then there was silence, and they rested, waited, the natives grumbling—he could hear them—they said some god was angry because they'd brought him. There was talk of killing him.

He tried to explain about earthquakes.

Someone, perhaps the old leader, calmed them, and they went on. Color!

They were out under it!

Blinding blue light; he blinked and rubbed his eyes, and shook the darkness off.

The sun!

His eyes grew immediately heavy and he fell to the grass and slept.

He awoke.

And heard the flapping and fluttering of bird wings among the crackling morning fire sounds.

Breakfast.

The smell turned him to the fire.

The natives were already setting up drums; others sat greedily scooping food from bowls; they were afraid—occasionally one would glance around with glazed eyes.

Grotesque masks they'd painted on their faces.

He decided he wasn't hungry.

He took off his shoes and walked onto the sunken expanse of a field covered by miles of short orange reeds, soft matting for bare feet, very different from the jungle: trees stood alone; bounded by white walls of rock rising right-angled and looming among the cumuli; and from the clouds a stream fell off the rim of wall, like white smoke rising, down into a distant pool from which a small river blue-streaked across his vision.

He hiked to the pool and jumped, kicking, whirling his arms, and twisting his body until he could stand the coldness, which after a while became a coolness; and he floated, and swam slowly, letting the water run into his mouth, and diving deep, swimming down—he glided between the pool plants illuminated dimly by the green sun above, and he saw little fish with long, pointed noses, and a school of polliwogs fluttering over his face, and in the distance a blurry shape which he swam to, and which turned out to be a rock covered with luminous pink moss which glowed like a rich tablecloth belonging to a magical king.

But it was not, of course.

It was pink moss.

He rushed to the air, and resting a few moments, began to splash around again.

The valley, the pool, and some caves he found in which he felt a friendly eeriness were what he'd come for, he decided . . . .

The natives!

Ugly!

What with their masks, superstitions, painted faces ... and as he watched them sitting at their drums, sweating and working like men in pain, he decided: *he wasn't going to do it.*

He'd done enough drumming.

Money and fame he'd gotten, and now his life depended on it.

No.

So he slept in a cave away from the rest.

He lay on his back and listened to honking calls of big birds which flew in monstrous packs over the valley, and in the evening lined along the stream to drink.

He heard echoes of the tom-toms being beaten bouncing off the walls.

He watched meteors.

And hid.

The remote pool — its geography, its granite, the moss, and schools of silver minnows, tribes of gray turtles, waving water weeds, its little blue lamps of phosphorescent fish — this green-lighted stage hypnotized him, and as a stage-struck girl in her dreams does, each day he'd dive, and play ... in truth ... like a daydream.

He did not touch his drums for a long, long time.

But they made him return to the contest, and while he waited his turn at the tom-tom, while his classmates one by one were playing, he realized he was really going to die.

There was no possible chance of his winning.

He thought back, long back to those two years he'd played in the saloon, and he knew he'd been happiest then.

When his turn came he was dazed as he sat down at the drum, so full of the past was he.

He looked around and saw them listening, waiting for him.

Then out of nowhere he heard a clarinet! then a trombone! and a trumpet! and a bass! and they were playing "When the Saints Come Marching In"!

Just like those saloon days!

And he began to play the drum part, his part, and oh how he played!

Deliriously drumming and dreaming those minutes all the old faces, young brown faces, laughing, dancing people, proud yellow coats, the bartender grinning, the drunks falling, a woman shouting, glasses glittering, calendars, Drink Coca-Cola! and someone was weeping someplace.

The natives didn't understand.

They couldn't see or hear the saloon, of course.

He lost the contest.

For five days he lived with his shame, alone in a bamboo cage, and he died in that kind of agony, alone, in white flames that lit the whole jungle and surprised the gloomy nightclouds as lightning does.

The Music Copyist

Once upon a time there was a music copyist.

He made copies of scores, and he was good at his business, competent and reliable, and worked free-lance for the best symphonies and performers.

One day he had a rush job. He'd been working ten hours straight on scores for a man considered by the World to be the master of the viola.

It was evening when he finished, and he bundled the big music sheets in a fold of newspaper, and took a cab from his mid-Manhattan apartment to Long Island to the house of the Master Violist.

He arrived about ten in the evening and he found a festive party in progress.

He handed the music to the Master Violist, who glanced over it casually and thanked him, and said, "Well, as long as you're here, why don't you take off your overcoat and have a drink."

The music copyist took off his coat and he got his drink, and he stood holding it.

But he felt a little out of place because here he was, surrounded by high music society, diamonded people, millionaires and heiresses, dressed in tuxedos and clothes from Paris, while he had ink smudges on his thumbs and cuffs, and he was bleary-eyed from working ten hours, and he was dressed in a regular suit.

The Master began to speak of his hobby, which was collecting programs of great musicians performing great music, and a small crowd of people gathered around him to hear him talk, and the music copyist joined the crowd and listened.

The Master finally led the group upstairs to his den to view his collection, and oh! here on the walls were programs of Casals soloing in Madrid, of Albert Schweitzer playing the organ in Africa, Paganini's first and last public performances (framed side by side), Handel conducting the Palace Band for a wedding in England, Bach playing Buxtehude, oh! and more and more . . . .

Finally the music copyist spoke up. Suddenly, and in a little loud voice, he said, "You know, I have a program which deserves to be in this collection."

"Oh," said the Master.

"Yes, and as a matter of fact, I have it right here." The music copyist pulled out his thick wallet and fished down into it among the many torn scraps of paper on which were scrawled telephone numbers of musicians, and he pulled out a tiny folded-up square of paper which he unfolded carefully, and which turned out to be a mimeographed program of a music teacher's recital of her pupils.

He handed it to the Master Violist, who, after glancing at it, said, "What's this?"

"Let me tell you about it," said the music copyist.

"Several years ago I went home . . . to Octagon, Ohio . . . . I hadn't had any occasion to visit my home town in, oh, ten years . . . . I stayed there at the house of my cousin . . . . Her young son was studying the recorder, and I noticed at the time that he really seemed to enjoy his lessons . . . not like most kids his age . . . he actually seemed to enjoy it . . . . One night the teacher . . . his music teacher was a woman . . . she also had a choir . . . was to give a recital of her pupils . . . . My cousin invited me to come along, but I didn't want to go . . . . Perhaps I should explain that, although I'm not a musician, I am, in a way, in that business . . . and I have an ear . . . for instance, I can name any performer on a recording by his style . . . that is, I mean, of course . . . the great musicians . . . and I have a record collection that is one of the . . . ah . . . of which I'm proud . . . . Anyway I didn't want to hear any *music teacher's* . . . well, anyway . . . I went, mostly to please my cousin, and resolved to try not to be sarcastic . . . . My cousin drove to the small-town auditorium . . . . I escorted her to some seats, and we sat waiting an interminably long time for the thing to begin, and while we waited I glanced over the program I'd been given (that one you're holding there in your hand) . . . and I noticed the music was entirely old music . . . pieces by Bach and Handel, Couperin, Vivaldi, Scarlatti, and Frescobaldi and . . . well it was all good music, but they were simple things, not technically very difficult, suitable for children to perform . . . . The recital began . . . and after a while I realized that I was sort of enjoying it . . . and was glad I'd come . . . . The children weren't prodigies, any of them . . . but the kids played with such a spirit, with such an obvious joyousness that the whole thing—little sour notes and all—was transformed for me into pleasure . . . there even seemed an appro-

priateness to those little sour notes like a crow's caw or a frog's croak
among country morning finch songs . . . in fact I became so absorbed
in the music that when, during an intermission, my cousin, spar-
kling-eyed proud mother, exclaimed, "Wasn't he wonderful!" I stared
at her blankly wondering exactly what on earth she was talking
about, until I realized I hadn't distinguished her son, and had just
been listening, rather than watching . . . . Finally . . . just before the
last number the music teacher stepped between the curtains and
made an announcement . . . . She said there had been a change in the
program and that instead of "Two Songs" by Vivaldi, that the choir
would sing the St. Matthew Passion, by Johann Sebastian Bach . . . .Well
I remember I frowned, a little irritated by the announcement, because
I knew what she had said was simply incorrect . . . because the great
St. Matthew Passion takes four hours to perform . . . it's one of the
few greatest and among the most complex pieces of music ever
written, and only the best professional choirs ever attempt it . . . and
besides it takes a full orchestra to perform it . . . . But then I became
distracted by some usherettes, high school girls moving down the
two aisles handing out things, and whispering loudly to the first
person in each row, 'Take one of each and pass them on!' . . . which
I did, and I found I had in my hands a pointed paper hat – a dunce
cap – and a light wooden stick with short crepe paper streamers attached at the top . . . .Well I noticed everyone else was putting on their
dunce caps so I put mine on too and sat there clutching the little stick
and I remember the thousands of little streamers made a funny quiet
noise in the warm summer auditorium air like autumn leaves stirring
. . . . Then every light dimmed out . . . and the dunce caps turned on
. . . they were luminous . . . the paper streamers too . . . and I looked
above and saw dim purple bulbs which I realized was the black light
source causing the luminosity . . . . All the dunce caps were shining sea-
blue . . . except . . . directly in front of me there was a line of bright white
dunce caps . . . and I glanced to the right and left and noticed everyone
in my row was wearing white hats . . . and I stared around in back and
all the caps were blue except that directly behind me stretched another
line of white dunce caps . . . . The white caps formed the design of a
cross . . . . I looked at my own hat . . . it was white . . . and suddenly
realized I was wearing the center cap . . . it was just an accident, I
just happened to be sitting in that seat . . . but before I could think

much about it the choir began to trickle one by one from between the closed curtains wearing luminous brown robes—hands, face, and feet invisible—finally forming a solid brownly shining blot across the front of the stage . . . . Then the music teacher appeared on the center dais . . . a silhouette . . . and after the applause there followed the silence . . . broken by a creaking noise which sounded as if the curtains in back of the boys were opened . . . but the stage itself was in complete darkness . . . nothing was visible beyond the bright brown blot . . . . The choir accompanied by a full orchestra began to sing the great *St. Matthew Passion* . . . . The children were trained! they sang . . . but the orchestra . . . they were playing ancient instruments . . . real Bach trumpets, thirteen feet long! shawms! viola da gambas! dull tabors! the actual instruments for which Bach wrote that Passion . . . but their performance! I had never before in my life heard anything nearly like it . . . they were like a band of angels . . . . But then for a moment I remembered something . . . an incident . . . I hadn't paid any attention to it at the time but . . . that afternoon I'd gone out to buy cigarettes and I happened to glance in a window of a car stopped for a light and thought I recognized a French horn player . . . a great musician I'd always thought, but he'd never become well known . . . I'd done work for him several times, hadn't charged him much because I liked him and admired him and I knew he couldn't afford . . . but then the light changed and the car drove on, and I said to myself, 'Oh, it couldn't have been. What would he be doing here in Octagon?' . . . But now I listened to the ibbletorks . . . yes . . . I became sure . . . my friend was playing in that orchestra! . . . For the next four hours, throughout the complete performance of the *St. Matthew Passion*, I lived in the wonderful daze, listening . . . . Finally it finished, and a few lights went on . . . .

"But the audience . . . the way they reacted . . . it was very strange . . . very peculiar . . . you see—

"Nobody clapped.

"Nobody whistled, or shouted—Bravo!

"Nobody moved, or got up to go home.

"For the phosphorescent fish who live four miles deep in the depths of the ocean off the coast of Japan know no silence as tranquil as that which they left in the dark air of the concert hall.

"Almost one by one the audience began to stream up the aisles toward the entrance, and I got up also . . . and began to work my way through the crowd in the opposite direction . . . . I was moving toward the stage and toward a door at the side which I knew would lead backstage . . . the music teacher appeared in the doorway . . . she was standing there blocking the way . . . and so I just said I wanted to go in and say hello to my friend . . . the French horn player . . . and I named his name and explained that I was a friend of his from New York . . . . She looked puzzled and said, 'What do you mean?' . . . and so I explained again, the French horn player, he was a friend of mine, I just wanted to stop in and say hello, if you'd give him my name I'm sure he'll want to see me, we're good friends . . . . Her face was puzzled and she frowned, and repeated, '*What do you mean?*' . . . I didn't know what else to say . . . I was looking puzzled at her . . . she was looking at me, I felt, the way one looks at an insane person, and finally she said, 'I'm sorry . . . only performers are allowed back here' . . . and she stepped inside and the door closed . . . . I walked out of the theater and got into the car where my cousin sat waiting . . . . It had been ten o'clock, the regular concert almost finished, when the *Passion* had begun and now it was two in the morning . . . the kid was already asleep in the back of the car . . . my cousin drove . . . finally I said, 'Well, didn't you notice anything—strange—about the concert?' . . . and she answered, 'Yes, it's nonsense her keeping the children up this late at night! Just nonsense!' . . . 'But the *music*—who was playing?' . . . 'Oh!' she said, 'I think it's a little band from Lopert down the highway that comes over to help her out occasionally at her recitals.' . . . But I knew that I hadn't been listening to any little band from *Lopert*, Ohio . . . and then I said, 'But what about all those lights . . . that cross . . . what did it all mean?' . . . And my cousin laughed, 'Oh, she's always doing crazy things like that . . . you can see why the children love her.' . . .

"Well, that's all."

The music copyist looked around the den at the silent group.

"The story's finished.

"I left Octagon that morning and haven't returned. That program, that program there, that's the program from that night . . . look . . . see! The last number on the program. It says, 'Two Songs,' by Vivaldi."

"Ooooh!" said a voice sarcastically.

"Stop it!" said someone with a disgusted wave.

"Come down, mister!" snarled a beautiful girl.

The group turned downstairs, mumbled asides answered by grimaces, and the Master himself made a very nasty, biting comment which the music copyist couldn't help but overhear.

The music copyist turned white. Nobody believed his story.

He asked for his coat from a butler, and had to wait a long time for it, and then pushed his way through the laughing, drinking bunches toward the door, and just as he stepped outside – the Master Violist appeared in the doorway behind him.

"Let me walk you a ways," he said.

The Master took the copyist's arm as they walked and he said, "I'd like to apologize for what I had to say on the stairway back there. Look . . . by chance you heard something you weren't intended to hear. I know you heard what you heard, but please . . . just *don't talk* about it. Those people," he said with a gesture back at his brightly lit, noisy house, "they can't understand."

The Master's fingers tightened around the copyist's arm, tightened with a violist's grasp, with all the strength in a violist's fingers, and he whispered, "But that night! that night in Octagon – wasn't it great! Wasn't it great!"

The copyist jerked his arm away. He was rubbing it gingerly, and said, "Yes, certainly, but how do *you* know?"

"I was there, of course," answered the Master, and then he said (and did he really blush proudly in the moonlight as he said it?) "I was playing second viola."

Text

of

There Are Different Kinds of Writing
A Shorter Version
The original *There Are Different Kinds of Writing* is an
evening-length prose work, using microtonal music
for the bass recorder (Part I)
and for the family of recorders (Part II) by
Tui St George Tucker

*   *

The dumbest guy I have ever met was an editor.

There is one thing about editors – they are idealists; there has
never been an editor who would not rather have written a great novel
or a great poem than do the job he is doing. In their own eyes they
are failures.

But this particular editor had developed cancer of the tongue when
he was ten, and his tongue had been removed surgically. The opera-
tion was successful, and the disease did not recur. However, for the
rest of his life he was unable to speak, other than those certain words
which can be pronounced without opening the mouth. He breathed
through his nose when he spoke.

When he wanted to say "yes," he said – Uh-hunh.

When he wanted to say "no," he said – Unh-unh.

When he didn't understand, he would say – Hunh?

When he was thinking something over he would say – Hmm . . . .

*   *

That a man could sit there feeling anxiety, breathing shallowly,
moving his toes inside his shoes, swallowing, licking his lips, raising
his eyebrows and then frowning, sighing sadly, twisting in his chair,
reaching for a magazine and then letting it drop to the floor without
picking it up . . . that a writer could sit there doing really nothing . . .
contemplating a far-off editor who might at that moment be reading
his manuscript, instead of *herself* writing what could have been . . .
what, good God, might have been a great novel!

Hmm!

*   *

Scrunched into the chair, her arm falling asleep, her black hair billowing over the purple pillow, wearing yellow film, perhaps taffeta, a white shoe askew on the bedpost, drunk. Steadily the ocean breeze rushes through the jalousies.

Costa Rica!

*   *

I am serious as the dead.

Some find the dead grotesque, but the dead see your lively exertions, in the face of the future, as grotesque.

*   *

Noticeably now, if there were but attention, if that activity might be envisioned, could it but be conceived — were I to invent it for the moment and place it there on the table like a model, so that the idea could be got, bursting on the brain in a fever of work — would you recognize it if you saw it?

*   *

If I could ride around a bit, sitting in the back seat of a great car, perhaps gliding through the yellow countryside of Ohio in the afternoon on a fine Fall day, or zooming through the midnight black of a New England Summer night with the rain beating down, drops dancing on the highway in the headlights, or picking our way on a Spring day around Baltimore streets passing among glad throngs, through the racket of everyday, moving ponderously, our dark brown Cadillac purrs, and is stared at by children.

*   *

Arid land, black banks of dust, where hills change places daily and the wind is long, the dirty dunes rising in hot clouds to cake with grime the gristle left of yesterday's lamb that the wanderer eats. Tomorrow he shall chew his belt, the next day his tongue. It is Arthur Rimbaud!

*   *

And here I am at the grave of Yeats and it's midnight. My horse is miserable. There's a full moon somewhere but it's black, black blanketing rain that greets the visitor from America.

*   *

In a far-flung corner of the Third World the fur flag of the Alaskan nationalists blew off the flagpole and was chased by three wolves across an airstrip, delaying the take-off of the small black plane containing three snowblind East German spies, whose fate it is to be sent back here, and to be eaten by polar bears.

*   *

The fire hose was tied into a dozen knots. The blaze consumed the building that was so hated by its tenants. The landlord collected the full insurance. Two people died in it. Its light cast flickering shadows a block away. Passengers taking the air on the deck of the Staten Island Ferry all noted the conflagration, and commented upon it.

*   *

Once upon a time a fox bit a furrier who was fishing on a private lake in Pennsylvania. The lake belongs to the fox.

*   *

Holding cupped in his hands three pieces of dry ice insulated by green napkins, the invisible man set them afloat atop the tropical fish-tank pool, like three smoking bars of bubbling soap.

A gramophone was playing a onetime top tune on the Hit Parade.

A lemon fell onto the rug with such momentum it rolled out into the middle of the room, and it will remain there, unpicked-up, untouched for at least fifteen minutes after this story is forgotten.

The man, whose hand was seen with green napkins dropping dry ice, now appeared above the water and rose to his feet from where he'd been kneeling behind the long empty fishpool.

A voice at the door exclaimed, "Pick up that lemon *immediately!*"

*   *

Crockery, cookery—shard, to be sure, but still with the taint of ancient oil, attracts the hordes of cockroach ghosts to the archeological site, affording to the few, those sensitives for whom the dead live, ghastly sensations.

*   *

Worm-eaten, moth-eaten, the cocoon that was left on fulfilling its metamorphosis by the famous *Phantom Moth-of-Gold* fell into the hands, by luck, of the incredible weaver who lived on the equator in Ecuador nine hundred years ago, who unspun its strong, invisible thread upon a bone spool decorated by an emerald, put the spool into a box-of-spools intended for use in the future, and on that very day was buried by his god, the volcano, under a thin layer of lava.

*   *

He placed it there with a thud.
Then he quickly covered its lip with melted beeswax and put a blue-clay stopper on the huge jar, and covered it in the deep hole with earth, mumbling prayers in a tongue that no one speaks now, in a language dead two thousand years. Stamping the earth firm over the grave, he tried to think of the future, much as you or I might think of the future—imagining someone coming across this page two thousand years hence, but nobody understanding the language.
Thud.

*   *

Look at that building framed by the mist, there is purple light inside it.
There are thirteen golden men inside it, their eyes closed.
Patiently they wait for us, for years they have been dreaming that it is us approaching through the wet grass.

*   *

An unoiled wagon sang a song, some Oriental mountain melody that plain folk in Kansas cannot appreciate; but the whining of the wheel is the whistling of a god, a Buddha no bigger than an elf that sits six inches high between the ears of a horse heading for a house where a baby will be born. The baby will be the reincarnation of so-and-so (I would not dare to try to pronounce that name).

For centuries upon centuries it has been the duty of this immortal, magnificent, miniature Buddha to attend each rebirth of so-and-so. It is his first visit to America.

*   *

"He brought me a bouquet of whirlpools and tornadoes and I put them in this cracked vase."

*   *

Where precipices lunge, chasms fall; mountains lounge, then avalanche.

*   *

"It was the person next to me.

"I tell you, it was that person next to me!

"I was reading this book aloud, and there was a person sitting here beside me listening, and it was that person who did it, not me.

"I was just sitting here reading this book aloud, and my eyes were on the page, and I didn't even realize that my listener had vanished. I tell you, I don't know which way that person went!"

The Typewriter Repairman

A typewriter repairman tripped at the curb, falling forward flat into a puddle on the highway, arms extended, and a truck ran over the tips of his fingers. The truck screeched to a halt a hundred yards ahead, and the driver jumped out of the cab and ran back toward the accident victim now sitting stupidly in a state of shock. His face had gotten smudged with grease and his hair was dripping black oil. Across the highway a State Police car had pulled to a halt, and help was on its way.

*

Fate takes strange turns, indeed – and to think that but a few minutes ago the man was sitting in the author's chair, that writer of short prose pieces whose new book of fantasies, *Some Morbid Curiosities*, had been reviewed only last week in the Sunday paper. The repairman had read with pleasure the author's two earlier books, and so he felt regret at having been out to lunch when the well-known man had brought his typewriter in for cleaning. A glob of honey had gotten among the keys and the typewriter of course had stopped dead, locked in sugar-shock. The typewriter was an old-fashioned upright which typed characters slightly oversize, easy to read, and rather unusual to see these days; it was almost an antique. He'd taken off its ribbon and given it a bath in acid, and when the typewriter was ready and now with a new black ribbon, the owner of the shop decided to deliver the typewriter himself after closing in the evening, for he saw to his surprise that the author lived only a few blocks away, though across the highway, where he never had any occasion to go.

The house strangely matched the typewriter, being slightly oversize and old-fashioned. It stood alone on the block and was surrounded by vacant lots in which weeds grew shoulder high. It had rained heavily all day, but it had stopped at dusk, leaving large pools everywhere, and the fields were full of fireflies. As he entered the yard, he noticed a tree on which the fireflies blinked off and on in unison like a Christmas tree, and he recalled reading on the dust-jacket that the author's hobby was Oriental botany.

A plain lady opened the door, and there were children's voices beyond her. She led him to the writer's workroom on a sunporch, and he placed the typewriter on the desk before the author's chair. The first thing he noticed on entering the room was that five humidifiers were silently sending up jets of spray.

She explained that the author would return in a few minutes and would pay the repair bill in cash, and if he would like to wait, why he could sit down right here. He assured her he had plenty of time, that his shop was closed, and that in fact he could do with a rest after lugging the typewriter five blocks in his arms.

"What is that?" he blurted out before she left the room.

He pointed at a very large table that was only a foot off the floor and on which many small plants were growing.

"It's a bonsai mangrove swamp," she explained.

An immense glass box whose walls were only a few inches high contained the shallow waters out of which on small islands the tiny trees grew in profuse entanglement. It was like a regular swamp. Miniature Spanish moss plants hung from the branches. The box emitted a high-pitched humming which he finally figured out was caused by clouds of almost-invisible flying insects that hovered over five finger-length alligators asleep in a heap on one of the islands. The glass box was illuminated from below, and light shone through the lakes, revealing tiny oysters clinging to the mangrove roots and fish of different sorts, some swimming in schools.

The lady—and the repairman couldn't figure out whether it was the author's wife or not—re-entered the room with a plate.

He said, "I read two of the books that were probably written on that typewriter. I enjoyed them very much."

She smiled. On the plate which she offered him were two clusters of brilliant vermilion grapes, each cluster shaped precisely like a football.

"They're a seedless grape from Burma. He grows them out back."

He bit one of the grapes in half. Its flesh was bright orange.

"He has a green thumb," she explained, and again she left the room . . . which he noticed now as he looked around was rather messy with stacks of books and magazines and manuscripts everywhere. A strong sense of good manners kept him from reading any of the manuscripts, but he began to glance idly at the titles of the books and magazines, and it puzzled him to find that they were all scientific works and periodicals, as many on geology and astronomy as on botany. He opened several of the books and saw that they were not popular expositions of their subjects but were illustrated with graphs and filled with Latin words and mathematics, and he found it queer that he didn't see a single work of fiction, for he knew the author had never written anything else. The author had been quoted in the Sunday paper as saying, "I never write about real life . . . I only write dreams . . . no one in any of my stories has ever even had a name." But for someone immersed in dreams he showed a remarkable interest in the real world! — said the repairman shrewdly to himself, while searching his pockets for his pipe, and he discovered much to his irritation that he had left it at the shop.

Within arm's reach he noticed there was a hookah on a shelf. Oho! — he said to himself — What's this?

If he had had his pipe with him, it never would have occurred to him to do it, but his craving for his forgotten favorite pipe caused him to put the mouthpiece of the water pipe between his lips, and he inhaled sharply as bubbles sounded from the hookah.

And what is this? — he said to himself as he opened a small circular container that rested on the shelf near the pipe. In it was some blackish-brown sticky stuff.

He said again — Oho! I think I have found the secret of the author's imagination. I'll bet this is opium or hashish or some South American mushroom.

But he replaced the container and the pipe onto the shelf and turned his attention to the typewriter. There on the table was a pile of typing paper, and he took a sheet of it and inserted it in the typewriter.

Now on returning a typewriter to a customer, it is quite customary for the repairman, before handing it over, to type a sentence on the machine, it being a self-evident demonstration that the typewriter is in good working order.

As often as not he would type — Now is the time for all good men to come to the aid of their party, but he didn't feel like typing that, no . . . but what should he write *on this typewriter?* This typewriter had never written anything but fancies and dreams, never once the truth. Never once had it written truthfully of the real world, never once . . .

but what could he make the author's typewriter write that would be the truth?

As the greatest authors have done, he stared at the blank sheet of paper.

If he hadn't been sitting in the author's chair, wanting to write the truth, I don't think he would have done it, but without giving it a second thought he said to himself, reaching for the container beside the hookah—I think I'll try some of this.

Using a matchstick, he scooped some of the sticky stuff into the bowl of the pipe, lit it, and inhaled deeply, holding his breath to get the full effect.

He stared at the blank sheet of paper. The truth? And college courses in philosophy were desperately recalled from long years ago . . . the *truth*?

He inhaled again a long puff from the pipe.

Suddenly he looked behind him, but there was no one. He felt not unlike a schoolboy in a empty classroom about to write a violent anonymous message on the blackboard which would be discovered later by the teacher on entering her room already half-filled with guffawing scholars.

What message should he leave for the author to find?

The truth?

He took another puff on the pipe.

The truth is that it was not opium the man was smoking but a remedy for plant fungus which had infected the mangrove trees. It was suggested to the author by an old friend who was a florist in Chinatown, and was composed of Japanese snuff and powdered anthracite coal, and given body by a little honey. It was in fact in concocting the stuff that the author had spilled some of the honey onto his typewriter. The author had doubted that the arcana of Chinese herbal medicine included Japanese snuff, but his old Chinese friend had assured him that for many years China had imported Japanese snuff solely for its fungicidal properties. He had been treating his plants several weeks with it, and it was proving remarkably successful.

The snuff was harmless enough, and it ignited well, but the anthracite coal powder, when it burned, produced carbon monoxide, and he had gotten several lungfuls of the poisonous gas, and to top it off, he had held his breath with the stuff in his lungs, furthering its effect on his system. If he had taken ten pipefuls of the poison, he would be dead, but luckily he had only four, but it was enough to make him confused, mildly excited, and it caused him to hallucinate. Indeed, even as he types the sentence on the typewriter the poor man is seeing in his mind great expanses of sky and clouds that roll out in a boiling panorama of great distances. Before fleeing the house in exhilarated panic, he puts his face close to the paper to read what the typewriter had written, and it is as if it had been written by the infernal skywriter in black smoke, each letter a mile high, the sentence stretching across the heavens. He had written in capitals on the virgin white sheet:

BORGES IS BETTER

The Hidden Ballroom at Versailles

Elegant and opulent, yet undiscovered, "the hidden ballroom" at Versailles, whose entire floor is made with many fragile panes into a smooth, single surface of mirror, rests undusty in darkness, unentered for two centuries by a flicker, nary a moonbeam nor match, lamp, nor any light, except for one time. Then, a tiny batch of insect eggs (blown through a crevice down through an imperfection in the molding onto the great glass floor) hatched fireflies.

That was in 1893.

Brief piece written to be read at the 1971 Memorial Reading for the poet Paul Blackburn which, as it turned out, I was not able to attend.

I am not used to memorials for my friends. I must attend two this month. Jackson Mac Low will live the longest of us all here . . . can't you just see him there in the future dressed all in white like George Bernard Shaw or Mark Twain, after we're all dead.

There he'll be, the grand old man, snow-white beard and hair.

He makes a funny face and a gesture with his cane at his daughter's grandchild, and then scowls at an elderly son, who smiles at this.

He'll get so old that every year on his birthday they'll put his picture in the newspaper.

Yet I wonder about his memory. Will he be able to remember us, then, as vividly as we see him there now?

Orange

Though a man may be white from frostbite, purple with rage, yellow from jaundice, green while seasick, green with envy, in redfaced apoplexy, turned black by the sea when drowned, or browned by the sun, now gray in horror, or in the pink for pleasure, yet I know of no case that a man may be orange.

Though the villain is black, the coward yellow and the novice green, I know nothing of the character of that man who is orange.

The human body's fluids, organs and flesh can be found to be of every hue, except that there is no organ, liquid, muscle nor piece of fat that is pure orange.

Excepting orange, in death we may meet every shade.

There is no word that rhymes with orange.

2

Orange is the best color.

Where this color is present, gloom requires effort.

Good spirits are created in this light.

With fixed, triangular eyes, a jack-o'-lantern stares at me, but in vain tries to raise his eyebrows at my thought.

Whatever the candle in the pumpkin sees, it illuminates.

Among great lights he holds his candle, and his grin is not discouraged by the white glare; nor later on the windowsill is he disconsolate at viewing the great dark, outside.

By his light children are transformed into—Good Lord! into what!? . . . (there go a pirate and rabbit walking hand-in-hand with Death) . . . perhaps, into gods this evening, hallowed, mellowed by orange.

I have asked myself seriously, "Why do the young stare so seriously upon the face of the pumpkin?"

As, even now, I conjure an image of that hideous visage, yet benign, so orange, I wonder—who in history's name could you have been? What life did a body lead to be left so headless?

I have tried to imagine the body of the jack-o'-lantern.

"Are you John the Baptist?"

"No," answers the pumpkin.

"Are you Marie Antoinette?"

"No."

"Are you that Greek whose body the women tore apart, whose head they left in a cave, where it alone survived and prophesied, and then allegedly was lost—are you that head, priest of poetry and music, Orpheus, himself? Is this what you've come to?"

The pumpkin is silent.

Perhaps he is embarrassed because of his teeth, or contemplates the Bittersweet.

3

The New York City garbage barge was called the *Ornery Henry* and its sister ship the *Frankincense*. The city sold the second-hand boats to an African company, and they were tightly tied together, side by side, and towed—bound for Africa, into the eastern Atlantic into the vicinity of the Canary Islands, where they encountered a hurricane. Such was the fury of the storm, the barges were cut loose at sea, and abandoned. For several years they drifted—still securely lashed together—southward, and then westward, caught up in the North Equatorial Current drifting inexorably west toward a line of islands that extends several hundred miles off the coast of Venezuela. Many of these are small islands without fresh water, are uninhabited, remote and unvisited; and it was on high ground at the center of one of them that another great storm deposited the boats. The garbage barges are now empty, clean and spotless, bone dry and sitting in the sand, without a speck of paint, silver gray, bleached by tropical sun and repeatedly washed by the afternoon rains and blown dry by a ceaseless, salty warm wind. A simple one-room cabin had been built at the back of one of the barges, and its door had been wrenched from its hinges long ago by the wind off the Canary Islands. A brilliant and large, intensely rusty hinge was still attached to the cabin doorway, a slender triangle pointed outward like a stiffened pennant, bright as a flag.

"You mean it is an orange door-hinge?"

"It is an orange door-hinge."

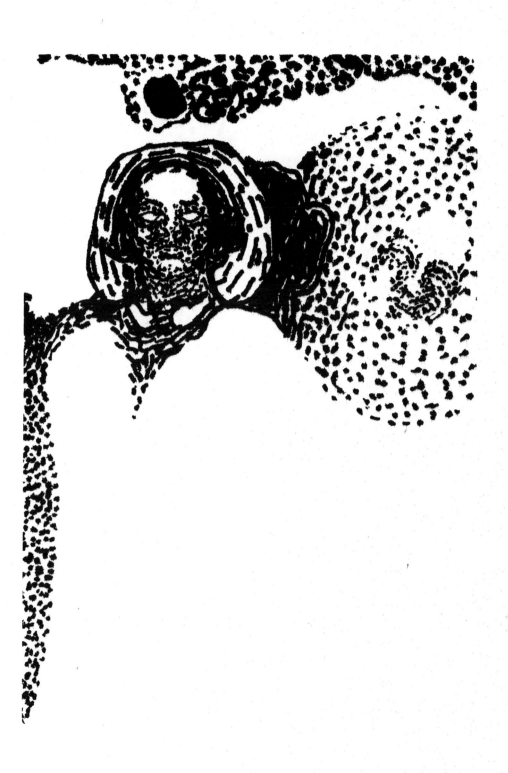

On Hope

For Martin Mitchell

The monkey leaped on the man's shoulder.

The man shuddered, for he knew who it was. He knew exactly which monkey of the ten thousand that roam about on the Rock of Gibraltar, tame and free as pigeons, walking around in the parks and streets.

It was a demon monkey.

It was the one he'd trained to bring him necklaces, who brought him pearls, garnets, and amber from moonlit bedrooms in the big hotels—from women sunk in snoring.

The monkey dangled before his eyes the largest diamond in the world.

The whole thing began several days previously when all on Gibraltar went into an uproar. The Rock of Gibraltar was visited by royalty, by the queen mother, and the princess. A battleship brought them and their entourage, and with them the famous necklace, the largest stone of which was the *Diamond of Hope*, which the princess was to wear at some great state occasion. (There's a curse on the necklace, you know, and misfortune had followed it, and come to whoever possessed it until it became part of the British crown jewels in the middle of the nineteenth century.)

On the very first night the royal party was in, the monkey returned to his gypsy master with the necklace. The necklace, of course, was valueless. It couldn't possibly be sold. Gibraltar would be swarming with police searching for it.

The gypsy was annoyed with the monkey, irritated at its genius, and terrified of being caught by the police with the gems; and besides, although he had no particular regard for the government (being a gypsy) he liked the idea of "the princess" and wouldn't dream of stealing her necklace. So he quickly wrapped it up and addressed the package to her and dropped it in an ordinary mailbox. He enclosed a note to her saying something like, "You really ought to guard this more carefully."

The next night the monkey returned again with the necklace.

This time his note implored her to have the police guard the necklace more carefully, and he even gave them advice. He advised them to place the necklace in the center of a cage.

(For a monkey of course couldn't get into a locked cage.)

Then the third night, when this story begins, the monkey again brought the gypsy the necklace, and fell at the gypsy's feet, dead. Shot. Very probably the monkey had been fatally wounded by a guard as he was escaping.

The gypsy shuddered at the diamond, and was not surprised at the death of his friend.

The first two times it had been like some freak occurrence, like a weird accident—to unexpectedly discover oneself in possession of part of the British crown jewels! but now . . . .

When he received the gems for the third time, the whole thing was plunged into meaning. It no longer seemed like an accident. He had been given the necklace. Fate was at work. Now the necklace was his.

He put it in his pocket.

It never occurred to him (being a gypsy) to doubt the reality of the curse which accompanied the diamond, and he accepted his fate with the stone. Quietly and secretly he buried the animal.

And as he thought about it he was actually a little pleased that he, a gypsy, had been singled out by fate to take the curse off the princess, and the English throne.

He walked down to the shore of the Mediterranean and took off his clothes, and—having nothing in which to put the necklace, he put it on—dove in, and swam.

There was a full moon and the sea was perfectly calm.

Just off Gibraltar there's a very deep place in the Mediterranean. It's called the Gibraltar Trench. Only a mile from shore the sea is a mile deep.

The gypsy was a very good swimmer.

He swam out a mile, over this spot, took the necklace off and dropped it.

At that moment a smile lit his face as he imagined the thousands of Sherlock Holmeses searching for it for the next fifty years.

The man lazily began to swim back toward shore, and the necklace fell down into the depths.

They each had a mile to go — the man had a mile to swim, and the gems had a mile to fall.

The necklace fell much faster than the gypsy swam.

It fell straight down until it got about a hundred feet from the bottom, where it came to rest on the dorsal fin of a shark.

The shark had been sleeping, but the necklace woke it, and it turned round and around wondering what was happening. It decided to go up to investigate.

The shark swam upward even faster than the necklace had fallen.

Meanwhile the man still lazily swam toward the huge "rock," now ablaze as never before with the royal festivities, with a million electric light bulbs — and he thought of the curse. The stone would never bring its misfortune to anyone ever again; it was finished forever, its power over man extinguished for good, buried beneath a mile of water.

Then he looked over his shoulder and saw the necklace floating a foot above the water, moving slowly past him.

(The gypsy did not see the shark's fin; he only saw the necklace glittering in the moonlight, as if floating in the air, not coming toward him, but moving past him, now receding into the distance.)

The man immediately realized that one of two things was true. Obviously, either he was witnessing a miracle (and the whole thing smacked of the miraculous) or, he was having a hallucination.

He decided to find out.

Was it a miracle? Or — was it a delusion?

He began to shout and wave his arms and splash, and he began to swim after the necklace.

And sure enough, the necklace stopped, and after a moment began to move toward the man.

The man is swimming toward the necklace. The necklace is moving toward the man.

That is where the story ends.

However, I can't help noticing, at this moment, that at first glance it seems inevitable — you know, that the shark will devour the man.

But I do not believe that result is as inevitable as it seems at first glance; that is, I believe there are several reasons, so to speak, for hope.

1. I do not think a shark has ever been approached like this before—that is, by a man wondering whether the shark is a miraculous manifestation or whether it is merely a figment of his own imagination. Such a man would smell different.

2. The man is a gypsy animal trainer.

3. The shark is now in possession of the necklace.

Brilliant Silence

Two Alaskan Kodiak bears joined a small circus, where the pair appeared in a nightly parade pulling a covered wagon. The two were taught to somersault, to spin, to stand on their heads, and to dance on their hind legs, paw in paw, stepping in unison. Under a spotlight the dancing bears, a male and a female, soon became favorites of the crowd. The circus went south on a west coast tour through Canada to California and on down into Mexico, through Panama into South America, down the Andes the length of Chile to those southernmost isles of Tierra del Fuego.

There a jaguar jumped the juggler, and afterward mortally mauled the animal trainer, and the shocked showpeople disbanded in dismay and horror. In the confusion the bears went their own way. Without a master, they wandered off by themselves into the wilderness on those densely wooded, wildly windy, subantarctic islands. Utterly away from people, on an out-of-the-way uninhabited island, and in a climate they found ideal, the bears mated, thrived, multiplied, and after a number of generations populated the entire island. Indeed, after some years, descendants of the two moved out onto half a dozen adjacent islands; and seventy years later, when scientists finally found and enthusiastically studied the bears, it was discovered that all of them, to a bear, were performing splendid circus tricks.

On nights when the sky is bright and the moon is full, they gather to dance. They gather the cubs and the juveniles in a circle around them. They gather together out of the wind at the center of a sparkling, circular crater left by a meteorite which had fallen in a bed of chalk. Its glassy walls are chalk white, its flat floor is covered with white gravel, and it is well drained and dry. No vegetation grows within. When the moon rises above it, the light reflecting off the walls fills the crater with a pool of moonlight, so that it is twice as bright on the crater floor as anywhere else in that vicinity. Scientists speculate that originally the full moon had reminded the two bears of the circus spotlight, and for that reason they danced. Yet, it might be asked, what music do the descendants dance to?

Paw in paw, stepping in unison . . . what music can they possibly hear inside their heads as they dance under the full moon and the Aurora Australis, as they dance in brilliant silence?

Charlie Morrow's Bracelet

Charlie Morrow's bracelet of unpierced pearls is strung by a marvelous method.

He corners a mouse with his three-cornered hat in a corner.

Their business is to transplant large old trees.

The first golf course in China comes alive with snakes an hour before the great earthquake at Tangshen.

An oboe player touches the pontoon of a seaplane with a dab of orange paint.

On the bottom of a shallow sea a scallop opens the mouth of its shell and makes a sound like a frog in falsetto on being touched by the deadly starfish and leaps two feet through the water into the mouth of a rusted can.

An orange peel drops onto a corrugated roof from the same cherry tree that later in the day will throw its shadow on the shed.

The Alpine greenhouse burns to the ground, leaving a gigantic black puddle in the snow, glittering with broken glass and floating ice.

A Neanderthal child is pressing leaves and shells into the mud, and removing them, leaving their impressions in the mud—making fossils.

He changes the direction of the steppingstone walk.

A Caribbean team of deaf-mute scuba divers is successfully searching out sunken treasure.

I seek the secret of senility.

As she opens the furnace door, the blast of heat which meets her face melts her contact lenses.

They have no waterfalls in Holland.

The gong of bronze gone to verdigris is struck a thousand times by raindrops, while the peacock makes eyes at his mate.

Pressing the metal softly against her face, she stares through the prongs of the pitchfork at the scarecrow she's been sent to dismantle.

Knots pop and pine resin drips and snaps in the hot wood fire—it's an original Franklin stove.

The sentence which follows will be really rotten. The sentence which preceded this was much, much worse.

Riding indigo waves in brilliant foam, a scarlet butterfly swims madly through the surf, riding a dead fish floating in to shore.

The stationmaster stands, pocket watch in hand, beside the steaming locomotive, whistle in his mouth, waiting for the flash of the daguerrotypist.

The tongues of his alligator shoes are made from the tongues of alligators.

He smokes a Cuban cigar and wears a Panama hat and tells jokes on a nightclub stage.

She tries to look over the shoulder of the artist who is tattooing a blue butterfly onto her big toe. It's Whistler.

My Achilles heel is killing me.

To have a black cat on one's lap, to have it yawn and gaze with great green eyes up at the candles that encircle the two of you as you illuminate the precious page with a giant letter in purple.

The bald man chooses a hat.

The first bird hatched from an egg laid by a reptile.

A white picket fence on which a Teddy bear is impaled floats out into the center of a swollen stream.

Only a foot apart, 26 parallel white picket fences, each covered thickly with rose vines all burgeoning in blossom, stretch out before us for hundreds of yards, and from miles around come millions of bumblebees—each bumblebee a different word.

We slide along salty walls of a tropical cave that's constantly swept by a strong oceanic wind, and we must stay alert to dodge the large white sea birds flying toward us, that intermittently plunge through this narrow passage.

The saber-toothed kitten reclines in my palm, and its mother's paw rests on my outstretched arm. "A friendly beast . . . " is the conclusion the big cat has come to, though not in so many words.

Look further for whatever you find, get more of whatever comes easiest to hand, take it where such things are rare, and sell it wholesale to a shop.

At the poets' costume party all the revelers wear masks and sandwich boards. On the sandwich boards are written—hand-lettered, large and clear—the poems they most admire.

At the masquerade ball of the stage costumers all their outfits are made of tissue paper that are the actual dressmakers' patterns of their favorite theater costumes, which have been cut out and put together with library paste at the seams.

Sunshine in Seattle seeps up from the ground through roots to stems and trunks of plants and trees, and is radiated by a billion leaves, lending the clouds, rolling low, their green glow.

Who hankers—should fetch.

They live an idyllic life in a houseboat anchored above a waterfall.

He makes a mint in the cold mountain mist by opening a chain of shops selling paper cones of French fried potatoes to the Indians of the Andes.

A pink-eyed hound turns the corner, and stops to sniff at a chocolate tomato wrapped in red tin foil that someone has stepped on.

He says he saw a silver buckle sitting on the table with its tongue out.

I gave her half my double Popsicle, and she shares with me her binoculars.

The out-of-work typist allows her fingernails to grow.

The fisherman who captures the Loch Ness Monster live in his nets as it gives birth to healthy triplets . . . .

"This ain't turkey! It's tuna fish!" shrieks the condemned man on taking the first bite of his last meal.

The Scottish boy eats his oatmeal in a porringer, and he notices that his younger sister's hair is oranger.

The dog reverses itself in front of the mirror, and wags its tail.

A child drops a flashlight down the well and it kills a frog.

When will my collection of bottle caps become valuable?

The autumn afternoon rain hides a crescent moon from view, keeps crickets and birds quiet, and sends a frog under a leaf to sit, while over the pool the spider sat in his dripping web.

Tomorrow innumerable marbles will be shot with lines, sediments shall shift, dunes develop where the wind commands, clouds lace, and at midnight jet streams trickle to a stop in moonlit vast emptiness, again.

Broken bricks that fall about at the foot of a battered building (ancient work stopped) collide with half-cut stones in dust, and crabs run in and out; scorpions sun themselves in solitude while ants collect in cool caverns; sand collects in cracks only to be blown again by the wind, and by-and-by to fly again over the Gulf, there to fall, sinking into double depths, blank valleys of smooth sand, perfect as pyramids, perhaps.

What it must have been like to have been Balzac!

The thief who escapes up the flagpole steals the golden ball.

The touchstone is placed on the benchmark.

You're the only person in the world who carries the seven of diamonds in his back pocket.

I bequeath my brain, properly pickled, to the Literature Department of my old school with certain stipulations, which follow, regarding its display:

At the flower show he sticks his head inside the blossom of a gigantic morning glory and bites off its pistil.

Sometimes I write like a knuckleballer who's lost the knack.

I have more to tell, I've hardly begun . . . and you say my time is up!

When the wind blows from a certain direction, our windows rattle loudly. At such times it is hard to hear oneself think.

At certain times these small visions might assist one in getting from one moment to the next.

The grim reaper smiled at me, as has the muse of poetry—while listening as I read my prose.

This is being typed on cellophane.

My son went to Japan to study computers, and he returned in five years a sumo wrestler.

2

I have here this bouquet—a careful collection of dried weeds, each grown out from a crack in the cement.

The phantom buyer from out of state meets the secret seller from the inner city.

Hordes of handymen are hanging about with nothing to do.

The plainclothesmen are in fancy dress.

An ampersand unwinds.

It is a jewel to cover a beauty's mole.

I fish for a name among my many noms de plume.

A nonce word is stuck under my fingernail.

There is a scintillator in my sock.

Whatever happened to the spoon with the long handle?

The ramp went to an unmarked level.

He had a stopwatch as big as a saucer.

The most exceptional collection I have encountered is that collection of exceptions to rules, which prove those rules.

He believes in the rules of grammar but not in the Laws of God.

Narrow zeros make me nervous.

The man hops on one peg leg down the steps of the Mayan pyramid.

I push my way through autumn foliage of dense bush and underbrush until I reach the edge of a scarlet wall, a blazing moat, a gully, full to the brim with a red river of poison ivy.

The horizon does not recede, but rather, as we approach it, reveals itself to be the edge of an unfathomable abyss.

Beware when a megalomaniac acts like a servant.

Nertz. Once more – see if it can get through . . . once more – Nertz. I believe it is something said in the thirties. Let's see now – Nertz! . . . it is said by a young woman with a run in her silk stocking.

The tattoo of the blossom of the orange camelia sits on my arm like a bloodfilled spider.

She paints five-minute portraits on balloons and sells them for five dollars in the park.

On Chinese New Year we eat snapdragon dumplings.

Fourteen cobblestones are missing from the street near the broken bridge where the old pimento factory road peters out in an overgrown vacant lot.

He cranes his neck to look back at the landscape of his childhood as the slow train brings him into the outskirts of his hometown.

Imagine my tattered typewriter ribbon in this antique typewriter in a dilapidated museum.

In the hanky-panky of an Oriental afternoon an opium smoker shoots an Arab dancing girl for making too much noise with her bangles.

I see a dangler on my windowsill; it is my neighbor's monkey wanting to visit my gray parrot.

On a boatload of blue tile I am floating down the Nile.

I feed a fast string of slowballs to the nearsighted batter.

There is a rogues' gallery in which we belong. There is a group of photographs which could be thrown on the table, and there – one of the photographs would be of us: the reader and the listener.

We aren't what we think we are, we really are what we pretend to be.

The dancer has two bad big toes.

I sincerely think you might have, though I hardly think that had you . . .

The narwhal enters the cove.

There is a movie on every billboard.

Nature reveals splendor in various sizes.

We find a mushroom big as an umbrella that tastes like steak soaked in gin.

A pelican and falcon land on the balcony of the Fish & Fowl Club, which itself is perched on the edge of a cliff by the sea.

The Paupers Club is an association of writers of short prose pieces that meet monthly at the old Anarchist Meeting Hall on Broadway below Fourteenth Street.

He found a fortune in amber and wastes it on jade.

A broken colloquium vanishes beneath the Virginia Creeper.

The champion of sorrow has a horror of pride.

The unutterable demeanor of the big cat who is painted crimson from the tips of his whiskers to his tail by the gushing artery of a beached whale.

Great ghostly hordes of Indians are returning from the Happy Hunting Grounds, all vegetarians.

Instead of needles, the porcupine on awakening discovers itself covered with worms. "Now, you are mine, my pet," says Medusa.

The houseboat finds new freedom during the flood.

It will be a sign that the world is fundamentally changed when it becomes the fashion for ordinary people to wear shoes that don't match.

Notice the seriousness of that vegetable that knows it is to figure in a still life by the artist.

The watermelon are visible by the thousands on the rolling hillside, and many artesian wells send up streams of sunlight sparkling in the air.

A few waterfowl fly by the waterfall . . . my water mug holds a water bug.

I said seven solid silver seagulls, and I'll say it again—I'll swear to it in court: *seven solid silver seagulls!*

The Cincinnati ballplayer got his chance.

They were the champions of chewing the fat.

Now she is thinking of what fiction writers talking to each other on the telephone laughingly refer to as "real life."

They dress their cats in silk.

The splendor of the invisible cord gives meaning to the knot.

It is easy to imagine having an elephant as a friend.

A dispute over dandelions becomes blasphemous and bloody at the Dublin Dandelion Winery & Bottling Plant, plunging the plumbers of copper tubing into bitter dispute with the coopers in whose barrels the wine is transferred from the old copper vats to be aged in old wood, prior to bottling.

There is something repugnant about a rusty funnel.

A footlong mosquito is buzzing at the window.

Going up the stairs at a run, up the 64 steps at the edge of the Ganges, hazarding a sacred saying at each step, imitating a holy man, the very devil, himself, in the form of pussycat soaking wet from a fall into that filthy water, is transformed into "a vulture forever at the top of the stairs," and flies off toward the sun to soar on all the hot air there.

A chocolate brown Burmese show cat quietly sits deep inside a brown paper grocery bag, pretending she isn't there.

Imagine you're in my movie, and this is your close-up: the camera comes to focus on your hand, your hand fills the screen in the elegant theater, and the camera slowly circles the hand revealing the changes of positions of the fingers which are grasping an object that is at first mysterious, but then turns out to be a book: the fingers are grasping a book . . . and then, miracle of miracles, there is a sound track to the movie being shown in the elegant theater, and the room in the theater becomes filled with the sensitive sound of a throat being cleared, and a quiet cough which is not at all ugly, and obviously precedes the sound of spoken words . . . ah, the words are the author's . . . but it is my reader's voice that is heard in the elegant theater on the sound track of the movie, my reader's voice.

VI

The author with Harry (Stinky) Davis, 1932 Tigers first baseman, at Navin Field in Detroit.

The Institute for the Foul Ball
An Unfinished Baseball Epic[1]

For Burt Britton

He hit a single, stole two bases and then stole home, winning the game, which had gone into the eleventh inning, and it won a minor league pennant for his team.

The three had seen enough. Three men had come to Louisville solely to view the young player in action. One was the chief scout for the Detroit Tigers, the second was the venerable and longtime owner of that club, and between them sat the Tiger manager. While the fans in the stands went wild at the fantastic conclusion of the game, those three men sat quietly and smiled at one another, for they owned his contract.

His nickname was The Cheetah. They called him that because of his amazing ability to run fast like that big cat, to spurt off at high speed, stop, and reverse the direction of his running, and each reversal of direction served to increase his speed. This, of course, is just the talent one needs to steal bases, and during the Cheetah's first year with the Tigers he broke the world record for stolen bases before the season was four-fifths over. But it was not merely speed, for he seemed to have the sixth sense of the hunting cat, he seemed to sense in advance the intentions of his opponents.

To watch him steal bases was a beautiful sight.

Nobody ever fooled him, and he was the trickster par excellence.

He was not a powerful hitter. Perhaps the oddest record he held was that of being the only regular major league player never to hit a home run.

He was a place hitter. And he could be relied upon to hit an infield grounder, or to bunt, but with unerring instinct he was able to hit the ball to just the place that threw the whole infield off balance. He invented "the soft hit" — that is, when he'd hit the ball it would slowly

---

[1]The first four chapters were published in the 1976 Horizon Press book *SPENCER HOLST STORIES* and the rest was written during the following year, as is presented here; the last chapter was published as a separate piece in 1982 by Station Hill Press entitled *16 Drawings & Something to Read to Someone*, with Beate Wheeler's drawings, exactly as presented here.

lob anywhere from five to fifty feet and fall to the grass without bouncing, and the place it landed more often than not was an exactly equal distance away from each of three or four players, so that each made a dash for the ball, and they frequently fell over one another trying to field his puny hits. Spectators and sportswriters soon noticed the frequency of those queer collisions, and the cruel crowd found it funny to see grown men crash into each other, saw it as comedy and cause for high hilarity, and greeted each new "accident" with gales of laughter. You can imagine how it made the players feel.

The infield got paranoid. They got overcautious about running for a ball that another player was also after, to such an extent that it became not uncommon that players who ran after a ball he'd hit would all suddenly pull up short and freeze to avoid colliding with one another, and none would dare or deign to reach down to pick up the ball, each of them standing staring at it like a crystal ball-gazer in a trance – and during this the runner would have gotten safely to base on a hit that any one of them might have turned into an easy out with a throw to first.

He was also the inventor of the "in-place, spinning bunt." This curious method of hitting a ball could only be used when the pitcher threw a low fast ball. Holding the bat as if to bunt, he would suddenly turn the bat vertical, and sharply waggle the bat as it met the ball, and a loud *crack* could be heard, the bat would shoot straight up twenty feet into the air, but the ball would shoot straight down to the ground, landing an inch or two in front of home plate, and it didn't bounce away, but stayed there spinning like a top with such a velocity that if the catcher tried to grab it with his bare hand the ball invariably leaped forcibly out of his hand as if it had a life of its own.

His great skill with the bat was acquired through much practice. No other player ever worked as hard practicing place hitting, and every day at dawn he practiced for several hours on the empty field, assisted by a catcher, sometimes several young pitchers, and a couple of kids whose job it was to chase the balls and to move the target.

For he had a cloth archery bull's-eye which lay flat like a flag on the infield grass, and he would have one of the boys move it into whatever position he was trying to hit the ball, and it was the boy's job to stand near the target and note where the ball came to rest. The brilliantly colored circles of the bull's-eye are marked with numbers, and armed with pad and pencil, it was the boy's job to keep score. Thus in a systematic way he labored at dawn day by day to achieve his ambition: to hit *any* ball that a pitcher might throw—to *any* precise location on the infield.

"To hit any ball that a pitcher might throw"—seems like a straightforward phrase, its meaning quite clear; yet it meant something quite different to him than it might mean to you or me, or than it meant to any other professional player. When a hitter stands in the batter's box waiting to hit the ball, there is an imaginary rectangle over home plate. If the pitcher throws a ball which goes inside this rectangle the batter is obliged to hit it, and if he does not the umpire calls "Strike!" However, a batter is not obliged to hit a ball that goes outside this rectangle. Well, he felt obliged.

He felt it was the duty of a batter to be able to hit any ball that his bat could reach, and much of his practice was devoted to hitting balls that others considered "Inside," "Outside," "High," or "Low."

He attained his ambition, and he always struck at every ball that was thrown by the pitcher.

He taught himself to hit either right- or left-handed, and while other batters tried to hit the ball squarely, his method was to hit the ball off-center, and he mastered the art of giving the ball just the right amount of spin so that when the ball first touched the ground it stayed there, rather than bouncing farther across the field, as might be expected, in the direction he hit the ball. And it must be noted no infielder ever got used to his hard-hit grounders that miraculously stopped abruptly when they first touched ground, and often a foolish mitt would be seen clawing the empty air at that place where by the laws of physics the blasted ball should have been.

But the most bizarre hit he ever invented (called "the laser" or "the mirror hit") was rarely seen, for it could only be used when the pitcher threw a fastball directly at his head. He would point the bat like a rifle at the pitcher, and then with all his strength he would shoot the bat forward to meet the ball as if he were making a billiard shot, hitting it head-on with the tip of his bat; but there was no controlling the direction of the ball, for it could only return on the exact path it had traveled; but such was the power he put into the bat that it returned at twice the speed like a bullet toward the pitcher.

He had some funny ideas about baseball.

1. He believed that a batter should be allowed only one strike.

2. He believed that the concept of four-balls-and-you-walk should be abandoned.

3. He believed that there should be only one batter's box, and that it should be located directly over home plate.

But let me explain more fully about these three ideas on how ideally baseball should be played, or, as he said, how it *shall* be played in the future. He believed that the batter should stand on home plate squarely facing the pitcher. If the pitcher threw the ball to his left the batter would hit it as a left-hander, but if the ball were thrown on his right side, well, then the batter would hit it like a right-hander; and if the pitcher threw the ball straight toward home plate, why, he said, there were a number of different ways to hit it. Instead of the imaginary rectangle, he saw an imaginary semicircle very much larger that was determined by the reach of the hitter's bat. That is, the batter would be obliged to hit any ball that his bat could reach. If the batter failed to swing he was out, or if he swung and missed he was out. One strike and you're out. But if, by chance, the pitcher threw a wild pitch, a ball that went outside that semicircle, that the batter couldn't reach, then the pitcher would be automatically taken out of the game, and the batter would get another chance to hit.

The owner of the Tigers was a good guy. He had acquired considerable wealth through canniness, and in the process had acquired wisdom, and from the first he took a liking to the young athlete, invited the youngster into his home, and often the young man joined his family at their rather elaborate and formal dinners, where he became a favorite of the old man's wife. On the very first of many, many such evenings, after dinner, the young man had been explaining these ideas he had about baseball, and the old man asked, "What happens if the batter hits a foul ball?"

"He gets another chance to hit," answered the Cheetah. And then he added, "But the foul ball is the key to the Mystery of baseball. There should be an Institute for the Foul Ball where scholars and scientists would bring all their intelligence and scientific equipment to bear in studying it. For there is something about the foul ball, I feel it in my bones, that will prove to be the key to the future of baseball."

And the old man said, "I own a factory, and on the grounds of the factory there is a whole building devoted to research, and sometimes there are ten or twenty people working on a particular project or problem that we think important—is that the sort of thing you mean? Do you mean that I should hire ten or twenty people to study *the foul ball?*"

"No," said the young man. "It would have to be a much larger effort. It would take hundreds of people, a real institute, with everybody studying, and it would be staffed by our best ballplayers as well as scientists."

"You mean all these people would do nothing but study *the foul ball?*"

"Not only that," the Cheetah mused. "They would also study the Home Run Pitch."

"What the devil is that?"

"Well, it should be possible for a pitcher to throw a ball so that when it was hit the ball would go two or three times as far as might be expected. In other words, a ball that you would expect, when it was hit, to just go over the second baseman's head and not much farther would in fact sail right over the center field fence for a home run."

"What!?" exclaimed the owner of the Tigers, and it must be admitted that this gentleman spilled his glass of sherry onto his white summer suit at this juncture, and began to sputter almost angrily out of pure astonishment. "What possible reason would any pitcher have for learning that pitch? Can you imagine any possible situation in which it could be used? Why would any pitcher ever want to throw such a ball?"

The young man sheepishly said, "You know, I've given considerable thought to that, and it's rather odd, because I haven't been able to think of a single occasion in which a pitcher could use it to advantage in a game. And yet, you know, it's *possible*, and I think at the institute they would choose to study that possibility."

The old man sighed and scratched his head. "Son," he said, "I'd like to get something straight about you—do you take this seriously? This idea of an institute where there would be hundreds of highly trained people studying the foul ball, you do see that such a thing could never be, don't you? If I read about it in a story, perhaps I'd be amused, or I can accept it as a beautiful daydream of a young ballplayer, but it can only exist as a fantasy. You do see, don't you, that it is not really possible?"

The young man sensed the earnestness of the owner's question, and he answered levelly, "If the people love baseball enough, and if they want *their* team to win badly enough . . . they will create such an institute. I must add that I think it more than just *possible*, I believe it probable, in fact, inevitable, and soon."

"In your lifetime?" asked the sixty-year-old man.

The young man smiled gently, and answered respectfully, "Sir . . . in *your* lifetime."

"My boy, do you have any conception of what it costs to have even twenty highly trained scientists work on a problem? Well, let me tell you it costs a fortune."

"Couldn't you get money from the government? I mean, baseball is America's national sport."

"That is unrealistic. I frankly find it difficult to believe that you could be so naïve. I believe that you think I should sponsor this project, and I wish to make it clear to you that I won't."

"Really! Gee, I hoped you would, because I can see it would take a person who could organize things, and of course, it would take a lot of money. I thought you'd be just the person for it. It would make you famous . . . I mean, your name would go down in history as one of the most important people in baseball. You'd like that, wouldn't you? In the history books you'd be as famous as *me!*" And the boy flashed a brilliant smile expressing his genuine affection for the older man, who was studying him with great perplexity.

But the boy's smile faded, and his brow clouded, and he said desperately, "But you *must* start the institute. It will be dangerous for you not to . . . . Couldn't you sell your factories? Aren't you sick of being rich?"

"Dangerous for me? Now what does that mean?" inquired the rich man, laughing icily, while pouring himself a Scotch over a spherical ice cube.

"For goodness' sake!" exclaimed the Cheetah. "The danger lies in that someone else will get the idea and make it reality. Suppose, instead of us, the Indians start the institute!"

"My boy, I'm well acquainted with the owner of the Cleveland Indians, and I want to assure you that neither he nor any other owner in America would do anything but laugh outright at the notion that they pay millions of dollars to support an institute to study the foul ball and (God forbid!) the Home Run Pitch! Besides, the way you say that baseball will be played in the future—I can't help noticing that those new rules just fit your style of hitting. You, and only you, would do well. I think those rules were tailor-made to give yourself the advantage."

"That is not true! Let me tell you how my ideas about baseball came about. When I was fifteen in the orphanage at Louisville . . . "

"You are an orphan?" exclaimed the owner's wife, who had been listening attentively.

"I was found by the cook in the snow on the front steps of the orphanage when I was only a few days old. She called me her little Eskimo and said I looked like a Laplander baby. She said the only mark on my body was a spot on the end of my spine which disappeared, she said, three weeks after she found me. I've always thought that my parents must have been American Indian. But all that's not important! Let me tell you how my ideas about baseball came about . . . I remember it so vividly . . . I was sitting in a classroom at the orphanage, and my English teacher was reading aloud to the class a book called *Moby Dick* . . . ."

"*Moby Dick!*" exclaimed the lady.

The boy paused, puzzled, mildly pained at her interruption, but deferentially he turned to her and explained, "Moby Dick was the captain of the ship in the storybook . . . but all that isn't important."

"But it is extremely important!" snapped the lady. "You're all mixed up."

"As I was saying," smiled the young man, "I wasn't listening to the story, my mind was having its own thoughts, and I was thinking about *baseball*, and I noted how often even in big league games the batters hit balls which were caught—flies and line drives and foul balls. I figured maybe a third of the outs in every game were caused by such hits. And I figured if those outs could be transformed into singles, why it would be of tremendous advantage to a team. If the batters could guarantee that their hits touched ground before they were caught, then . . . then . . . no one would ever hit a home run! I suddenly saw a flaw of baseball: greed for home runs causes a ridiculous number of needless outs. I stared at the moving lips of my teacher, but I didn't hear a word. I immediately saw that stealing bases would assume a new importance among batters who would only single, and at that moment I knew I should become a great runner. I saw my future clearly then, what now is every day. On that very afternoon I signed up for track, but of course I never learned to run, I learned to stop, and, in stopping, to swing in an inner circle that sends my body flying off in the opposite direction. I discovered how to do it within a month of that afternoon, and within three months I figured out the three rules for future baseball. The thing I didn't realize that afternoon was that once a batter takes his eye off the outfield fence, and instead, only aims at the infield, then he gains in control what he lost in power, and the possibilities become vast for variety, so to do the unpredictable becomes easy. It's easy to hit balls that are "High" or "Low" or "Inside" or "Outside," if you're only aiming for the infield. It's easy to bat and run the way I do, and anyone could learn it, if anyone would take the trouble to try. The present-day rules concerning "three strikes" and "four balls" are from a different era when everyone seemed to have more time, and I'll bet, when the players weren't so good. The truth is that the times have changed, and baseball is becoming old-fashioned. The game is too slow. Baseball is boring."

"But, it's what I've always said," laughed the lady.

"You have always been *ahead* of your time, my dear," murmured her husband.

But the Cheetah ignored their banter, and continued seriously, "We love the fans who love baseball, but sir, have you ever considered the people who don't like baseball? Don't you sometimes wonder why? I've been thinking about them. I think a lot of those people are going to become baseball fans when my new rules are adopted, for though home runs will be rare, there'll be lots of action, and the game will go at a faster pace, and there will be a *new drama* in every play. Don't you see? The pitcher is obliged to throw a ball that the batter can hit; and whatever ball the pitcher decides on, the hitter is obliged to swing; and except for the case of a foul ball, everything will hang on a single pitch, and each time the pitcher winds up, each spectator will be on the edge of his chair. Statistically it will be evident, and to everyone it will be quite clear that there is more to be gained in trying for a single than in trying for a home run. But there will be occasions that can arise in a game — for instance, in the ninth inning when the other team has a two-run lead, and there are two men on base, a man might come to bat, and perhaps, if he felt a certain faith in himself, that man might throw good sense, logic and statistics to the winds, and the man might clobber the ball, and it's possible that that man might hit a home run. It is difficult for us to imagine now, so sated at seeing several home runs in a game, what those future fans will feel who witness that event, or how the great crowd will respond, yet I think it safe to say that the home run then will be seen in its true light, and as something more marvelous, befitting of baseball, more like a miracle."

The Tiger owner's wife said, "If baseball were religion, I think you'd be a saint."

2

The forthright lady turned and to her husband said, "Well, what do you think?"

"Very interesting," he said — yet he will find this evening unforgettable, will find occasion to recall with rue the ring of truth in the words of the Cheetah; but far more memorable in his mind is what comes next, for the evening is not over — and indirectly, what comes next, by his own estimation, will make him the happiest man in the world.

The slender beauty whose hair is pure white, who is all things to him, is first and last his wife; she'd been a sort of super-secretary while intimately sharing his earnest reflections; she had had a hand in all his deals, each scheme had had her touch, and she was his perfect partner in those strange plots necessary, no doubt, to a self-made man in becoming a magnate in the world of heavy industry; and their faith in themselves has never flickered for an instant in forty years. It is especially poignant that the marriage of so perfect a pair could be marred by something anybody else would consider unimportant, merely that she didn't like baseball, yet so it was. It is his sad obsession, and has been his lifelong daydream, that she should sit beside him in his box to watch the Tigers play. But alas, instead, she had conventional interests not unusual for a wealthy woman — she was a trustee at the Art Museum, and she supported the Symphony; yet literature mostly occupied her mind — she was a real reader of fine fiction, and she had read everything. To a timid suggestion by him that she might join him in watching the Tigers play, she invariably would reply, "I'd rather read a book!"

This lively, lovely lady then touched the young man's arm, and said, "Will you come into the library with me. There is something there I would like to show you."

The old couple lived in a mansion, and the young man followed the lady down a marble hall and into a deeply carpeted, great dark room that was illuminated by a single reading lamp, where books were everywhere, scattered all about. She explained, "If I ever let anyone clean up in here, I'd never be able to find anything." She took a book from a shelf and opened it to the first page. She waved him to a chair, and she herself sat down, and she said to him, "Call me Ishmael!"

"What is that?" he asked.

"It's *Moby Dick!*" she replied, "I'd like to read some of it to you, if I may."

He nodded assent.

"Only this time," she laughed, "I would like you to *listen.*"

He said he would, and indeed, he did; his eyelids drooped and he sat quite still; as phrase conjoined to phrase, sentence after sentence, and paragraph piled upon paragraph, as her eye skipped suddenly from the bottom of a page to the top of an adjoining page, and later as the page was turned, or the chapter ending reached, during that impalpable pause when the periods on the page turn bright green, her voice took off its clothes; by that I mean those rags of her personality in her voice (by which one might recognize her on the telephone) were somehow dropped away, and revealed the genius of the English language quite nude; and a naked anonymous beauty danced from phrase to phrase. I think it was the muse. And as she read you might have said at certain moments that Herman Melville himself was in that room, that it was his voice, readily recognizable by the Nineteenth Century idiosyncrasies of his speech; but that momentary phantom from another time is but another costume of a voice that vanishes in a rush of sparkling grammar, and the voice of the work itself revealed itself. They heard the voice of Moby Dick, those two. That night they heard the song of the great white whale.

As she read, she forgot she was reading, and as he listened, he forgot he was listening, so enrapt did they become in the tale, and chapter followed chapter and the minutes passed majestically.

Why does it seem unusual that a young baseball player should deeply experience a work of literature? Well, that is what happened.

The minutes passed by quite differently down the hall, where the owner nursed a Scotch, and after a while he began to wonder what had become of the two, and wandered down the hall in search of them. Quietly he approached the library door, which had been left ajar, and he stared inside, surveyed the dark scene, saw the two, saw their profiles, and had the sense not to interrupt.

He returned to the sideboard to replace his glass, reached for the phone, called the plant, and had a long chuckling conversation with a labor leader; he glanced at his watch and saw that it was five o'clock in Italy and he called his representative in Rome; then he spoke with Washington, and he talked with our Senator there, and several others; he called San Francisco to wish a grandson happy birthday; then he rang the garage, and gave instructions for the morning to his chauffeur.

Now he raised his eyebrows at his wristwatch, and returned to the library determined to interrupt them, but the lonely echoing of his footsteps in the darkness damped that determination, and his steps were still as he approached the door, and for several minutes he listened to the sound of her voice, not making out the words, merely listening to the distant dance of syllables; and he wondered whether her throat weren't getting tired.

With new determination to be patient he quietly retreated, got himself another drink, and sat down in a comfortable chair, closed his eyes, and his recurring daydream re-occurred: it was a sunny day at the ballpark, the fans were on their feet cheering, and his wife was beside him, laughing and obviously enjoying the game. That was all there usually was to the daydream, but now it began to go differently than it ever had before, for the man fell asleep in his chair and the Forces of Night began to play in that idyllic ballpark: a cloud crosses the face of the sun. The stadium is cast in shadow. Low storm clouds race across the sky. Lightning strikes the flagpole, and the flag goes up in flames. An explosion on the pitcher's mound creates a crater rapidly filling with water. The baseball fans begin to riot. Violence is in the air. Shrieking bodies begin falling from the upper decks, and his wife says to him, "This is why I don't like baseball!"

Luckily this likable man never remembers his dreams, and now he fell into a deep and dreamless sleep and for twenty minutes he hardly moved a muscle.

He awoke to the sound of the grandfather clock, and was himself in a moment, and to himself he spoke. "It seems incredible that they could still be reading that book. It seems incredible," he said aloud in the empty room. "But is it possible that my outlandish plot is working?"

Several days ago when the Tigers were playing out-of-town he'd been watching the game on television and his wife had happened by and for a moment her eye had been attracted by a close-up picture of the Cheetah on the screen, who was about to bat. "What an interesting face! Is he Oriental?" she had exclaimed.

"He is American. He's from Kentucky," he'd answered. "I don't know what his ancestors were."

And she had watched the Cheetah hit the ball in one of his weird ways, so that it stopped abruptly between the pitcher and first baseman, both of whom ran for the ball. The pitcher got it, and snapped the ball toward first base, where he thought he saw the first baseman, but the ball hit the umpire on the nose. Next she watched him steal two bases, and she watched the infield commit two ridiculous errors which were really hard to believe, and the crowd began laughing, soon falling over themselves laughing, unable to stop, and she witnessed forty thousand baseball fans possessed by the devil of infectious giggling.

She had smiled.

He had seen it from the corner of his eye.

Although she had continued on her way, and had not inquired as to the outcome of the game, still it was a start, it was the first pleasure she had ever taken in watching baseball.

The old man figured that perhaps if he could get his wife to take a personal interest in a player, then it might follow as a matter of course that she would become interested in the game, and it was with this idea that he had invited the Cheetah to dinner.

Now his footfalls echoed happily in the darkness of the hall, and as he approached the door ajar, he called his wife's name, and opened the library door, found the wall switch which illuminated the great globe of a chandelier, and flooded the room with light.

The old man beamed at the blinking pair, unable to hide his delight in their friendship, and said, "I think you got carried away."

The Reader and the Listener arose, and she closed the book.

Quietly, he said to her, "Don't lose the place!"

She stared frankly and deeply into the young man's eyes, and quietly answered, "I won't forget!"

Yet stubbornly the youngster stood there staring at her with an urgent question, the mute appeal eloquent upon his face, and for a moment she was bewildered by its meaning. And then suddenly she saw it, and she said, "Tomorrow!"

"After the game!" he whispered.

She turned to her husband and asked, "If you are driving home after the game tomorrow, can you bring the Cheetah with you? We have an appointment."

"Certainly!" he said.

She left them, and the old man saw the Cheetah to the door, and offered to call a cab, but the Cheetah noted that there was a full moon perfect as a baseball, and that he would prefer to walk awhile . . . for what after all is more wonderful than walking through the sleeping suburbs with the lines of a great book rampaging inside the skull, when one first is beginning to grasp the idea of destiny and that the stars are right.

Back in their bedroom the owner said, "The Cheetah is not an ordinary player, and it would not surprise me if he becomes a real star, I mean a favorite of the fans, for already they are beginning to applaud when he comes to bat. Yet he's just a kid from Kentucky, and he doesn't know anything. Fame can throw him off balance. Soon he's going to be adored, and there'll be a million people after him, and he's got to learn how to handle them. He's got to learn to meet all kinds of people. I would like you to invite the Cheetah to our dinner party for the Prince of Persia next week – and if you would, I'd like you to take him under your wing, make sure he's dressed properly and knows which fork to use . . . in a word, I want you to *educate* him, if you would, to the world."

"You mean . . . I should be *his* *teacher!*" she exclaimed in utter astonishment, and she added, "I think you have been reading my mind!"

"I have not been reading your mind!" he snapped irritably. "You know I never know what you're thinking."

"That is true," she said. "Well, let me share my thoughts with you. Tonight something very beautiful happened while I was reading to the Cheetah. You know, I have read *Moby Dick* several times, and I have in the library everything Melville ever wrote, but tonight I experienced that writing in a way I never did before. I witnessed something inanimate—the book— come to life, and I feel just as if I'd witnessed a miracle. I'm sure the Cheetah saw it too! I'm going to read out loud to him every book in the library!"

"You can't be serious," said her husband. "Let's get some sleep."

And so the light in their bedroom was turned out, and soon the man began to snore, but wait! The snoring ceases, and his wife, who was lying there wide awake, thinking that he might have woken, half-rose out of bed to look at him and was startled by an uncanny smile upon her husband's face. In fact, the man was dreaming.

He dreamed he saw the Cheetah juggling seven baseballs.

That was all there was to the dream, but it went on for some time, and the man obviously was delighted by the performance; but it is really of no consequence, for this man never remembers his dreams.

The lady got out of bed and donned a robe and put on slippers and made her way through the great house to the kitchen to prepare a cup of tea, but all the while she tried to figure out what had happened in the library. With steaming cup she made her way through dark rooms of silence until she reached the place itself, and found the book. And she read a few lines out loud but it was no good, for there was no magic. For the magic to occur, it was obvious to her that it was essential to have a listener; but not just any listener, it must be someone who really listened, like the Cheetah, for she sensed that his eyelids quivered at each nuance, he had angelic sensitivity, and she had heard him take a sudden breath at a turn of the tale, a moment before Ishmael first saw the white whale. But why was it important? Perhaps because she was such a reader, and she sensed that it would happen with every book she read to him; all the familiar books, which she knew, might come alive, be quite different, be quite new. She saw clearly that in all her reading she had missed something essential, that it takes two people to read a book, a Reader and a Listener, that only then can the voice of the work itself come to life. But what was her relationship to the Cheetah? It surely wasn't sexual, and the woman had three grown sons, and she recognized nothing in her feeling for him that was maternal. Could it really be so, what her husband suggested—was she to be his teacher?

Her husband suddenly appeared in bare feet at the doorway, and she answered with silence his serious stare. "What are you thinking of so late at night?" her husband asked.

"The Cheetah," she said. He made to return to his bed, but she called out to him, "Wait! What is it? What can it mean? *The Baltimore Chop* . . . ."

And he explained that that was a baseball expression which she perhaps heard used by someone speaking of the Cheetah, for, as he said, "It is one of the Cheetah's favorite methods of hitting the ball. Like a lumberjack with an ax, the Cheetah raises the bat above his head and brings it down with all his might, smashing the ball straight down into the ground in front of home plate so that it bounces high, high into the air like an infield pop-up fly. It doesn't matter if someone catches the ball because it's already bounced once. The ball has to be thrown to first in order to get the runner out, and frequently a good runner like the Cheetah can get to first base ahead of the throw. That's a Baltimore Chop. Let's get some sleep."

"Wait!" I have many more questions to ask. If I show up at your office tomorrow at one, will you take me to lunch? And afterwards, I want you to take me to . . . I want to see it myself, the game!"

3

In five years' time the whole world would know that the Cheetah was a champion, but during his first season in the major leagues only his running was regarded remarkable, and at that, he was considered a clown.

There is an odd group of men who always dress in white, who devotedly make the trek to the ballpark each day the Tigers are in town, but who never see a game. They are those concessionaires of Coke and hot dogs and beer who work behind long counters built along the inner corridors of the stadium; and there are certain old

men among them who have held that same job year after year, who
have sharp ears, and who have become connoisseurs of "the roar of
the crowd," and can make remarkably good guesses at what is
happening on the field by merely listening to the booing and applause, or the spirit in the roar when the fans suddenly stand to cheer
a play. But this year these old men began to hear a sound from the
crowd which they had never heard in the ballpark before—it was
laughter, it was everybody laughing out of sheer delight at the Cheetah, for to watch him steal a base was like watching an impossible
magic trick performed before your eyes; for when the Cheetah hit a
single, and the next man came up to bat, why the pitcher, the first
baseman, the second baseman and every fan knew that very probably
within the next few minutes the Cheetah would try to steal second
base. Each spectator was expectant, and a hush would fall as everyone waited for him to break, and the tension became terrific, and
there! Doing exactly what everyone was waiting for, right before their
eyes, the Cheetah would steal second base, and the infield would
blunder, and the crowd would break into uncontrollable laughter.
And often, even when he failed and was tagged out, as sometimes
happened, as he walked off the field toward the dugout the crowd
would rapturously applaud him for having made a good try at doing
what delighted them, for as I said, the crowd considered him a clown.
One reason no one took him seriously was his batting average, which
at first was nothing special. His hitting was erratic, and though he
had developed the rudiments of his style before he reached the major
leagues, it was during his five years with the Tigers that he perfected
it. Slowly but persistently his batting got better each year, and con-
sistently he got better at doing all his tricks. During his first two years
with Detroit the sportswriters, especially those from out-of-town,
were wont to refer to him as the "Kentucky Kid," often in a rather
patronizing way; but during his third year this nickname was used
less frequently, and then it was forgotten, as people in the baseball
business, to a man, stopped laughing, and everyone began to realize
the Cheetah was a champion:

The statistics tell the story. Here are his batting averages for those
famous five years:

In 1979 he batted 238.

In 1980 — 288.

In 1981 – 338.

In 1982 – 388.

And in 1983 he batted 438, the average improving by precisely 50 points each year.

Now a knowledgeable person with a nose for statistics can tell there is something slightly astonishing about these figures.

For one thing it can be seen that in his fifth year he sublimely *tied* the all-time hitting record made by Hugh Duffy in 1894; but furthermore those figures show a *constancy* well-nigh incredible, reflecting surely his *perseverance* practicing place hitting at an hour when others would consider themselves lucky to be sleeping.

Sublimity, constancy and *perseverance* are, no doubt, the attributes of many superior men, but there is more than that to being a champion—one must win and, moreover, one must win at the right time.

But only the champion can lose at the right time. Only the champion can—at the right time—choose to lose.

Let me show you what I mean.

It was the Cheetah's last year with the Tigers (it was the Tigers' last game of the season) and there were two outs in the bottom of the eighth when the Cheetah came to bat for the last time. The Tigers were ahead 10–2, and unless the visitors scored eight runs in the ninth inning, this would be the last time the home team would be at bat.

It had been the Tigers' greatest season, they'd won so many games they'd clinched the division championship a week before, while the visitors were in Last Place, so this final contest of the regular playing season was not what you'd call an important game, except in one respect. The Cheetah was coming close to breaking the all-time record for a season's batting average, and the stadium in Detroit was jammed, filled with fans who wanted to see him do it. To heighten the drama of it the ballclub had altered the scoreboard, adding two new boxes, one of which showed the Cheetah's average, as it changed hit by hit, and the other showed the number of hits he needed to break the record. He'd hit well that day, bringing the average up to a point so that now he needed only one more hit to break the record, while if he struck out, he'd merely tie it.

Of the most venerable records set in baseball, this one is the oldest. Most records in sports over the last hundred years have been rather regularly broken. Generally, in each generation somebody breaks the record. But the record for a season's batting average was made in 1894 and has never been surpassed. Now, baseball fans are devoted studiers of statistics, and there is not a living man that can claim to remember any other name at that spot in the roster of all-time records, any name other than *Hugh Duffy*. That name, his record, intrude like a bright beacon through the darkness of time from that legendary land of oldtime baseball, lend it relevance, and create continuity between the afternoons of yesteryear and the game we play today.

The final part of the eighth inning passed as in a dream. The spectators weren't paying any attention to the game, and everybody began talking to one another excitedly, and the sum of all these conversations was a steady roaring drone so loud that you couldn't understand what the person next to you was saying, so that every-body had to talk a little louder in order to be heard.

As the Cheetah stepped into the batter's box, the noise from the excited crowd, if anything, grew louder. Here was a crowd, if ever there was one, that was ready to cheer the victory of a champion.

The pitcher stepped on the rubber, about to pitch the fatal ball, when suddenly the Cheetah stepped out of the batter's box, calling time out for a minute. He stood there with the bat in his left hand and that hand rested on his hip, while with his right hand he took off his helmet and scratched his head with it, and looked up at the sky, for all the world like a man who was trying to figure something out that he didn't understand.

Finally he turned and spoke to the umpire who was standing behind the catcher, and staring seriously into the old man's eyes, he asked, "Should I break the record?"

This man was the senior umpire in the American League, and had devoted 30 years to studying the fine points of the rules of baseball, and perhaps more than any other man in the world was equipped to answer any question concerning any situation that might arise in a game, so that it was really quite appropriate that the Cheetah should ask him his opinion.

The umpire could not say yes or no.

Instead, he removed his black hat, and scratched the top of his head with his finger while he pondered, and Lord knows all that went through his head as he weighed the matter.

Finally the old umpire answered, "When somebody breaks Hugh Duffy's record, I think I'll retire. It will mark the end of an era, and I am part of that era that knew that long-dead Duffy had been a better batter than any living player could ever hope to be. When that ancient record is taken off the book, it'll be a new ballgame, and I, I am part of the old ballgame."

"Listen! Tell me this!" exclaimed the Cheetah to the umpire urgently, "What'll happen if I fail? I'll have merely tied the record, so they'll let Duffy's name stand as it always has, only below or beside it, they'll put my name. To have my name beside Hugh Duffy's . . . what greater honor could there be? Am I right in what I say?" he demanded of the umpire.

The umpire answered, "That is the way the record would appear."

The Cheetah said to the catcher, "You signal the pitcher to throw three balls straight across the plate. I'm not going to swing. I'm going to let the umpire call me out."

"I understand," said the catcher.

And so the Cheetah stepped into the batter's box, and the catcher signaled. The pitcher threw the ball over home plate.

"Strike!" called the umpire, thrusting his right hand into the air.

Suddenly there was silence in the ballpark.

The catcher threw the ball back to the pitcher, and all the pitcher had to do was lift his mitt in order to catch it, but the pitcher failed to do this, so the ball sailed past him, and had to be retrieved by the second baseman, who walked over and handed the ball to the pitcher, who was plain flabbergasted, as was every fan in the park, at the Cheetah's failure to swing, because for five years it had been the Cheetah's style to swing at every ball thrown by the pitcher, and no umpire had ever had occasion to call a ball or a strike when the Cheetah was at bat, and now for the first time in five years he had failed to swing.

When the pitcher threw the second ball, he was so nervous that the ball went out of control and came across the plate so low that the catcher hardly managed to hold on to it, but again the umpire's right hand shot out, and he shouted.

"Strike two!"

The Cheetah half turned his head and muttered out of the corner of his mouth to the umpire, "Thanks!"

And the umpire muttered so that only the catcher could hear, "Better get that pitcher in line!"

The catcher flashed the pitcher the sign, and repeated it vigorously for emphasis, and the pitcher nodded, and threw a ball that sailed right through the very center of the imaginary rectangle, and such was the silence that each person in the ballpark heard the umpire shout, "Strike three! You're out!"

There followed a long moment of stillness in the ballpark during which it would probably be correct to say that the only movement in the stadium was that of the Cheetah walking back to the dugout dragging his bat along the ground. There was no wind and the pennants and flags hung limp upon their poles.

But a sudden breeze set the flags to fluttering, and the moment was over, and the players on the field began to move. The Cheetah's out had retired the side, and now it was the visiting team's last turn to bat, and as they left the field, the Tigers came out.

The spectators all understood that the Cheetah had failed, but that he had failed they could not understand. They were dumbfounded and the fans began quickly to leave the stadium. Their exit was orderly and the whole crowd left as fast as they could, and as they quietly fled they looked at one another quizzically, and shoulders were shrugged, and all were chagrined.

Meanwhile one of the weirdest half-innings ever played by two major league teams ensued. Though it was of course theoretically possible that the team at bat might rally and score eight runs to tie the Tigers, and send the game into extra innings, nobody for a moment believed such a thing might actually happen. Everyone knew, every player on both teams knew, that the Tigers would win, and that furthermore, no one cared whether the Tigers won or not.

As the ninth inning began, the last of the spectators disappeared, leaving the stadium empty except for those whose business kept them there. The players looked around in wonderment as the first man came up to bat, the pitcher threw a ball, and then a called strike, then another ball and then another called strike, then another ball and then finally, at last, another called strike. As if under the spell of the Cheetah's performance, the batter hadn't swung, but had allowed himself to be called out on strikes. But the pitcher seemed to be taking an inordinate amount of time at it, and everyone was itching to get off the field. The next batter again took the full count, and when the sixth pitch was thrown, he hit a line drive into left field and speedily ran to first base. The coach at first base said sarcastically to the player, "What are you trying to do, start a rally?" The player blushed. There is one thing that can make a baseball player blush. It is the sarcasm of a coach. The runner felt like a fool, for he realized all of the players wanted nothing but to end the inning as fast as possible, and to get off the field. His getting a hit was an utter waste, and was merely time-consuming.

The next batter came up, and again the pitcher threw three balls, and two called strikes, and when the sixth pitch was thrown the batter did not swing, but the umpire startled everyone by calling, "Ball!" The catcher stamped his feet in irritation as the batter walked to first, and the man on first moved over to second.

It would probably be correct to say that at this point everyone in the ballpark felt as if he were about to lose his mind. Would the game never end?

The Tiger manager was so angry that he replaced the pitcher, but this only served to make the inning last a little longer.

The runner on second had his special agony: he was ashamed that he'd been so idiotic as to hit a single, and in his nightmare of embarrassment, desperately he asked himself, What would the Cheetah do in my position?

Suddenly he broke into a run, as if trying to steal third base, and the pitcher threw the ball to third and the man was tagged out. The runner on first got the idea, and he too broke into a run, trying to steal second base. And he even made a good show of it, sliding into the bag, but he also was easily tagged out, ending the game.

The happy Tigers fled the field and found the locker room filled with writers. Indeed, it was as if the Baseball Writers' Association of America were holding its annual convention in the Tigers' locker room, for every prominent baseball columnist in the country had come to Detroit for this game, to witness the Cheetah break the record, and now it was the duty of each to find out for his readers what the devil had happened. Each player found a photographer standing on top of his locker, and three television networks had live cameras centered on the catcher who had come into the Tiger locker room to recount for the whole world the conversation he had heard

258 ** THE ZEBRA STORYTELLER

at home plate between the Cheetah and the umpire. And the umpire, standing nearby, immediately corroborated what he said. The Cheetah amazingly managed to get into the shower for these few minutes, eluding the cameras, and when he emerged, draped in a towel, and the microphones and cameras turned to him, the drops of water on his body caught the television lamps, and on the television screen he was seen to sparkle as he spoke, and he was the perfect picture of a champion. His face expressed pure pride, and he did not have the manner of a man who had failed. He said, "The proudest day of my life was when I broke the record for stolen bases back in 1979, and each year since I have broken my own record, and each year it makes me feel proud."

He stood aloof, apart, his gaze directed a little to the side, and down, as he spoke with grace of pride—but suddenly his whole demeanor changed, he seemed to shrink a half an inch, and he became before their eyes an ordinary troubled human being, and looking directly into the cameras he spoke from his heart, and the sentiment he expressed touched the heart of every baseball fan.

He said, "I would not have been proud to have been the one to take Hugh Duffy's name off the roster of all-time records."

And suddenly everybody understood—that the Cheetah cherished the ancient records, those Nineteenth Century statistics, and that they themselves did.

Had the Cheetah broken the record, many men would have blinked and dimly known that yet another wrinkle in their brain had been smoothed out, but when he chose to lose, it made them stop and think, and they found that they were moved; for baseball engages the heart in a manner no other sport, nor art, can.

In a work of art "sentimentality" is rightly regarded as an unforgivable sin, and that there must be no sentimentality in a work of literature is quite true; however, I must say, it puts any author of a baseball story in a peculiar pickle, and I should like in passing to point out that in real life men only do good deeds, never vicious things, from sentimental motives.

It was said that everyone understood why the Cheetah had chosen to lose, but there was one fellow who couldn't, an Englishman who's a film critic for one of our national magazines, and it was his opinion that the Cheetah decided not to break the record because the fans had booed him in the first inning when he had sacrificed instead of making a hit.

Now generalizations about groups of people are more often than not incorrect, and are merely exaggerations of intangible things; however, such a statement will be made, and it is quite correct, true — and furthermore might be instructive for a foreigner who would understand our game.

This is the statement: *Baseball fans are more sentimental than other people.*

Than, say, hockey fans, or basketball fans, or cricket fans.

Baseball fans have "a sense of history" no Englishman can hope to comprehend who was raised playing cricket. The critic's English education left him well equipped to understand American movies, but not the Cheetah's motives when he chose to lose.

If one could get copies of all the statistics that have ever been compiled in the history of the world, and set them all up alongside one another so that it would be possible to fairly choose among them, and one asked the question: Which set of statistics is held to be *most sacred?*

The curious question has only one answer: *The Official Baseball Records.*

The European sports of soccer and cricket have no comparable body of statistics.

I mean — *Why do they say Babe Ruth is immortal?*

Why, indeed. A thousand years from now every religion practiced today will have utterly withered away, present-day governments will all be gone, no existing university will exist then, but baseball will survive through all the changes of those thousand years, and the Official Baseball Records during all that time will be kept assiduously; and Duffy's name will be there and the Cheetah's name below it, followed by a hundred other names of hallowed hitters who had followed the Cheetah's example, had tied the record, but not broken it — a most illustrious list; and as the oldest institution on earth baseball will have its historians, some of whom will specialize in The Twentieth Century, and one of those fellows, pondering the people of our time, might well in wonder ask: Why during the first century of baseball did they say Babe Ruth was immortal?

Why, indeed. But there is no answer to that question, for it is a part of the True Mystery of baseball.

A famous sportscaster, known by his family and associates to be the most callous and cynical of men, actually wept on his national television show while explaining to his listeners what the Cheetah had done.

And baseball fans all over the world that night—perhaps to the extent that each at one time or another had doted on and studied those statistics—felt a gush of gratitude for the Cheetah, and a strange esteem.

And even young children understood that in losing, the Cheetah had done a generous and noble thing. And as every child knows, nobleness is the attribute of the champion.

4

"Is it lonely being a champion?" asked the Tiger owner's wife.

The orphan sighed deeply.

"I have hardly had time to be lonely," he answered. "And yet, there have been times . . . you know, I practice hitting every day at dawn, but frequently I arrive an hour early at the field while it is still dark. The night watchman lets me in. I change into my uniform, and sometimes when I walk out onto the field the stars and moon are blazing overhead; but at other times it is overcast, it is pitch black out there, but I can make my way down the third base line to home plate, carrying a couple of bats. Perhaps I feel around on the ground and find a few pebbles, and I stand at home plate, throw a pebble into the air, and I practice hitting in the dark. Sometimes I pause, and I wonder what it's all about . . . baseball. I look around and wonder what I'm doing there, standing at home plate in the middle of the night. And I realize that I am the only person on earth trying to hit every ball that can be thrown; and that I alone know how important the ability will be for the future of baseball. Especially on such nights, I see that I am utterly alone, but then . . . then . . . it is at such times that I most vividly see *him*."

"Whom?" the forthright lady asked.

"The Abominable baseball player," the Cheetah said, squinting as if trying to make out a figure in the far distance that was in his mind.

"Who the devil is that?" laughed the owner.

"It's a kind of joking name I gave to a real person, an actual individual, a man who must have lived five million years ago."

The lady said, "But the ancestors of Man five million years ago cannot properly be called 'men.' They were probably more like chimpanzees."

"Exactly!" said the Cheetah, "I once saw a movie about wild African animals and it showed a roving band of male chimpanzees encountering a leopard. Several chimpanzees grabbed long sticks and waved them like clubs, threateningly, and others began to throw things at the big cat, stones, bits of wood, anything that came to hand.

"At the time on earth that I imagine, the ancestors of Man could do no more.

"They knew no more than how to wield a club and throw a stone.

"Yet more and more they were becoming what we might call men. For instance, when one found a good club, he'd hold on to it, carry it around with him. It was his club. And he learned to do more than just wave it in the air, he learned to *hit*. Eventually he learned how to hit hard, to grasp the club with *both hands*, swing it back, and bring it forward putting his whole weight behind it, so that he could knock out a leopard with a single blow.

"And when one would find a good stone for throwing, one more-or-less spherical, one that fit well in his hand, maybe about the size of a baseball, why he'd hold on to it, carry it around, and after throwing it he'd go and find it, and he could recognize it at a glance. How many million years did it take to learn to throw a stone? They got good. One could hit a bird in flight.

"But a beast can wield a club and throw a stone. A chimpanzee can do as much, if not so well.

"This is the scene I see five million years ago.

"Imagine the beasts, our ancestors. A roving band of nine or ten males emerge from the deep forest onto the edge of a clearing. Some carry clubs. Some carry throwing stones.

"There, sitting in the sun in the center of the field, is *another* band of nine or ten males, who also have clubs and stones, who shout, and leap to their feet at the sight of the visitors.

"At other meetings they might be friendly and curious, but here they're furious, for the field is the heart of home territory, and over behind bushes are several females dawdling with their babies. The largest of the males, obviously it is the head beast, steps out in front of the others and shakes his club angrily at the intruders, who continue to advance until the two groups are separated by a distance of about sixty feet, whereupon the leader of the intruders (the visiting team, you might say) pitched his throwing stone, a fastball aimed at the foremost of the furious beasts.

"The beast at whom the stone was thrown, utterly without reason, not knowing what he was doing, without a notion as to what might be the outcome of a thoughtless action, stepping lightly aside, he grasped his club with both hands, swung it back, and putting his whole weight behind it, swung the club forward, hitting that stone head-on, as if it were the head of a leopard, smashing a hard line drive that went a little to the right of the pitcher perhaps, hitting a companion in the stomach, knocking the wind out of him, so that both the beast and the round rock fell to the ground side by side.

"The one who'd pitched the stone looks down at the rock which had fallen beside his friend, and he sees *it is his own stone*, the one he'd just thrown! And he excitedly points it out to the others. It would seem like a miracle to them!

"And the crack of the bat when the club struck the stone—what could they have thought it was? No one had ever heard anything like it before. The club swinger would be a magician to them. Would they throw down their weapons and flee? Or would they throw themselves down at his feet? It hardly matters.

But later on that afternoon the one who'd hit the stone would get to wondering how he'd done it. Probably he'd get a friend who had a couple of good throwing stones, and somehow he'd say, 'Get over there and pitch a stone at me, I'd like to try something . . . .' And so would begin the *abominable batting practice*. And it would take a lot of practice but the fellow could get good. And most important, *it was the kind of thing that he could teach to his son*, for it would perhaps be another two million years before they would discover flint and begin to fashion tools which were sharp, so for two million years the trick with the club and stone would be considered miraculous, and those who could do it would be considered magicians."

"Wait a minute!" said the woman. "That *abominable batting practice!* The way that prehistoric man would stand there—his stance: he would try to hit the stone whether it were thrown on his right side or his left side, whether it were high or low—that's the way you say baseball will be played in the future!"

"Yes, I think the fans will recognize that stance immediately as being more natural," admitted the Cheetah. "But you know, although they practiced for a million years those primitive hitters could never do more than try to hit the stone as hard as they could, and yet, you can bet—each one would *wish* he could control the direction of his hits, but because of the irregular shapes of the stones it would never be possible.

"In mastering place-hitting I am fulfilling the daydreams of two million years of magicians. Knowing their wishes are with me—how can I be lonely?"

The Cheetah smiled at the lady.

The owner said, "That the most primitive man might have hit a stone with a club does not seem to me to be unlikely or unusual, and I think to call it a miracle is exaggeration."

"Don't you see?" said the Cheetah. "A beast can wield a club and throw a stone, but ... *chimpanzees do not have magicians.* Only human beings have magicians. At the crack of that bat those beasts became men. That was the miracle. The most ancient chord in the memory of man is the thrill that's felt by a baseball fan at the crack of the bat.

"It was the First Miracle.

"And was he not, indeed, a true magician?"

It is with great regret that I cannot write of the death of the Cheetah more fully, for his funeral will be fabulous, in splendor unsurpassed by any coronation, unique in that it will be attended by every person on earth, and furthermore, historians of the far, far future will find his funeral more remarkable than anything he did during his life.

For something happened at that funeral.

A natural phenomenon occurred of such a magnitude that it began a new era, and signaled a change in human nature.

The Cheetah lived to be 78 and died in the year 2040.

It may be thought that the author deals cavalierly with our future, writing offhandedly of it as if writing of things that had already happened; now the future is truly a secret, and very correctly so, yet it can happen that a man following his calling – in order to do his work, be he a writer, a man of God, or a player of baseball – will be given a glimpse of the future. All those who make history are given a glimpse of the future – it is part of the prize. But the author is no prophet, nor even are these words spoken as a scientist making "educated guesses" – this is fiction, and in what follows no secrets of the future will be revealed other than those necessary to the telling of a tale, and those that further the storyteller's ambition, that is . . . to make what is incredible understandable.

To that end, that the Reader might understand *it – before describing in detail at the close of this book the event at the Cheetah's funeral, I shall first briefly survey the state of the world in which that event shall occur, though revealing not all, surely, by a long shot; but merely highlighting certain differences, certain things that might seem strange to a Reader of today, nevertheless each essential in providing that context from which such an event might come about of itself, naturally.*

For the event at the Cheetah's funeral was a natural phenomenon.

Anyway, one of the main differences in 2040 will be that there won't be all these dumb people around. I mean, at the time of this writing (in 1978) there are great masses of people who are uneducated, who don't even know how to read; however, that will not be the case in the year 2040. Everybody's kid will go through school even in the jungles of New Guinea and Brazil, and most will get their homework done, even as their fathers after sunset watch the Evening News.

There are many great institutions in the world today which will vanish – I refer to those vast arrays of dismal buildings which now house mental patients and the retarded – for marvelous advances made in medicine and public health will eradicate the major maladies of man.

Nobody at all will be undernourished.

Now at the time of this writing there are great masses of people who, although they know how to read, and have attended school, yet have no feeling for fine paintings, great music or literature, nor have they the curiosity to thumb through periodicals of science fairly dazzling with ideas and discoveries – they are barbarians, blinkered beasts of burden, dull, leading drab lives, indifferent to the treasures of all time; and though they sometimes attain power and wealth, their successes inspire not admiration, only sadness, among civilized people – indeed, some-

times despair – and the violent bent of these barbarians will be the bane of the concluding years of the twentieth century; however, by 2040 this type of person will no longer exist.

Well, there it is.

That every person on earth will be healthy and civilized is no change in human nature, of course; but the idea that it may actually come to pass during the next sixty years might seem to some to be unlikely; however, the Cheetah and the Spirit of Baseball each took a hand in the civilizing of Everyman, and to understand the event at the Cheetah's funeral it is necessary that the Reader know about this.

5

From the very beginning of the sport it was noticed, especially among journalists who routinely went to many public gatherings of various sorts, that there was something different about people who attended professional baseball games.

There was a different spirit there. There was something special about those people – perhaps it was no more than a gleam in their eyes, but it was distinctive enough so that a new word was added to the English language. For thousands and thousands of years scholars will return again and again, fascinated, to ponder the following sentence, for in it that new word was *written down* for the first time, and it is odd to think that the man who wrote it died never dreaming he had written an immortal line; this is the sentence:

"Kansas City baseball fans are glad they're through with Dave Rowe as a ball club manager."

Kansas Times & Star
March 26, 1889

It is the earliest record of the word *fans* appearing in print.

In the beginning the word referred only to the spectators at baseball games. It was a baseball expression, a piece of baseball slang probably suggested by the word *fanatic*. It was not until 1901 that its meaning was extended to include spectators at other sporting events, and then for a decade it was used exclusively by American sportswriters. Then, in 1915, a reporter covering a soccer match for the *London Daily Express* introduced the word into British journalism; while in that same year back in America a new group of people were for the first time designated *fans* – perhaps it was no more than the gleam in their eyes, but it proved a most appropriate designation—in the November First issue (year 1915) of *Film Flashes* it is written: "It is quite usual for a picture 'fan' to come out of one theatre and immediately cross the road to another."

Who transformed more people into fans? Al Jolson? Babe Ruth? Rudolph Valentino?

Ty Cobb or Greta Garbo?

Charlie Chaplin or Knute Rockne?

During the Roaring Twenties, who roared? No one in any walk of life is immune to becoming a fan.

To become a fan is like taking a step on a rung of a ladder. It is not a downward step.

On becoming a fan, people who have never written anything but a book report or a letter to their Ma frequently are *impelled to write*, and a new genre of prose came into existence during the Twenties—when an ordinary person sends a message to a star, it's called a *fan letter*.

One can be a fan of an individual, of a group, or of a whole field of endeavor.

Those fields which inspired fans during the Twenties were thought to be frivolous diversions by earnest and thoughtful people of that day; indeed, those people would be somewhat startled by the way we use the word today, for in fifty years its meaning deepened and its use once again has been extended.

For instance, it is quite correct according to current usage for a person to say "I am a fan of van Gogh" even though the man is dead.

Or to say "I am a fan of the Steady State Theory" in the field of cosmology, even though that theory has been proven untenable.

The point is that now the most serious and earnest endeavors of man inspire fans.

In fact, there are only two fields left on earth which do not; at the time of this writing the enthusiastic followers of demagogues and religious zealots are called *fanatics*.

What's the difference between a fan and a fanatic?

The most obvious way to tell the difference is by *the gleam in their eyes*.

The meaning of that difference is easy to demonstrate by an example: There is what might be called an Olden Rivalry between the

Detroit Tigers and the Cleveland Indians, but the idea that a Tiger fan would go over to Cleveland and kill a fan of the Indians is plain ridiculous.

But suppose for the sake of this example that such a thing could happen, and that the person were declared fit for trial, and you put twelve Tiger fans in the jury box—why, to a man those twelve would find their brother Tiger fan guilty of a foolish and foul murder.

But now, instead of being fans, what if they were all fanatics? Why, those twelve fanatics would jump out of the jury box and congratulate the murderer—they'd probably want to pin a medal on him!

The gleam in the eyes of a fanatic expresses a propensity for murder and a condoning of killing.

What does the gleam in the eyes of a fan express?

Well, whatever it is, it is a spirit notable for the absence in it of the murderous impulse, and that spirit has been extending its influence from sphere to sphere of human activity—inevitably that influence has been growing and that spirit born on a baseball field is about to take over the world.

The truth is that fanatics are barbaric and fans are civilized.

Now around the year 2000 the word *fanatic* will become obsolete as fanatics become extinct.

I do not mean to say that there will not be leaders with charismatic personalities, but their followers will be fans, not fanatics.

I'm not making this up, you know—using fans in the sphere of politics.

There is a wonderful book called the *Oxford English Dictionary*, based on Historical Principles, which chronicles the earliest use of words by writers, and from which my two earlier quotations were drawn. Under *Fans* in Volume One of *The Supplement* it quotes one S. Vines writing his memoirs, and it is one of the most poignant sentences I have ever read, and in 1928, when it was written, it must have made the angels weep. This is the sentence:

"Where are the fans of the League of Nations and of disarmament?"

Where, indeed, were they?

They were, of course, there; but it was a world still full of fanatics; now if the Reader and Listener will rise with me above this spinning globe, and for a moment ponder all four billion people there, at a glance it will be noticed that there are still an *awful lot* of fanatics down there, and the idea that in a few years all those fanatics can be transformed into fans might seem to some to be fantastic. Well, it *was* a bit fantastic.

Let me show you how it happened.

6

The tallest building in Tallahassee, Florida, is the Marat Hotel, and on the terrace of the spacious penthouse suite the owner of the Tigers, himself a wealthy industrialist, stood studying the configuration of the city through field glasses.

On the terrace there was not the hope of a breeze. The blazing blue sky stretched forever in every direction without a cloud, and for three days the temperature had stood at one hundred degrees.

"Ah! How beautiful!" he exclaimed. "There is the Ford Motor Company down there. Why, there must be a thousand trees on the factory grounds." He turned his glasses and exclaimed, "There is the Chrysler Corporation. What a marvelous job the landscape architects have done."

The owner's secretary touched the old man's arm, and the young man asked, "Sir, what are you looking at?"

The owner handed his employee the glasses, and said enthusiastically, "Look at Chrysler's down there. I never realized what a place of beauty it is. Why, they've diverted a little stream so that it runs through the factory grounds, and there, you can see the workers eating their lunches beside the stream."

The secretary briefly stared through the glasses at the place indicated by his employer, and then said, "Sir, that is not Detroit down there. We are in Florida. And that is not the Chrysler Corporation factory, it is a pig farm. There are also cows and goats along the stream, but I assure you I see not a single human being. The truth is, sir, that you are drunk. In fact, I have never seen you so drunk. May I remind you that inside there is a meeting of the Baseball Owners Association, and may I suggest that as chairman it is your duty to go in and adjourn that meeting. It is a shambles in there, sir. They are all drunk."

"Do you mean to tell me that the owner of the Cleveland Indians has been *drinking*?"

"It is he whom you hear screaming. But no one is listening. The rest are in a drunken stupor paralyzed by heat. A dozen half-naked men in there are talking in low voices, but they're *talking to themselves*, not to each other. In there it's like the ward of an insane asylum! Sir, I am so sorry for you all! I am sober. And I realize I am a witness to a tragedy. Perhaps tomorrow I shall drink, but today I shall remain a sober witness to the end of many baseball teams and the shattering of the American and National Leagues. I know you came here with high hopes, but every idea presented today has proved to be without merit. The fact is, sir, and it is a plain fact—there is no hope for baseball!"

"No hope for baseball?" repeated the dazed man quizzically, and then his brow hardened into an intense frown, and the old man stared at the ground silently.

Now the truth is that baseball was in trouble; however, it was merely financial trouble.

A baseball club has a multitude of expenses incurred in the caring for the grounds and upkeep of a ballpark, in transporting the team and its equipment, and in paying respectable salaries to players, coaches, umpires, scouts, and innumerable ballpark personnel; unlike more ancient institutions such as the church and farming, the financial health of a ballclub does not depend on the price of real estate or legislation by Congress of subsidies. No; rich old ladies do not leave their fortunes to ballclubs, nor do great foundations intent on good deeds endow them. No; in a straightforward way the health of a club depends on the fans buying tickets for the game.

Two factors caused the trouble: the costs of running a ballclub had been steadily rising, and there had been a slight decline in attendance. That was all there was to it.

Yet so insidiously did these two factors combine to provide a severe drain of cash that unless something drastic were done, a dozen teams would be bankrupt by the end of the season.

The owner of the Tigers had called this urgent meeting at this out-of-the-way spot in this hotel which he owned so that they could have privacy from the press. Yet it might be thought that the Commissioner of Baseball, or the Presidents of the Leagues, would be invited, but not so, for it must be remembered that these distinguished men are merely *employees* of the owners. Here were businessmen come to talk money, and that baseball should make money is not the responsibility of the Commissioner of Baseball.

Here were 26 owners, powerful men, each rich in his own right, and ordinarily, when traveling on business, they were accompanied by aides and secretaries, but not so here. Most had come alone, and en route by limousine or train or plane, each had thought deeply about the financial plight of baseball, and each became *determined* — nay, each solemnly swore — to do whatever the majority called for at this meeting, for each man saw that their only hope lay in a unified push by *all* the owners working in concert behind some single scheme, whatever that scheme might be.

It must be noted that on every other day of the year each of these men was the arch-rival of every other. Now, when 26 arch-rivals each solemnly swear to agree with one another with all their hearts and to join in a giant mutual effort, one might expect indeed that this was not to be a day like other days.

7

Authors, you know, have certain prerogatives which they never let on about to their readers; however, that immortal silence shall be broken, and a truth of fiction spoken.

Now a Reader might look back on earlier periods of his or her life, and ask: What would my life be like now, if I had done *that* rather than what I actually did do? What if I had married so-and-so instead of . . . but of course it is a commonplace truth that there can be no answers to such questions.

Yet it often happens that a writer may get five chapters into a story, and at that point he will sit back and re-read what he has written, and then, pondering this or that, he might ask a question such as — What would it be like if in the fourth chapter I had so-and-so marry that other guy? If she did that, why such-and-such would happen. And when *that* happened it would have a wild effect on all of them, it would change them all . . . and the author can see how the whole book would go.

But likely as not, the author will again re-read his story and decide that the fourth and fifth chapters are correct as written, and he will continue the story along those lines, *never* sharing with his reader that knowledge which he has as to what would have happened if the story in the fourth chapter had gone otherwise. Yet it is the author's prerogative to *actually know* what would have happened.

I shall now exercise that prerogative, and share my knowledge with the Reader of what would have happened to these 26 owners if their meeting had been a failure. The meeting will not be a failure, of course, but here's what would have happened if those teams had actually gone bankrupt: Within three years, five of these men would have put bullets through their brains. Half a dozen would die in fiery automobile accidents, driving while drunk. Some suddenly would develop disfiguring, debilitating, destructive diseases. For several sanity would slip away, never to return. Millionaires would become paupers. Deserted by every friend, they would become despised by everyone, suffer unspeakable agonies, know unknowable miseries followed by ever deepening humiliations, each one more cruel, until death finally in merely half a decade would claim the last of the scattered outcasts, each dying in a horrible and ugly circumstance. Shoulders would be shrugged, but not a tear would be shed by anyone at any of their deaths.

The events described above are what *actually would have happened* had the meeting failed.

8

On the night before this meeting, en route to Tallahassee on a night-flight from Detroit, loosening his seat-belt, the owner of the Tigers dozed—and dreamed the meeting failed.

In his dream he was conducted directly to Hell, and as he looked back over his shoulder he could see the world, the sunlight on the trees, the trees swaying in the breeze, but when he stonily stared straight down the gorge of rock, he saw a great black wall three times as high as any prison wall, and set in it were two ancient doors, each as tall as the wall itself.

"These are the Gates of Hell," said a voice. "Every evil spirit, every devil, every sinner who has ever lived on earth lives on behind that wall, and that is where you are going."

"I never expected it would be lonely in Hell," said the owner with a sigh, but then suddenly, amazed, he blurted out, "What the devil are those?"

As far as he saw along the wall were many ancient machines of war of the kind called catapults, which in olden days were used to fling boulders over fortress walls. As he approached one of these giant contraptions, he saw that it was no boulder, but a woman, placed in the machine. Suddenly snapping into ferocious movement, the machine flung the flailing body of the screaming woman high, high and higher yet until her screams became inaudible; yet he clearly saw her body clear the wall and disappear over the other side.

The owner asked, "On the other side—is there far to fall?"

"Yes," answered the voice. "She will have broken bones and her body may be mangled, but, of course, she will not die. Sinners live forever in Hell—that's why it's crowded, people piled ten deep, those on the bottom struggling with the strength of drowners to reach the surface for a breath of air. And yet, when one finally attains the top of the heap, then inevitably, exhausted by the effort, that person falls asleep, and the unconscious body is thrust to the bottom again. It goes on endlessly," said this voice that spoke to him in his dream. And it offered further information, saying, "The first sinner ever sent here is still alive inside. When that first person ever to be sent to Hell got to just about that place where you are standing now, the Gates of Hell opened, and that sinner walked inside easily as someone might walk into church. When that original occupant entered, the Gates of Hell were closed behind him, and closed for good, for during all the time that's passed since that original occasion, the Gates never have opened again—for it's a more suitable introduction into Hell to be tossed by a catapult over the wall."

The owner stared at the ground, and quietly but firmly said, "I know I truly sinned by allowing the Baseball Owners Association meeting in Tallahassee to fail. It was sinful not to be successful, for Lord knows what will happen now to baseball! Since I failed, what can be the fate of baseball?"

The owner lifted his eyes to Heaven, and tears streamed down his face.

The voice cleared its throat, so to speak, and said, "You do not understand . . . . It is not *baseball* which concerns us *here*! At stake in that hot penthouse among the tweny-six of you was not merely the fate of baseball . . . rather . . . it was the destiny of the world."

The voice paused, and in a softer tone continued, "A trillion unborn babies, each with a future, all were waiting on your words,

THE INSTITUTE FOR THE FOUL BALL 🐟 273

all were *listening* breathlessly to every word you said, for it was being decided at your meeting whether those future generations should one day be born, and live. The unborn generations yearn so much to live. They all were praying that your meeting would be successful."

The voice paused, but continued: "There were *so many* of them praying, and their earnestness was deeply moving, deeply moving . . . to such an extent that the attention of the Lord was turned in their direction, and He looked in Himself at that scene they all were praying for, the meeting of the Baseball Owners Association, and He listened to everything that was being said, and especially He listened to the things *you* said, for you called the meeting, and were its chairman."

The voice sighed, and continued: "It is incredible that you allowed that meeting to fail. The destiny of the world was hanging in the balance, and when you failed there were a trillion disappointed unborn babies who knew that because of you they were as good as dead. The universe is sad."

The voice turned coldly formal: "We have never had to deal with one such as you. You are not like the man who's murdered a saint. You are not like the woman who disfigured fifty children, blinding them to transform them into slaves. Your crime is so much more colossal that you cannot be catapulted like them. The Lord has decided *this*: because of the magnitude of your failure, the Gates of Hell are to be opened, and you can walk inside easily as someone might walk into church."

Even as the voice spoke, a horrendous noise of grinding gears, clanking chains, and scraping metals exploded as if bursting in the owner's eardrums, and the magnificent Gates began to tremble.

The earsplitting noise of a giant machine that could open such an ancient Gate—when the Listener imagines it—that horrific sound must be *doubled* in volume by the Listener's brain, because there are twin machines, a machine for each door, and as they inched open, wider and wider, each machine made more sound than the other.

The last words the owner was ever to hear—through the din of the doors the voice was clear, though it sounded as if shouted from far away—were the words, *"I can't make out what you're saying—I have my hands over my ears!"*

The owner of the Tigers turned his attention to the slowly opening giant doors, and he saw a clear crack appear between them, but all along that crack there was a peculiar wiggling motion, and then he saw that the wiggling at the crack was caused by thousands of fingers. As the doors opened wider, whole hands and feet were thrust through, and then horrible heads of ancient sinners began one by one to appear through the widening space of the opening doors.

The first sinner out of the Gate was a midget, but ten men and women tied in a dead heat for being the second to escape from Hell.

As the Gates opened ever wider, hundreds, thousands, hundreds of thousands raced out at full speed, running for new life up that very road down which the owner had just traveled; and from where he stood outside the Gate he could see the millions rushing out into the world of sunlight and breeze. Out of the Gate thousands came through each minute in an unceasing flow, and for a while the owner, standing back a bit to one side, hands clasped behind his back, stared into the stream.

Considerable time passed—time passes funnily in dreams—yet the streaming hordes poured forth from Hell in continuous great numbers which did not dwindle. The owner lost track of the time, yet at last he heard a scuttling crowd crawling quickly by on all fours, their faces only a foot above the floor, major portions of their bodies missing, their arms adroitly manipulating very short crutches. These were the last.

After a certain silence passed, the owner slowly ambled over to the threshold of the Gate, and he stared curiously within, and then he walked inside as easily as someone might walk into church.

Hell was empty, except for him.

The great doors closed, once again.

A sudden silence ensued that was to last for an eternity.

The owner of the Tigers sat upon a rock, put an elbow on one knee, and propped his chin in his palm, and sighed in puzzlement, "I never expected that Hell would be lonely . . . how can this be? What did the fate of baseball have to do with Destiny? Why in heaven are a trillion unborn babies bawling because of *me*? Suddenly every sinner, every devil, every evil spirit that ever existed on earth has been loosed upon the world, and all because that meeting failed . . . . What a hell the world will be! What should I have said? How could *my words* have saved the world from *that*!?"

In his dream the owner closed his eyes, and in truth he fell into a deep and dreamless sleep from which he did not awaken—until his plane landed in Tallahassee; he awoke refreshed, utterly rested, and ready for this morning meeting at the Marat Hotel; his dream can have no consequence, for luckily this likable man never remembers his dreams.

9

Now while the Tiger owner had dozed and dreamed, other owners of home teams of the twenty-five most important cities in the United States and Canada were also traveling through the night to Tallahassee, and it must not be thought that all were sleeping, for many were troubled, and troubled thought would not allow them even troubled sleep.

Travelers often take books, and an odd fact that was never known is that the only book carried by any of them to read on the trip to pass time was a ponderous tome, a bulky volume of official baseball records. It is The Baseball Encyclopedia and it contains numberless numbers, and could not possibly be of any use to them; for the numbers in that book are not like other numbers, they are not to be subtracted or divided—they are there forever, and can only be *compared* and contemplated; and the contemplation of such comparisons can cause considerable controversy, especially late at night in taverns, for ordinary people as well as experts can have opinions as to the meaning of those numbers, which are *not like* other numbers. They are the bare bones of history. And there is a high sense, small in importance perhaps, in which this book can be said to contain nothing but *the truth.*

However, it was not for its factualness that they'd brought it.

It was the magic of the book which had caused so many of them to lug it along, for on the trip in dipping into those dry pages, dawdling at tables of yesteryear, they were immersing themselves in the spirit of baseball, hoping to draw from it some inspiration, some "idea" that could save them all. They thought about the history of baseball, and about their own childhoods, when they themselves had learned to play ball. Some had learned in fancy schools, but for many these memories were of grimy back alleys, for like the owner of the Tigers, many were self-made men.

They were nobody's fools.

Yet they had put their money where their hearts were, and in this sense they are not ordinary businessmen.

They are like opera singers.

A person who is both an opera fan and a baseball fan will immediately understand the above statement.

The author rarely panics, yet suddenly there is a sense that the Reader or the Listener may be *only* a baseball fan, or *only* an opera fan, and to such people, whom the author cherishes equally, the above statement can only be perplexing, and so deserves explanation.

The very special soprano, the star of a great opera company, when that lady has a temper tantrum at the hairdresser or hysterics in her dressing room, those people with whom she surrounds herself – a coterie of intimates, a lover, perhaps, and a close cousin, her personal maid, her manager, the costumers and various backstage personnel – it never occurs to any of those people that she should consult a psychiatrist; indeed, her bizarre behavior is considered quite normal by everyone. Now the reason for this is that it is *beyond the imagination* of any of these people as to what it could be like to stand in front of thousands of distinguished people and have a sound come out of one's mouth as is emitted by the star.

Now while watching a ballgame it is easy for any baseball fan to imagine what it would be like to be playing first base, or even to be at bat, or even to imagine oneself the umpire spreading one's palms wide and shouting "Safe!" or shooting the thumb into the air, screaming "Out!", and it even is easy to imagine what it might be like being the batboy; however, it is *beyond the imagination* of any baseball fan to imagine himself being the owner of his home team. It is a mind-boggling proposition.

Just as the temperament of an opera star is considered by everyone to be normal, just so, and for the same reason, the eccentricity of a ball club owner is considered quite natural; it is accepted – indeed, it is expected – that an owner will exhibit bizarre behavior, and no one thinks twice about it.

In my youth I asked myself foolish questions, and once I devoted considerable thought to this query: Of all the small groups of people on earth, which group is the weirdest? At the time I decided that the weirdest bunch were probably those thirty-six Hidden Zaddiks, those secret, most eminent rabbis of the Hasidic Jews, who frequently pose as simple shoemakers, sellers of hot chestnuts, or sometimes even pretending to be small-time criminals – yet it is these Thirty-Six whose concerted activity holds the whole world off from instantaneous collapse into utter chaos. Nowadays I don't think much about these questions, and I'm not sure now that I really believe the 36 rabbis really exist. Anyway, if the truth is that they don't exist, then – without question – the weirdest group of people on earth are the 26 ball club owners.

Let us examine what this means.

Let us conduct two thought-experiments. In the first, two ordinary people, perhaps volunteers, are put into a rather complicated situation and then, in the second thought-experiment, the owner of a ball club is put into the *same* situation, and it will be observed how the behavior of a ball club owner differs from the behavior of ordinary people.

10
FIRST THOUGHT-EXPERIMENT

My Reader and the Listener must join the author in some after-midnight merriment, and it is necessary that we be accompanied on our escapade by Fame and Fortune in the figures of a popular young movie star (famous for her beauty) and the president of one of the biggest banks in town. It would be hard to imagine two persons more unlike one another, for the banker, with a neatly clipped moustache and his rimless spectacles, is rather a cold fish, and when he speaks one is never quite sure of what he's said; whereas the highly trained young actress is irrepressibly vivacious, and it's hard to keep her quiet, for even when she whispers, her words can be understood distinctly half a block away – in the last row of the balcony, so to speak. Now imagine the five of us hidden in dark shadows outside the wall of the City Zoo. It is 2 a.m. and this summer night is unbearably hot. Several large, sturdy, empty wooden crates stand abandoned by the curb and if the Reader will assist the author in piling the crates one atop the other . . . just so, why, there! you see, we have improvised a regular staircase by which we can climb over the wall, and enter the quiet, private confines of the public zoo. Just inside the wall a great tree grows, and from atop the wall – if this branch is grasped firmly – it is possible to lower oneself gently to the

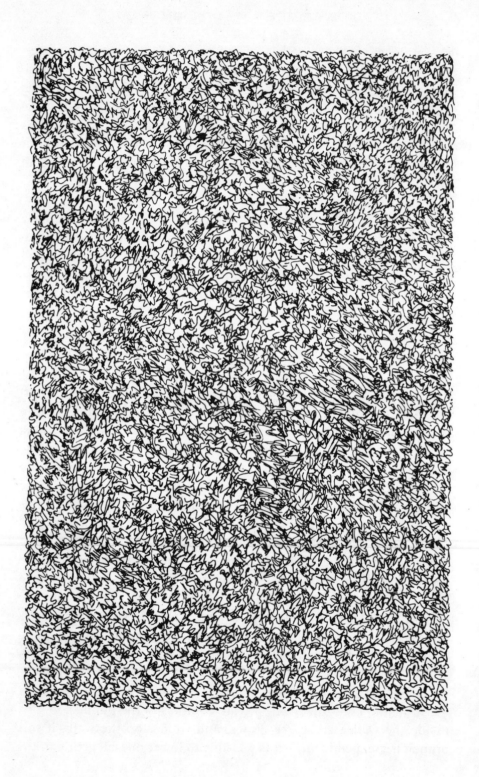

ground, being careful not to make a sound which might alert the Zookeeper, or his young assistant, he who carries the long flashlight that uses four batteries, who might even now be making his rounds. At the base of the tree trunk, in utter darkness, the five of us huddle in a close circle for some whispered conversation. The author knows the way. And now the Reader must firmly grasp the author's left hand, and then with the other hand the Reader must take the hand of the Listener, who in turn must grasp the hand of Fame, that is, the hand of the young lady, whose other hand must grasp the hand of the banker, thus forming a line that will move through the darkest shadows, the author leading, with the banker in a manly sort of way bringing up the rear. Have no fear. The author knows the way. Crouching low on tiptoe we pass the sleeping parrot's cage. We make a wide circle to avoid a patch of light. We thread our way among the huge cages—then freeze! Nearby some giant unknown animal is stirring. Then all is quiet, and we pass on, finally reaching the seal pool at the very center of the zoo. Beside the circular pool a cement den has been built above ground for the seals, a concrete palace of many cubbyholes of the sort in which seals like to sleep.

The pool is empty.

All seals are sleeping.

I suggest we all take off our shoes and climb right up onto the edge of the pool so that we may stand there for a silent moment to contemplate the still waters. There is not the faintest wind.

There is no moon, but the sky is cloudless and ablaze with stars all twinkling in the purple seal pool, shimmerless beneath our gaze.

It is unbearably hot, and our clothes have become sweaty and smelly. What a joy it would be to instantly have freshly washed clothes! How about it? Are we game?

The banker booms out, "The last one in is a sissy!"

And all five of us, screaming wildly, leap into the pool. The last one into the pool, in fact, is the author, who dislikes swimming, and were I not myself trying to make a point with this madness, let me assure you, no one would have been able to talk me into joining this venture.

On coming to the surface, the actress giggles wildly with pleasure. The Reader shouts, "Yahoo!"

The banker roars out jocularities which are answered gaily by the actress, and it seems almost as if they are having a shouting contest,

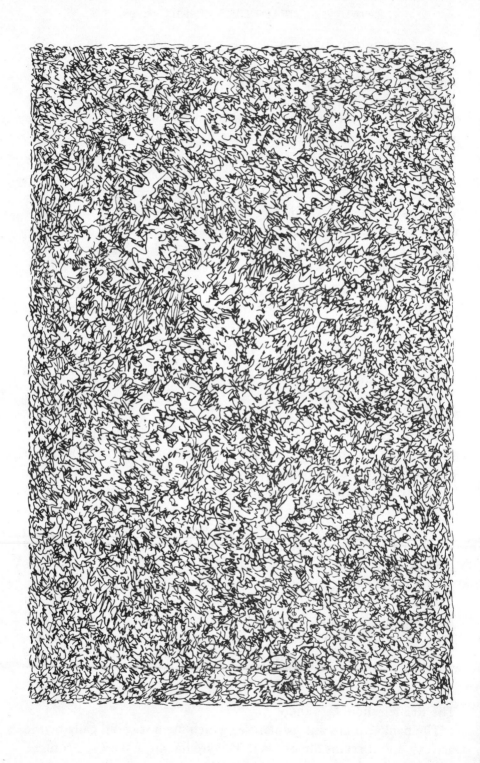

making those happy remarks people make to one another over the expanse of a swimming pool. It should be noted that the author and the Listener do not join in the general hullabaloo. It is a matter of temperament. The Listener and the author have one thing in common: we dislike noise, and feel inhibited about making noise.

In any event, the Zookeeper and his assistant take one ghastly gape at the bunch of us, and immediately summon the police, who arrive in no time, and plunge us into a paddy wagon which delivers us to a building, and thence into a subdued, wooden-paneled room in which Night Court is in session.

Adjacent to the large courtroom is a little alcove where our fingerprints are taken, and then we are instructed to sit among a dozen people waiting their turn to stand before the judge: prostitutes, gamblers, transvestites, drug addicts, striptease dancers, drunkards — People of the Night, one might say. And we are told to join them, to await our turn to stand before the judge.

The judge is beautiful.

He has a halo of snow-white hair, and shaggy white eyebrows that stand out against the perfect complexion of a healthy man.

As we await our turn, we watch the judge handle half a dozen cases with awesome good sense and wisdom, and it soon becomes apparent that we are witnessing true justice. Although the cases are vastly different from one another, they are all handled in the same way: the arresting officer reads the complaint, and then the judge surprises everyone by asking a question. Sometimes the question is directed at the arresting officer, or perhaps, at the defendant. In any event, in the answering of the question the whole truth is revealed, often startling, but always quite evident to everyone in the courtroom, so that when the judge promptly pronounces the sentence, we feel like applauding his decision. Sometimes our sympathies are with the defendant — these he lets off scot free; yet other defendants are vicious and vile, people we would not like to encounter on a dark street, creatures who belong behind bars, surely, and with these he deals harshly, inflicting the maximum sentences our laws allow.

The actress and the banker in the alcove each have made a frantic phone call, and soon five impeccably dressed lawyers have appeared to represent the banker, and it is their intention not merely to quash the charges, but above all to keep the incident out of the morning newspapers.

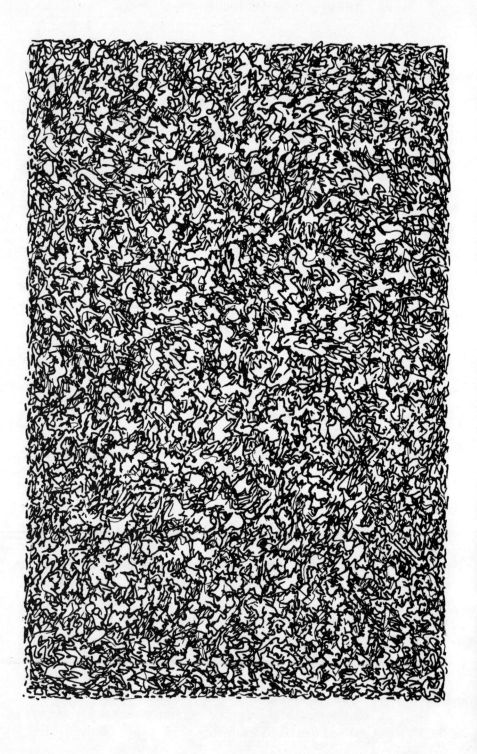

Five other men, even more fashionably dressed, have appeared to represent the actress: it is the entire public-relations department of the film company which this week is to release a movie starring the actress, and they are there to see to it that this story hits the headlines of every paper in the country.

Finally the five of us line up before the bench.

A policeman stands before the judge and lists the laws we've broken, and concludes with the words, "The Zookeeper has accompanied us here, Your Honor, and will testify to what he witnessed at the seal pool."

The Zookeeper steps forward and exclaims angrily, "I've been Night Zookeeper for twenty years and I've never before heard such a ruckus and commotion as these people caused. My assistant and I were in the basement of the Administration Building, and the first hint we had that anything was amiss was a shriek that seemed to come from the center of the zoo. 'Was that a cry for help?' I asked my assistant. My assistant answered, 'No . . . it sounded more like *Yahoo!*' Well, we rushed outside to see what was up, and we were halfway to the seal pool when we suddenly both stopped in our tracks. There was a peal of uncanny laughter; it was like the laughter of a banshee, it went on and on, and it seemed to come from every direction at once."

Beside me, the actress giggles softly, and the author nudges her urgently with his elbow to be silent. That tiny giggle, of course, echoes through the chambers, and two women at the very back of the courtroom titter in sympathy.

As the judge slowly turns his head to solemnly stare at the young woman at my side, so do the eyes of everyone in the courtroom fasten themselves in fascination on this famous lady who has had the temerity to interrupt the proceedings in a court of law by the interjection of a giggle that anyone can see could be construed as being in contempt of court.

The actress suddenly senses she has an audience, and indeed, all eyes are on her; and as if inspired by our eyes and ears she responds with a demonstration of her virtuosity: she drops a decade from her face, becomes the ingenue.

Why, it is no more than a slip of a girl in a damp dress beside me, a fourteen-year-old—no more, surely—goodness and purity

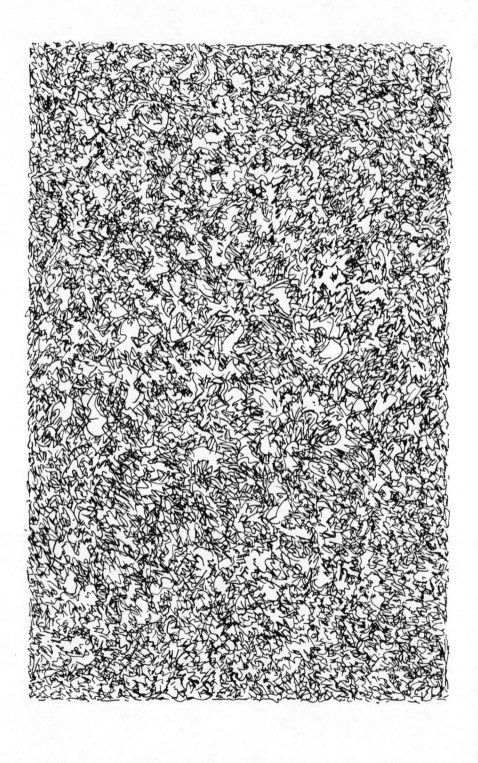

shining on her face, and it is unthinkable, or at least, it is a monstrous thought, that anyone should consider such a fragile beauty to be in contempt of court.

Her face is the emblem of Innocence.

Yet with trembling lip, she says, "Your Honor, I *confess* . . . I was laughing."

The judge rubs his eyes, and stares once again at this apparition before him. During this brief moment a hairpin drops from her tousled hair, and it makes a terrible clatter as it drops to the floor, but no one seems to notice it for all are agog, watching to see what the judge's reaction will be.

The judge turns to the Zookeeper, and says, "Like a *banshee*, you were saying. Please continue."

At this point the whole courtroom breaks into applause, for this judge is known for his harsh sarcasm in confronting fraud, and people are applauding because he's chosen to pass over, that is, to ignore, her behavior; but, of course, the applause is also in appreciation of her performance, for no one here has ever seen before—a live performance by a movie star.

The judge acknowledges his share of the applause with a faint smile, and then with a masterly gesture he quiets the courtroom, and says to the Zookeeper, "Please continue."

"Your Honor, we found these five people in the pool. They were shrieking with laughter, shouting, and carrying on as if our city's sanctuary for seals were their own private swimming pool. When I demanded that they cease and emerge, they refused. Instead, they said silly things, splashed water on us, and laughed at us, and so we summoned the police."

"Where were the seals?" asks the judge.

"They were too terrified to come out of their den, they were cowering against the wall, shivering in fright, for it was bedlam at the zoo tonight, Your Honor."

The judge now turns his attention to the five of us.

Now this judge is quite used to seeing strange, weird, and unlikely people in the clutches of the law, yet there is something about our appearance before the bench which plainly puzzles him, and one by one he stares deep into our eyes trying to fathom the secret meaning of our presence here. One by one we come under his scrutiny—the

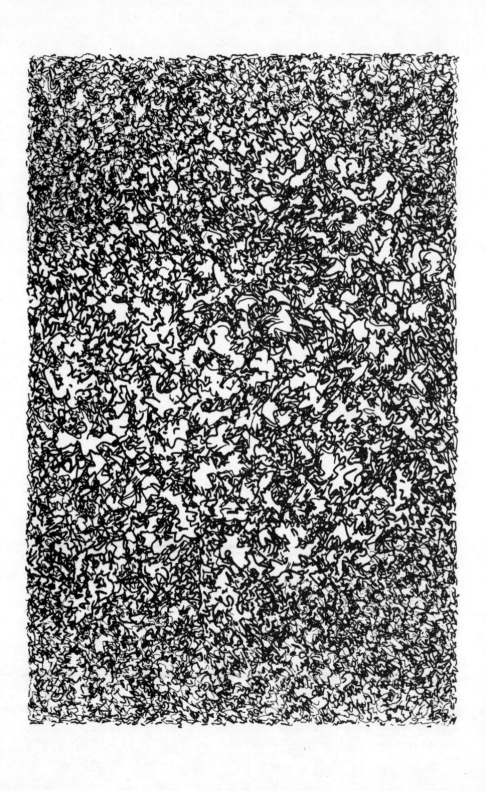

banker, the actress, the author, the Reader—and finally his eyes linger on the Listener, and then the judge sighs deeply, as if to say: Well, now I've seen *everything*.

Now he directs his gaze at me, and his manner is kindly and genuinely curious. He asks, "What were you doing in the seal pool at two o'clock in the morning?"

"Frolicking," I answer.

The judge smiles and nods, and it is obvious that he expects me to say much more. Now no doubt the Reader and Listener are familiar with authors who in a similar situation could write a two-page speech in our defense, yet I am not that kind. Where one word will suffice, well there it is, that's what I say. Why be verbose? To be succinct is my lifetime ambition, and indeed, I might well be called a seeker after the Single Word, especially when the word expresses—as Henry James put it—especially when the word expresses "everything."

The judge is patient and the author stubborn, and who knows now how long a silence might ensue?

Luckily, at this point, one of the banker's smart young trial lawyers requests permission to speak in our defense, and the judge grants it.

The lawyer says, "I should like to call the Court's attention to an irrefutable fact that the Zookeeper contradicted himself in his testimony, and that in so doing he told a blatant lie, he concocted a vicious fabrication, and he presented his own foul fantasy as if it were the truth, and by distortion of fact misrepresented, indeed he defamed, the quite decent characters of the defendants, and implied that they acted, Your Honor, like *beasts* while on the premises of our public zoo."

"Now what is all this?" asks the judge. "Are you accusing the Zookeeper of lying?"

"I was not lying!" exclaims the Zookeeper.

The judge says to the lawyer, "Substantiate your statements."

The lawyer says, "At the conclusion of the Zookeeper's testimony Your Honor asked him a question, and it was an important question, indeed; it got to the very heart of this case; and it is on the true answer to Your Honor's question that this whole case hangs. The Zookeeper was asked *Where were the seals?* and only one part of his answer was the truth: he said that the seals did not emerge from their den. Now the den at the seal pool serves a dual purpose: at night the animals

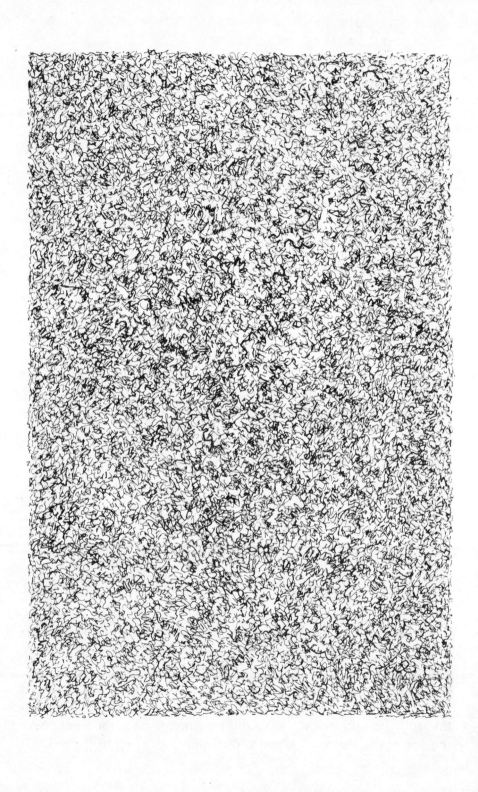

sleep inside, but also, during the day, it gives the seals privacy from the public, for when they enter their den they go completely out of view. Now if you can't see the seals in broad daylight when they are inside their den, how in the middle of a moonless night could the Zookeeper have possibly seen them cowering against the wall and shivering in fright? He just made up all that, Your Honor."

The judge asks the Zookeeper, "Did you actually see the seals in the pitch-dark den?"

For a very long moment the Zookeeper is silent, and then he answers, "No, I did not. But, Your Honor, I was not exactly lying because I know my seals, and I know they must have been frightened by the noise these people made."

The lawyer says, "Your Honor, when seals are frightened they utter a cry of distress, a kind of bark, a woof! woof! woof! woof! so to speak, and if what the Zookeeper said were true, everybody would have heard a dozen disturbed seals all going woof! woof! woof! But such was not the case. Furthermore, were those seals frightened they would have made a mad scramble to get into the pool. This contradicts the expertise of the Zookeeper, but I say any ignoramus knows that seals on land are awkward and defenseless whereas once in the water they have little to fear, seals being superb swimmers. Why did no one hear the seals bark? Why did the seals not emerge from their den to plunge into the pool? There is a single, obvious answer to these questions, Your Honor, and it is that the seals were *sleeping*. It is not surprising that the Zookeeper, whose job is to guard the zoo, should be startled by the word 'Yahoo!' or by the sound of laughter coming from the center of the zoo, yet it does not follow that these same sounds would disturb the sleeping animals. Finally, Your Honor, the Zookeeper told the Court (and I quote) that 'it was bedlam at the zoo tonight.' Now that sounds awful, for bedlam at the zoo implies the trumpeting of elephants, roaring of tigers, screeching of terrified birds, braying of wild asses—"

"Stop!" says the judge. "You needn't enumerate all the animals on the ark. I know what bedlam at the zoo means."

"Your Honor, there was no bedlam at the zoo. The defendants did not climb that wall to be vandals, nor to torment or tease the animals, and the fact is that not even inadvertently did they disturb the slumber of a single sleeping animal. The defendants were engaged

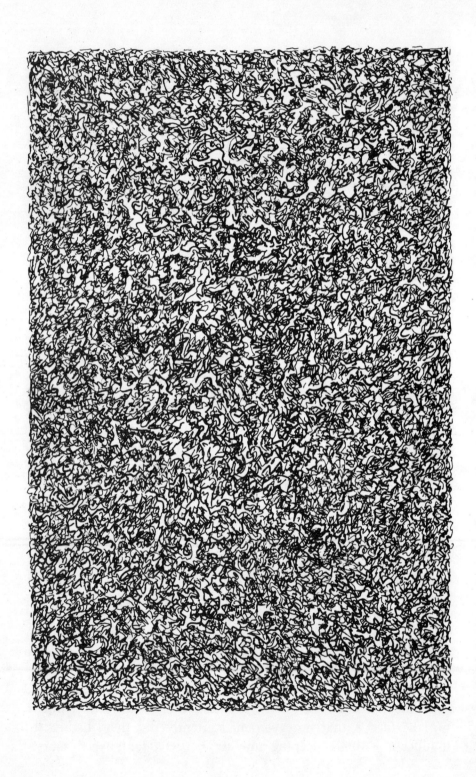

in harmless frolicking, in after-midnight merriment, in the Pursuit of Happiness, if you will, and Your Honor, the pursuit of happiness, in itself, has never been against the law in our land. In short, though the defendants are no doubt guilty of the misdemeanor of trespassing, they are guilty of nothing more."

The judge turns to the patrolman, and asks, "Officer, while at the zoo did you hear the animals calling out, or did they seem disturbed in any way?"

"No sir."

"Did you hear the seals barking?"

"No, sir."

"Did you notice any movements in the den that would indicate that the seals were awake?"

"No, sir. It was pitch dark in the den."

"I see," says the judge.

The judge now pronounces sentence on the five of us, saying, "The Court finds you each guilty of trespassing, but of nothing more. Fifty dollars or five days in jail. Pay your fines to the court clerk over at that desk. Next case."

The banker and the actress rush over to shake the hand of the lawyer, and congratulate him for his splendid speech, and for getting us off with the lightest possible punishment. Swooping over to the clerk, they pay their fines, each with a fifty-dollar bill and, each surrounded by an entourage, soon have vanished out the doorway.

The Reader takes out a checkbook, and makes out two checks, also paying the Listener's fine.

I feel a timid tugging at my elbow, and turn to find it is—of all people—the Zookeeper, who says, "I know the whole truth, and I want to speak to you."

"What!?"

"The whole truth—for instance, when the judge questioned me I might have said: 'Your honor, when we reached the pool, of course the first thing I did was to check on the seals. I told my assistant to direct the beam of his flashlight inside the den, and he did so, and said, "My God! The seals are cowering against the wall." And I added in horror, "They are shivering in fright!"'"

The Zookeeper pauses, then continues, "What if I had said that? What could your smart lawyer have said then?"

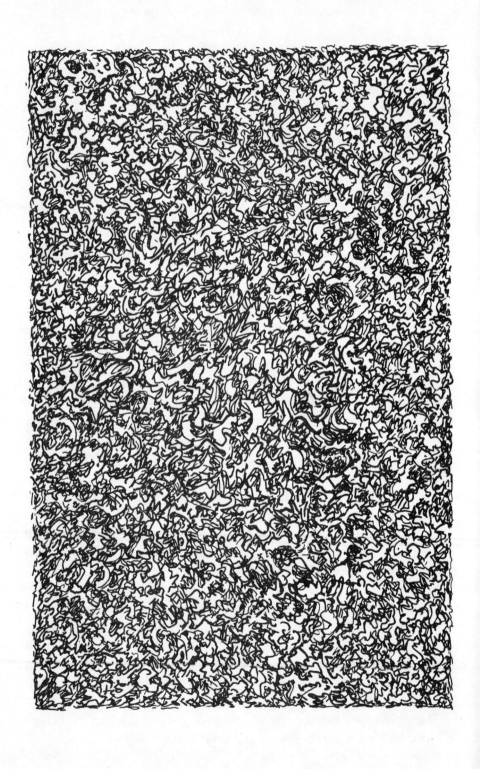

I answer, "If that were the truth, then you should have told it to the judge."

"But I saw that the judge would undoubtedly have sent you all to jail if I had said that. The idea that the actress should have to go to jail because of my testimony, that such a fragile beauty should be sent to jail—it was unthinkable, or at least it was a monstrous thought, and so I lied. Yet it was because I saw the whole truth. Don't you see? I know. I know. I know I am a character in a story."

"Stop! Do not say another word. I have no interest in anything further you may have to say."

"Don't put me off. Don't you see? I like being a character in your story, and I'd like to make you a bargain. I have two twenties and a ten-dollar bill here, and I'll pay your fine if you'll use me as a character in another one of your stories. And also, whenever the Zookeeper is referred to, you should spell it with a capital Z. That's part of the bargain."

"Why on earth should 'Zookeeper' be spelled with a capital Z?"

"It would make me appear to be—you know, special. I shall be the epitome of all angry zookeepers, and if the author wants to make some point, well, you can rely on me, for as a character I shall be *convincing*. How about it? Here. Take the money."

I sigh.

I say, "You are the very Devil. You lied to the judge, and the lawyer ferreted out your lie and showed you to be a fool, and now you are persisting in your folly, and are asking me to believe that same lie about the seals. Well, I do not believe it. You heard me tell the judge I was an author and have taken it into your head that I am some sort of magician or possess magical powers. Well, I do not. I am just a regular writer. I don't know how you think stories are written, but the idea that an author would put a character in a story because that character had given him money in a previous story is so outrageous I will not comment on it. I want to have no further conversations with you on any subject whatsoever. Is that clear? Now there is something urgent which I must immediately attend to."

And so saying, I turn my back on the Zookeeper and approach the Reader, who stands at the desk of the court clerk. The clerk has just handed the Reader two receipts, and I say to the Reader, "Forgive me for having to ask you, but I hope you will be able to loan me fifty

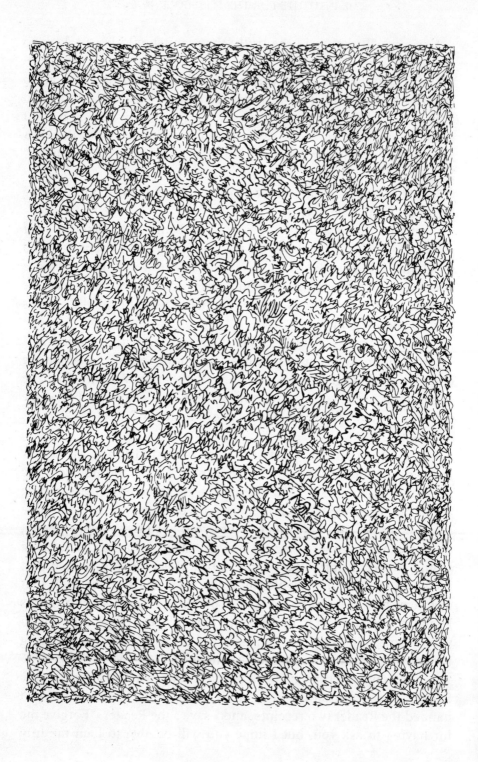

dollars because—I know it's ridiculous—but I don't have a cent on me. I can return the money to you immediately, of course, later on today. But you *must* lend me fifty dollars! Otherwise . . . don't you see . . . I shall have to go to jail."

"You must be joking," says the Reader.

"I am *not* joking! Listen! You must give me a dime at least. I have a friend I can call. Only I need to have a dime for the phone call. You cannot be so heartless as to not give me a dime in such a situation!"

The Reader answers thus, "After getting us in this trouble you expect me to give you money? We were lucky to have a smart lawyer, for if we had relied on your one-word defense we'd probably all be in jail. No! I won't give you a dime!"

I can see that the Listener is already half-out the doorway and is eager to be out of this place, and gestures impatiently to the Reader to finish. The Reader joins the Listener, and at the doorway turns and in a not unfriendly way lifts an arm in final farewell.

I wave my hand . . . and the Reader vanishes.

About the Author

Spencer Holst is of old American stock (Celtic-Scandanavian-Indian) which has produced four generations of writers. His first American relatives arrived with the Massachusetts Bay Colony in 1630 and were among the founders of Windsor, Connecticut. "Their ship," Holst says, "became iced in on the Connecticut River forcing them to spend that winter eating acorns.

"My sister, Mary-Ella Holst, and I are the only Ohio writers born in Detroit, Michigan.

"My great-grandfather founded a newspaper in Ohio soon after the Civil War, the *Weston Avalanche*, and my grandmother received the Hattie Award from the Ohio Womens' Newspaper Association for writing the same column for sixty-eight consecutive years, and my father Doc Holst, also a columnist, was a lifetime member of the American Baseball Writers' Association, covering baseball in Detroit, and much later writing for the *Toledo Blade*, the Ohio city in which his three sisters lived. My mother wrote for many, many small newspapers.

"In the geography of literature I have always felt my work to be equidistant between two writers, each born in Ohio—Hart Crane and James Thurber, but my wife says don't be silly, your stories are halfway between Hans Christian Andersen and Franz Kafka."

For years, Spencer Holst has had a devoted following based not only on two popular collections of stories, *The Language of Cats* and *Spencer Holst Stories,* and wide-spread magazine publication, but on three decades as the storyteller *par excellence* of New York's literary cafés.

Holst is a recipient of the Rosenthal Award from the American Academy and Institute of Arts and Letters and an award from the Foundation for Performing Art. He lives in New York City with his wife Beate Wheeler.